ANIMAL BEHAVIOR

AND OTHER TALES OF LYCANTHROPY

BY KEITH GOUVEIA

Published 2014 by Beating Windward Press LLC

For contact information, please visit:
www.BeatingWindward.com

Second Edition
ISBN: 978-1-940761-08-4

Cover Art by C.J. Hutchinson and Jesus Morales/Dark Riddle

"Lady of the Forest" originally published in Carnival of Wicked Writers *Raw Meat* anthology 2007 and reprinted in WolfSinger Publications' *Wolf Songs* anthology 2008

TABLE OF CONTENTS

INTRODUCTION

LIKE THE VAMPIRE, werewolves—or any sort of animal-shape shifter—have had a long standing in our history. Tales of lycanthropes have been documented from as early as the 18th century and can be found in all cultures across the globe. Some even consider vampires and werewolves the same.

It's no secret to those who know me that the werewolf is my favorite beasty. As a kid, nothing frightened me more than the half-man-half-wolf. The combined efforts of *An American Werewolf in London* and *The Howling* forever sealed the deal and forever changed my mind on the monster. Compared to other genre tropes, the werewolf is far more interesting and menacing.

Traditionally, zombies could be handled on a one-on-one basis with their slow motor skills and dim-witted mindsets. Even for the fast-moving zombies found in the *Dawn of the Dead* remake and in Brian Keene's *The Rising* series, any bludgeoning weapon will get the job done. Nothing about the walking dead ever scared me. Same could be said for vampires. They were far too romantic to be truly terrifying especially considering their numerous weaknesses, their ego being the greatest. But when faced against the ferociousness of a werewolf, one-on-one, you will surely lose to its killer instinct and those deadly teeth. Whether cursed or chosen, the werewolf is a monster capable of unimaginable brutality.

Over the years I've learned all I could about the myths and legends. Read numerous books, saw every film, and watched them slowly fade out of popularity, but my love and my fear never died. Though werewolves have remained a staple in the horror genre, there have been less leading roles for them.

With the werewolf's popularity on the rise again, A.P. Fuchs (the originial publisher of this book) approached me on whether or not I had enough material to fill a collection of werewolf stories. Both of us were surprised by the answer. At that time I had one story complete: "Lady of the Forest," and one I was currently writing, "War Dog." I questioned if it was possible to put together such a collection without rehashing too many ideas or plots and Mr. Fuchs's response was quite simple: "That's the challenge."

My first novel, *The Eternal Battle*, though flawed, has a unique spin on the werewolf genre and I was more than a little concerned on whether I could pull off such a feat again. I completed "War Dog" and the muse slapped me in the back of the head with inspiration for another tale, "The Beast of Garden Row." When that one was completed, I was blown away and before I could relish the fact that I had just written, in my opinion, my greatest short story, two more ideas popped in my head and I immediately went to work. This book is my answer to that challenge and whether I succeeded or not is up to you, the reader. I have taken some of the lesser known myths and made them my own, even created a few myself; "The Guardian" for instance. I hope inside these pages you'll find my passion for these creatures and that some of it will rub off on you.

With Universal Studios' release of *The Wolfman*, Lorne Dixon's *Snarl*, also published by Coscom Entertainment, two upcoming anthologies from Library of the Living Dead, W.D. Gagliani's Nick Lupo series (*Wolf's Trap* and *Wolf's Gambit*) published by Leisure and a few other projects, perhaps lycanthropes will see their resurgence much like the vampire and the zombie.

It's time to rip off your skin and answer the call . . .

Moonlight brightens the sky
I stare out into the night
My life has gone awry
Because of one fearful bite

Freewill bends to instinct
It scratches under my skin
It's too much, I can't think
Who will forgive me for this sin

Bones crack, lengthen and twist
Flesh reforms with a bestial cry
This is not a curse, but a gift
Tonight someone will surely die

THE BEAST OF GARDEN ROW

Father Malloy stared into the wild eyes of a once loving husband and father and called upon the strength of the Archangel Michael. "O God, come to my assistance. O Lord, make haste to help me. Glory be to the Father."

The man laughed as his wife and daughter wept.

The priest continued his sworn duties and recited the vade retro satana. "Let the Holy Cross be my light. Let not the snake lead me. Step back, Satan. Never tempt me with vain things. What you offer is evil …"

The man smiled, looking as though he was enjoying the exorcism.

Impossible . . . his teeth . . . it's unnatural, Father Malloy thought. *No . . . He is with me. I must be strong.* "In the name of the Father, the Son, and the Holy Spirit I cast you out. Devil be gone!" With the flick of his fingers, Holy Water splashed the man's face.

The smile faded, but the man did not flinch. Father Malloy expected the water to burn his sinful flesh. He threw more.

"Why are you men of the cloth so eager to blame the devil? Why can't you accept the evil that resides in all our hearts?" Spittle flew from the blasphemous man's lips while strands of saliva dangled from the corners of his mouth.

"Your thoughts are clouded. You are being manipulated."

"You are wrong, priest. Just as you are wrong in thinking you can save them, but for your efforts, I shall reward you."

The sound of fabric ripping echoed in the log cabin. The man dropped to all fours. Looking at his wife and daughter he said, "You better start running."

"Go!" Father Malloy said as the man's left leg snapped and twisted around at the knee.

Mother and daughter bolted out of the log cabin and Father Malloy was alone to face the beast. He performed the sign of the cross in front of his chest and spoke over the sound of cracking bones. "Even though I walk through . . ."

The right leg snapped and twisted.

". . . the valley of the shadow of death . . ."

Skin stretched and tore as the man's nose and mouth elongated.

". . . I shall fear no evil . . ."

Ribs cracked and expanded as his chest cavity increased in size and his shoulder blades lengthened.

". . . for Thou art with me . . ."

A low guttural growl emanated from within the man as hair sprouted from every pore.

". . . Thy rod and Thy staff they comfort me."

The beast stood on its haunches, towering over him. Hot breath, smelling of rotten meat, blew down on him.

Father Malloy trembled. "Forgive me, Heavenly Father. I have failed You."

Claws dug into his biceps and the beast lifted him off his feet and pulled him close to its massive maw. The monster's tongue reached out and licked the side of Father Malloy's face. It bit into his shoulder and he screamed.

"Huh!" Jim sat up abruptly, waking from his dream. He looked around and realized he was safe. He leaned back against the willow tree, perched atop a hill looking over Garden Row Cemetery, and thought about the two lives he failed to save. He prayed they reached Heaven's pearly gates.

The little girl had been so vibrant, so hopeful and happy to see him when he arrived to exorcise the demon plaguing her father, but he failed. Failed her, his church, himself, but most importantly, he failed his faith. He was tossed aside—

body broken—but alive as the beast stalked his beloved family and slaughtered them. Pieces of their bodies had been found scattered across the acre of property.

The beast had toyed with them, tortured them as he does me now a hundred years later.

A single tear streaked down his face.

The church had no idea what it was up against and when they realized their mistake, it was too late. Jim Malloy was a condemned man. Excommunicated by his peers and sent away from the Roman Catholic Church, he struggled with the beast within. Struggled to retain himself and not become the monster forced upon him.

I am alone, he thought, leaning his head against the tree and looking to the heavens. *Have You forgiven me yet, or have You forgotten me?*

"Jim, what are you doing up here?" his boss said, ascending to the top of the hill.

"Sorry, boss. I thought I'd beat the heat and take my break in the shade."

"Who're you trying to fool? I know you were sleeping up here again."

Jim stood up. "I'm sorry. I didn't mean to nod off."

"I know, you never do, you can't help it. Late night parties and such."

Wish I could say that. It's better than the gruesome truth.

"Have you finished digging the grave?"

"The grave site is ready."

"Then why you covering up? You know I don't care what you do as long as the work's done. Come on, I need you."

"What's the problem?" he asked as they walked back to the mortuary.

"Mrs. Jarvis is having a party tonight and she would like me to come over and do her make-up for her. I need you to embalm Mr. Moore and prepare him for tomorrow."

Perfect timing. "No problem. Is this business or pleasure?"

"Maybe a little of both, if I'm lucky." Mr. Jackson winked and nudged his elbow into Jim's side.

He managed a smile. "Good for you. Just make sure to take it easy on her. We don't want her becoming the newest resident here."

"No worries. She's a tough old bird."

Bile burned the back of Jim's throat. The thought of two elderly people fornicating disgusted him. *Perhaps all these years alone have jilted me? It's good that they have each other.*

Both Anna Jarvis and Don Jackson had lost their significant others. Hers to cancer, and his to a younger beau who now lived off money he had saved all his life. Jim could understand any woman wanting Don to do their make-up, he was an artist; you had to be in his profession. But to have sexual relations with the bulbous man, that was too much to comprehend.

"When are you leaving?" Jim asked.

"Now. You've got your keys, right?"

Jim pulled them out of his pocket and jiggled them.

"Don't be smart with me."

"Sorry, boss."

"Don't be nervous," Don said, obviously sensing something was amiss. Jim couldn't help the attitude: tomorrow was the full moon. "You've been practicing and you're getting good. Real good."

"Perhaps, but I can only do so much." He felt bad pretending that was the issue, but it couldn't be helped.

"No need to worry. Mr. Moore died of a heart attack. Just give him a little bit of color."

"Okay."

"Good. I'll see you tomorrow."

Jim waved Don off as he got into his car and drove down the gravel road. With a sigh he turned and entered through the arch-top mahogany front door, the weight of his deception bearing down on his soul. He walked through the viewing room, passed the casket showroom, and into the funeral director's office.

Forgive me, Father, he thought as he got to work on the paperwork. Though he had been doing it for years, falsifying documents was like swallowing a bitter pill. He knew it was wrong, but it was a necessary evil. *Better to defile the dead than destroy the living.*

With the paperwork done, Jim took the staircase from the office to the morgue. There, Mr. Moore lay naked in the supine position on the cold, metal slab with his head propped up on a cedar block waiting for embalmment.

Fortunately, Don used the modesty cloth. Have to remember to thank him, he thought, recalling all the times Don hadn't and how embarrassed he had been. Despite his years, and all he had seen, he still found himself uncomfortable around the naked form.

"I'm sorry, Mr. Moore. There's been a change of plans. I know you won't look your absolute best, but it's still early and you will be presentable. I promise you that much."

The man's clothes were neatly set aside along with his personal artifacts his family wished him buried with. Jim walked over to the nearby sink and washed his hands.

He put on a pair of surgical gloves. "Your turn."

As he washed Mr. Moore with a germicidal solution, he worked the muscles to relieve the rigor mortis and then he set the features using a photograph provided by the family.

"Now I'm just going to insert these needles into your carotid artery and jugular veins to give the impression you were arterially embalmed. Again, I am sorry for this, but I can't have the meat spoiled. It won't kill me, of course, but it's rather difficult to digest, believe you me."

Jim tossed the large needle into the sink and turned on the centrifugal pump so as not to throw off Don's inventory and raise suspicion. As the fluorescent yellow fluid went down the drain, he applied a moisturizing cream to the body, then dressed the man in his Sunday best.

"There, all ready for tomorrow. I guess I won't see you again 'til tomorrow night. I hope you understand it's nothing personal. You just came here at the wrong time."

He took one last look around, making sure everything was in its place. "Well, goodnight, then." With the flick of a switch the morgue was engulfed in darkness and Jim made the rest of his rounds.

* * * *

The next night, he walked out into the moonlight naked, his clothing stashed away. Jim had lost too many outfits over the years. Often times, the beast's razor sharp claws tore through the confining garments before the transformation was even complete. His expanding chest popped buttons off shirts, his twisting knees and enlarging thighs ripped pant legs and his toe nails tore through his shoes and socks. Under the pale light of the moon, he transformed into the monster that had taken everything away from him. As the beast, he had full knowledge of its actions, but control was lost. It was as if they were two personalities sharing a body, each had their time in the spotlight. After a hundred years he had learned to influence the beast, but in the end, it was a wild animal whose actions were unpredictable. As a former man of the cloth, he would never gamble with an innocent life, so he chose this existence: to live among the dead and allow the beast to release its destructive impulses on those it could not harm.

That's it. See where it leads.

The beast followed the trail of pig's blood that Jim laid out during the day to Mr. Moore's gravesite. With the concentration of the blood over the grave, the wolf began to tear into the earth.

Find it. Devour it.

Freshly packed dirt flew into the air between the wolf's legs and in a matter of seconds, the wolf's claws scratched against the fiberglass casket. Once its fingers punched through the material, the door was pulled off its hinges and sent hurling into the air.

Yes!

Clamping down on the corpse's head with its powerful jaws, the beast lifted its meal out of the hole and tossed it to the ground.

A scream echoed in the night.

The wolf turned around and saw two teenagers, a boy and a girl, staring at him over the tombstones.

"Run, Amy!"

Leave them. Your meal is here.

The wolf gave chase, snarling and snapping its jaws. The boy dropped the blanket and radio he was carrying and the beast stopped briefly to take in the scent.

It's locking in on them. It'll be able to track them to the ends of the earth now. Just let them go! The beast ignored his plea and sprinted after its prey.

"Hurry, Mike. It's gaining on us."

"Don't look back, get to the car!"

No. Please stop.

"We're almost there. Please, God, let us make it."

Yes, God, he thought, agreeing with the boy, *let them make it.*

With a few feet between them, the wolf leapt. Mike opened the driver's side door, jumped in, and slammed it shut. The wolf's face slammed into steel, stunning it for a moment.

Let them go. That's enough. We must run away.

With the girl safely in the car the engine came to life. Gears ground as it was put into reverse. Gravel shot into the wolf's eyes as it backed down the road. The wolf tried to slash the tire, but instead dragged its razor sharp claws along the tail end of the car.

Vision blurred, the beast relied on its other senses to track them. Following the scent of carbon monoxide, the wolf chased after them. The cool breeze helped remove the debris from its eyes and the car's tailpipe came into focus.

Don't do this!

The beast ignored Jim's orders and ran along the driver's side of the car. The girl screamed, only taunting the beast's frenzy. It drove its massive body into the car, rocking the vehicle.

"Hold on!"

"Watch out!"

The car swerved slightly, but the boy was quick and recovered. The wolf slammed it again. And again.

"Ah! Do something, Mike!"

"I'm trying."

The darkness gave way to a blinding light. A horn blasted. The girl screamed again and the beast was racked with pain as a semi-truck slammed into its face and continued over its body, crushing its bones.

Thank you, Lord, Jim thought as the wolf lay helpless on the road, watching the car fade over the horizon. Though the pain was excruciating, he knew it was worth it.

Twisted and mangled, the wolf dragged its broken body to the edge of the road and tumbled down the embankment. Darkness swelled, blanketing his vision. Both man and beast succumbed.

* * * *

Jim awoke to a burning sensation in his hands. They itched. *What am I going to do? Do I leave town, or do I stick to the plan?*

He looked around, trying to decipher his bearings. He wasn't too far from the cemetery, but the sun was well past the horizon. *I don't know if there's enough time to put everything in its place and pretend nothing happened.* He looked down the long winding road and thought about how far he could get. *No! I have to try. I've worked too hard here.*

When he arrived at Garden Row, the first order of business was to get dressed. His clothes were right where he left them in the tool shed. Once dressed, he grabbed his shovel and searched for Mr. Jackson. With no sign of the old man, he headed toward Mr. Moore's plot.

Seeing everything just as he left it and no one around, Jim looked to the sky and mumbled, "Thank you."

He dropped his shovel and hoisted Mr. Moore on to his shoulder, then carried him back to his casket. With the body in place, he walked over to the lid and carried that back too, placing it back in position the best he could.

"What are you doing?" asked a man in uniform. Jim squinted from the sting of the sun, but he made out the figure: it was Sheriff Williams.

Act cool. "Just cleaning up after some vandals."

"Well, I've just come from the station after hearing the damnedest story."

"Really."

"Yes, really. I'm going to have to ask you to step out of the hole, sir."

"All right."

Jim climbed out of the grave and stepped aside. The sheriff jumped in, looked around, then opened the casket. The hinges were busted and Jim had only been able to lay it in place and not fix it; anyone could see it wasn't closed properly. It fell to the side and leaned against the wall of dirt.

The sheriff said nothing upon seeing the teeth marks in Mr. Moore's face. He turned toward Jim. "You weren't going to report this?"

"I'm just doing my job." He didn't know what else to say. The thought of beating him to death with his shovel and burying him with Mr. Moore crossed his mind, but he quickly dismissed it.

"So you've done this before?" asked the sheriff as he climbed out of the grave.

Jim rubbed his fingertips into the palm of his hand. "No ... I .... This kind of thing doesn't happen around here."

The sheriff turned back to the casket, then back to Jim. "What's wrong with your hands?"

"They're just a little itchy."

His eyes narrowed. "What's the casket made of, fiberglass?"

Jim swallowed hard. "I ... I'm not sure."

"Save it. I'm going to have to ask you to come with me to the station for questioning."

"I meant no harm. I just wanted to save the family some grief. Think of what it'll do to them. They've suffered enough."

"I understand that, I can even respect it, but I have a sworn duty to protect the living. And from what I've heard and seen here, there is something extremely dangerous threatening my town. I didn't want to believe the boy, he sounded crazy, but ..."

"What did he tell you?"

The sheriff placed his hand over his gun. "We'll talk about it at the station."

"There's no need for that. I won't give you any trouble."

"Glad to hear it. Let's go."

Jim sat in the back of the squad car and prayed for both strength and forgiveness. There was no denying he needed to get out of town, but where would he go? He finally had it made, but he survived before and he could do it again. He knew a small town like Madison, Virginia, would band together tonight and he couldn't afford to go toe-to-toe with a lynch mob. *They would never survive. There's always Europe. I hear their embalming practices leave much to be desired. The beast could have its fill of untainted meat. But first, I have to get through this.*

"So, tell me about these kids. You sure they're not the ones that dug up Mr. Moore? Some kind of initiation prank or something?"

"Whatever it was or is . . . these kids had nothing to do with it."

"What were they doing in the cemetery?"

"They're teenagers. What do you think they were doing?" *Should have known. Damn kids.* "Were they drinking?"

"After hearing their story the first thing I did was give them a breathalyzer. No, they're on the up and up, which is more than I can say for you. You've got an awful lot of questions for someone who says he was just doing his job."

Jim folded his arms across his chest and looked out the window. *He's right. I'm acting guilty.*

"Is there anything else you want to tell me?"

"No, Sheriff."

The rest of the ride was done in silence and once they arrived at the station, Jim saw the maroon '68 Dodge Charger parked outside. Sweat beaded on his brow as he took note of the long claw marks on the rear quarter.

"Look familiar?"

"Never seen it before."

"Not the car, the marks. Same as that casket."

"So I see. Some kind of large animal. Bear, perhaps?"

"Perhaps. Let's go."

He was pushed from behind and escorted in, then seated at one of the cluttered desks.

"Who's this guy?" asked another uniformed officer.

"The caretaker of Garden Row. Call Ernie. Tell him to get his ass to the cemetery. I want an investigation before the scene is compromised any more than it has been."

"How long do you think this'll take?" Jim asked.

"As long as it takes."

"Someone needs to inform my boss. Don't want to lose my job over this."

"Don't worry. We'll take care of it."

"When can we go home?" Jim recognized the voice of the sex-crazed teenager.

"Why don't the two of you come out here? I've brought the grounds-keeper of the cemetery."

The young couple stepped out of what looked like an interrogation room and took a seat across the desk from Jim.

"Do you recognize this man?" the sheriff asked them.

They both shook their heads.

Mike looked Jim in the eyes. "Did you see it, too?"

"No," said Jim. *Forgive me, Father.*

"Consider yourself lucky," Mike said.

The girl still appeared to be in shock. She sat there; quiet, with Mike's right arm tightly wrapped in her arms as she rocked back and forth.

"Sheriff, I really need to get her home."

"Her parents are on their way. They should be here any minute."

"I called Don Jackson. He's on his way, too," said the deputy.

"All right, then. Everyone just sit tight," said the sheriff.

Jim looked to the clock. *A little after noon. Where did the day go?*

"Somewhere you need to be?" the sheriff asked.

"No, sir."

"Keep an eye on him," he said to his deputy. "I'm going to the john."

I can't believe how this day is flying by. I lost too much time this morning while my body healed. Worse, I have no preparations for tonight. Nothing to keep the beast occupied. If I don't get out of here in time, the whole town is in jeopardy.

"There she is!" a hysterical woman said, running to Amy.

Amy finally released Mike's arm to embrace her mother. Mike pumped his hand several times; obviously the limb was going numb from her clutching so tightly.

"I'm not happy with the idea of what you two were up to, but thank you for keeping my little girl safe," said Amy's father, offering his hand, which Mike shook cautiously.

"When can we take her home?" her mother asked.

"The sheriff will be out momentarily. He'll let you know."

"Are you sure you saw what the sheriff says you did?" Amy's father asked them.

"Yes," Amy said.

"Yeah," Mike said.

The man ran his hands through his salt and pepper hair. After a hundred years, Jim hadn't come across anyone who believed the tale of the beast at face value. The rational mind was the main reason why he managed to live for so long.

"Where are your parents, Mike?" he asked. "Are they on their way?"

"No, sir," Mike replied. "They don't give a hoot about me."

"Ah, Mr. and Mrs. Torres, I presume," said the sheriff as he entered the room.

"I'd like to take these kids home," said Amy's father.

"And you may. I have all I need. Their statements have been taken, and Mike already knows he must leave his car here."

"Thank you," her father said. "Come on, guys."

"Not a word of this to anyone," the sheriff said as they started walking out the door.

They nodded and left.

At least they're safe now, Jim thought. "When are we going to get started?"

"All right, Jim. Now that they're gone we can talk freely. Did you try to scare those kids out of the cemetery?"

"No, sir. I had no idea they were there. I heard nothing."

"Where were you last night?"

"I was in bed."

"And you sleep at the mortuary?"

"Yes."

"That would drive me crazy," said the other uniformed officer who Jim thought to be a deputy.

"Is that what this is about? You think I'm crazy?"

"No one's saying that. Those kids said they saw a werewolf. No mistaking it. Now—"

"Who's crazy now?" Jim said, trying to throw them off. *I need to get out of here.*

"As I was about to say, it was dark and shadows can play tricks on the mind, especially in a cemetery. There's no denying that a large animal is behind this, but your behavior it's . . . off. Why? What are you hiding?"

Jim looked the sheriff in the eye. "Nothing."

"You obviously got fiberglass particles under your nails. Were you inspecting the claw marks in the lid?"

"Yes."

"You know tampering with evidence is illegal, right?"

"Yes." *Come on, just let me off with a warning.*

The phone rang and the deputy answered. The deputy said nothing, only listened, then finally said, "I'll tell him. You too. Bye."

"Was that Ernie?" the sheriff asked.

"Yeah. He's inspected the scene and is bringing samples back to the lab. He'll call back as soon as he has something."

"Any idea how long?"

"No," the deputy said.

What kind of samples? "You can't keep me 'til you hear something. You know where I live."

"You're not going anywhere, so just chill out."

Jim crossed his arms and waited. Forty-five minutes later, Mr. Jackson finally showed up.

"What took you so long?" Jim asked upon seeing him.

"I had to go out to the site and see for myself," he said.

"Thank you for coming, Mr. Jackson."

Don sat beside Jim. "Please, call me Don."

"All right, Don. Can you tell me if anything like this has happened before?"

"No, never."

"Have you ever seen any animals large enough to do this in the outlying woods?"

"No."

"And how long has this man been working for you?"

"Going on twelve years now, why? You don't think, Jim, had anything to do with this, do you?"

"I can't rule it out. He was caught reburying the body."

Don looked to him. "Jim . . . why . . . you know the drill."

He said nothing and Don nodded.

"We need a lawyer present."

"That's not necessary, Don. No charges have been filed yet," said the sheriff.

Jim's stomach growled for everyone to hear. *No surprise. Haven't eaten since yesterday.*

"Since we're accommodating you by sticking around, how about some food for my friend here?" Don said.

"We can do that," said the sheriff, then walked away toward the phone. "Pizza all right?"

"That's fine," Jim said.

"I can't believe they think you did this," Don whispered.

"It's all right. I messed up."

"Don't worry. We'll get you out of here."

It may be too late, he thought, looking at the clock. *Quarter of two. Time's running out. What am I going to do? I can't let the beast hurt them.*

"What's wrong?" Don asked Jim.

Jim forced a smile. "Nothing."

"You know you got the wrong guy," Don said, looking toward the sheriff. "Jim volunteers at the soup kitchen every weekend and donates half his paycheck to the halfway house in Roanoke. He's a kind-hearted man who wouldn't hurt a soul."

"Thank you, Don, but it's not necessary."

"To hell it's not. It looks to me like they already have you pegged."

For good reason. Jim eyed the jail cell and wondered if it would hold the beast. Though it would expose him, it would be the only way to protect the innocent.

The phone rang and the deputy answered it. "Yeah. Hold on. Sheriff, it's Ernie."

Sheriff Williams picked up the phone on his desk and the deputy hung up his. "Go ahead."

What's he telling him? I should run. No. They'd gun me down and I'd wake up in the morgue as the beast. How many innocent lives would be lost then? Best bet is that cell. Pray they understand. Pray they believe I mean them no harm.

"Thank you for checking. Good work. Keep me posted." The sheriff hung up.

He has a look. What did he find out?

The sheriff approached him, hand hovering over his holstered pistol.

Got to act quick.

When the sheriff was in range, Jim leapt to his feet, shoving the sheriff and grabbing the key ring hooked to his pants. The belt loop tore and the keys came loose.

"What are you doing?" asked Don and both the deputy and the sheriff drew their weapons.

Jim ran to the jail cell, closed the door behind him and locked it.

"Does this mean you're ready to tell us the truth?" asked the sheriff, hand still on his pistol.

"What's he talking about, Jim? Did you do that to Mr. Moore?"

"Not me per se," he said. "You should all leave. You're not safe. I've never hurt anyone and I don't want to start now."

"Are you really going to stand there and tell me you're a werewolf?"

"Yes, Sheriff."

"The guy's crazy."

"Shut up, Bart. The kids said an impossibly large wolf attacked them. Claw marks bigger than a grizzly's were ripped into the side of their car and the casket. His hands itched from fiberglass particles stuck under his fingernails and Ernie says there were traces of DNA that matched both human and canine in the wounds on Mr. Moore's face. Add it up and you've got the irrational."

"Sheriff, there's got to be a mistake. I've known Jim for . . ."

"No mistake, Don."

"But, Jim—"

"Don, in the twelve years you've known me, have I changed one bit? Any gray hairs? Wrinkles?"

He took a moment, processing the question. "No," he finally answered. "It doesn't matter. He's a good man. In the same twelve years I haven't heard of one single animal attack."

"It doesn't mean I'm not dangerous. I can't control it. I can only manipulate it to a degree. Trick it into doing what I want, but it's too late. I made no preparations tonight. Nothing would stop the beast from going on the hunt. I have denied it the thrill of the chase and the rapture of the kill, but last night it got a taste of what it's been missing, and tonight it will be ravenous."

"So Mr. Moore's body isn't the first?"

"No. On the nights of a full moon I usually have a body lined up that hasn't been embalmed and I get the wolf to dig it up and feed on it rather than hurt anyone. I'm sorry, Don. I tricked you, too."

"I understand, and I forgive you."

"Thank you. It means the world to me. If only our Father could do the same. I've been cursed for a hundred years. I was once a priest, but I was excommunicated when the Church discovered I was cursed after a failed exorcism. I've done everything I could for redemption, but I've seen no sign of forgiveness from our Father. My penance is not complete. Please, you must go or it will set me back even further."

"We should just shoot him now, before he turns."

"Bart! You're not helping."

"It won't do any good, Sheriff. Your bullets will not stop it. Only aggravate the beast."

Bart looked around. "Silver! We need silver."

"We are not killing an innocent man. Besides, I need to see proof."

"Are you insane?" Bart asked.

"If you're afraid, then go, but I'm staying."

"I'm staying with you, Sheriff," Don said.

"It's not safe. I've never tried to cage the beast."

"We're going to find out. Together," the sheriff said and there was no more argument.

The men waited for nightfall with little conversation. Jim could hear the beating of their hearts grow faster with each passing hour. He didn't know what to say, so he just sat there not wanting to add to their anxiety. He feared the worst for them, but admired their courage.

If I was half as brave as them, I'd take my own life and end this nightmare. But I am afraid. Afraid the Lord our Father will cast me out, shun me as my peers have.

"It's happening," Jim said, feeling his insides twisting and contorting. "Ready yourselves."

The men stepped further away from the jail cell and watched wide-eyed as Jim pulled off his shirt to reveal bubbling, expanding skin. He dropped to all fours, hair sprouted over every inch of his contorted body. The sound of his bones cracking echoed in the jailhouse and his weeping moan turned into a blood-curling howl.

"Oh my . . ." said the sheriff.

Don made the sign of the cross over his chest and the deputy wet himself.

The beast roared and hit the bars with all its strength. It reached through the bars and swiped at the air.

Do not do this. Calm down.

The beast grabbed the bars with its clawed hands and pushed and pulled. Dust fell from the ceiling as the bars wiggled in the concrete.

"There's no way that cage is going to hold it. We have to go," said the deputy.

The sheriff shook his head and looked to his desk. "No, we'll have to put it down."

"How?" asked Don.

"There's a silver letter opener in my desk drawer."

"You can't be serious?" said the deputy. "You know how close you'll have to get?"

"It doesn't matter. This thing could kill the whole town. I have to try."

Stop struggling. I'm not ready to die.

The beast continued and one of the bars broke free.

Don stepped closer to the door. "Hurry, it's getting out."

Bart drew his pistol and shakily aimed it at the beast.

"Got it," said the sheriff with the letter opener in hand.

"You better hope that's real."

"Thanks." The sheriff approached the beast; it growled, but didn't back away as if it dared him to get close enough to use it. "Shoot it in the leg, Bart!"

Bart lowered the gun and fired two shots. The beast yelped as it dropped to its knees. Without hesitation, the sheriff jammed the silver letter opener in the beast's left eye. It howled in pain as it fell to the floor, the letter opener still in its eye socket. Smoke snaked into the air from the wound.

It burns. This is it. I can feel it dying.

"Great, our only weapon and you lost it."

"It couldn't be helped," Don said, backing the sheriff.

"Look!" said the sheriff.

Out of the beast's good eye, Jim saw the man pointing at him. There was a sudden chill in the air as if the warmth of the fur coat had fallen away.

I'm changing back.

Don knelt down in front of the jail's bars and reached in. "Jim," he said.

Jim reached toward his friend with his misshapen hand. The burning sensation in his eye was almost too much to endure and Jim knew all too well the power of a compassionate touch. For a brief moment it would calm the pain.

"What're you doing?" The sheriff grabbed Don by the shoulders and pulled him back as Jim's hand was a mere inch from Don's.

Don pulled free of his grip. "He's dying, can't you see that?"

"He's still dangerous," the sheriff said, and Jim couldn't deny the fact as he looked at the claws still exposed on his fingertips. His hand bubbled and oozed as it returned to its human form.

"Before today, you didn't even know who he was. He's my friend!"

"That doesn't change the fact—"

"Please … forgive me," Jim said, his naked body trembling.

"There's nothing to forgive, Jim," Don said, kneeling once more. "You didn't hurt anyone."

"But I put all of you in danger."

"Shh!"

Hot white light formed on the outside of Jim's vision and slowly consumed everything in his line of sight. As it did, the pain subsided. He could no longer sense the beast's presence. He felt peace.

Within the light a figure approached him.

Father!

LYCANTHROPY

"Come quick. He killed him. He ripped the doctor's throat apart with his teeth!"

Officer Chase looked over the hysteric nurse. His gaze traveled up and down her slender frame. *Something's off*, he thought. Even after the woman adjusted it, her white uniform was twisted slightly to the left and provocatively undone. "Calm down, ma'am. Where's the suspect now?"

"He was moved to the adjacent cell. The orderly sedated him and we put him in a straitjacket."

"So he's not a danger to anyone right now?"

"No," she said, then looked over her shoulder.

Chase followed her line of sight; the arm of a black man vanished behind a corner. *A few seconds too late. Should have known someone was watching me. Should have sensed it. Don't let her distract you, you're better than that.*

She faced forward and her hands shot toward the blouse to button it. "Are you going to come in or are you going to stare at my breasts?"

What the . . . I wasn't even . . . that's some mood swing. "One second." Chase grabbed the radio pinned to his left shoulder sleeve and leaned toward it. "Dispatch. Sixteen-twenty on the scene. Suspect subdued." He released the button.

"Copy."

"ETA on Homicide?"

A burst of static, followed by, "Ten minutes."

"Is the crime scene secure for the moment?" Chase asked.

"Yes."

Though it went against his training, Chase knew the scene had already been compromised and there was no point in wasting any unnecessary time, so he made a judgment call. "Ma'am I'm going to get some caution tape out of my car, then I'm going to need you to take me to the crime scene."

"Okay," she said, then turned back to look down the corridor again.

Suspicious, he thought, as he walked away. He remembered the way she fidgeted with the bottom of the uniform's skirt; she tugged it down when she opened the door. *She was having sex during working hours with mystery man around the corner. Had to have been. Duly noted.*

Chase popped the trunk to his squad car. With seven years on the force, everything he could ever need was stored in here. He saw to that. His hand roamed over the supplies: road flares, first aid kit, folded blankets, bottles of water, a couple of teddy bears for children that might need a distraction, and finally the rolls of yellow tape. *One should do it.* He slammed the lid shut and walked back up the hospital's stone steps. He looked upward toward the face of the building, then to the left and right. The brick seemed to go on forever, and with the light cast down from the roofline he could clearly see the Florida sun had stolen the brick's vibrant red coloring. Wrought iron bars covered every window and he couldn't help but wonder about the people locked behind them. As far as he knew they were always sedated to some degree; the need was lost on him.

"Right this way," the nurse said as he crossed the threshold. "Dr. Ebby was a pompous ass, but no one deserves to die the way he did. That awful gasping and gurgling sound as the blood spilled from his airway." The woman's shoulders twitched.

Chase pulled out his notepad. "Where were you when the attack happened?"

"Taking care of other patients. We have nearly three hundred here, you know."

"And what about the rest of the staff?"

"I'm not going to pretend to know what everyone was doing. Are you treating me as a suspect?"

"No, ma'am, these are just routine questions."

"Well, anyway, the hospital is understaffed and over budget, but it's not like the patients are demanding. Most are catatonic in their psychosis."

"I see," Chase said, jotting the info down. "The detective is going to need to speak with the entire staff when he gets here. Any precautions we need to take?"

"Not if he does it on an individual basis. Dr. Thompson has been called. He's on his way."

"Good to know."

"About time you showed up," said an orderly, standing by a door.

The man was dark-skinned and Chase stole a quick glance at the nurse by his side. *Definitely lover boy*, he thought, noticing the way she looked at him. *Suppose there's some truth to the old 'once you go black' adage.*

The orderly's eyes fixated on him. Chase looked the man over. He figured the guy to be at least two inches taller than himself and with the same muscular build. His hands were balled into fists and he gnawed on a loose piece of skin on his lip. Chase had seen this kind of behavior many times from those who had something to hide.

I could take him without the allotted protection of the badge. He stepped right up to the man, getting in his face. "Move aside."

The man stepped away from the door and Chase peered into the small window. A man lay curled in a ball on the padded floor, the straitjacket still secure. The man looked to the door, his chin and mouth stained crimson. He looked upon Chase with a distant gaze, then lowered his head.

Good. The drugs are still working.

"The doctor is in this room," the orderly said.

Chase turned from the glass. "Who's been in the room?"

"Just Julia, me and Franklin. We pulled him off the doc and sedated him while Julia tried her best to save him."

"And you are?"

"Name's Lamont."

Julia jumped in, "There was nothing I could do. The wound was too deep and I couldn't stop the bleeding."

There was guilt in the woman's eyes and he doubted she believed she'd done everything she could have. *That doesn't make her a suspect*, he thought. "Where's Franklin now?"

"Down the east wing. Francesca needed some help."

"With what?" Chase continued to write.

"The doc's screams disturbed a lot of the patients."

"What, did you guys forget to pass out meds before you dashed off to the broom closet?" As soon as he said it, he regretted it. Not because he was concerned with getting into a brawl, but because he betrayed his training.

Julia looked away.

"Hey, man!" Lamont stepped forward, stepping right up to Chase.

Chase unsnapped the strap holding his gun in its holster. "Back off."

Lamont pursed his lips, obviously thinking over his next course of action.

Julia grabbed his arm and pulled herself close to him. "Lamont . . . no."

The man's shoulders relaxed. "Look, man, no one told us what he was up to. The doc acted on his own. Everybody here has their routine. It's not our fault."

"Fine, I'm sorry for my outburst. This all just seems like it could have been avoided," Chase said, dropping his hand to his side. "I need you to help Franklin secure the patients and get him back here."

"A'right."

"Julia, I need you to go wait for the homicide detective and bring him back here when he arrives."

"Okay," she said and started to go.

"Before you go, where's the doctor's office?"

She pointed behind Chase. "Down that corridor, take a right, second door on the left."

"Thank you," he said. She and Lamont left.

Chase was tacking the caution tape across the door to the padded cell when his radio blared. "Sixteen-twenty do you copy?"

He pressed the red button on his radio. "Go ahead, dispatch."

"There's an accident on 14 with two lanes down. Homicide is stuck in the middle of it and will be there as soon as possible. Do you require backup in the meantime?"

"No, but you may as well call in the coroner. Get him over here."

"Copy. Over."

Seems every other day there's an accident on that highway, Chase thought as he walked down the corridors to Dr. Ebby's office.

With a silver plaque reading Dr. Wayne Ebby there was no mistaking Chase stood before the right door. The door was closed, but unlocked; he walked in. *Impressive*, he thought as he looked around. Framed certificates and newspaper articles occupied every inch of wall space, and bookcases from the floor to the ceiling were stocked with textbooks and plaques. Everything had a place except for a few pages of paper sitting by themselves in the center of the kidney-shaped mahogany desk.

Chase moved toward it, snatched up the bundle, and read:

> *If you're reading this, than I have made a grave error. One, hopefully, you can ensure never happens again. By now you should already know who I am and what I do, but I'll err on the side of caution.*
>
> *My name is Wayne Ebby, the leading psychiatrist at the North Floridian Mental Health Institution. I have aided Federal agents on high-class cases, been consulted by fledgling psychiatrists to the stars, and have published widely on all forms of psychosis. I am the best there is. And, unfortunately, you reading this now proves my ego was my downfall.*

Shaun Robbins came into my care twenty-three days ago suffering from paranoid delusions. He was found squatting beside the body of a young woman, naked and covered in her blood. The first officers that arrived on the scene reported he had been chewing on a sizable chunk of the girl's thigh, and defended his kill, growling and snarling as they approached.

Needless to say he was arrested on sight. It took two taser shots to bring him down. When he awoke in his cell they say he bounced around in an animalistic frenzy and didn't settle down until dawn. He was brought here to deem whether or not he was competent to stand trial. The District Attorney's office believed the man's rantings of being a werewolf were nothing but a farce to elude a prison sentence. It was left for me to decide before wasting taxpayers' money.

At first, Shaun was reluctant to talk to me. His demeanor was rational and non-violent. A far cry from the murderer the papers made him out to be. He showed no signs of remorse. That worried me. That is a classic sign of a serial killer who has been doing this for quite some time and grown desensitized to the act of murder. I implored the DA to have someone reevaluate recent unsolved crimes when Shaun finally confirmed my suspicion that he had in fact murdered many others. As of yet, the DA has not. I am aware of three human victims, but there is no way of knowing if Shaun withheld information.

Shaun's reluctance came as no surprise to me. It was natural behavior. Many before him cracked under my strong will and he, too, eventually succumbed. In the days leading up to him opening up to me, I studied the numerous myths and legends revolving around Lycanthropy. The Argentina and Brazilian belief of the seventh consecutive son being transformed into a werewolf on their thirteenth birthday; Norse mythology where one can become any animal one desires just by wearing the creature's skin; the Russian belief of a ritual *and incantation followed with stabbing a tree with a copper knife to invite the spirit of the wolf into one's being; bewitching, pacts with the devil, and surviving a werewolf attack are also commonplace in many societies. However, none of these came remotely close to what Shaun confessed to me, and that is why I dismissed the notion out-of-hand.*

As a child, Shaun's older brother teased him. He used the boy's fear of spiders against him and twisted that fear with lies and exaggerations. Shaun was made to believe that if one was bitten by a wolf spider, a common sight here in Florida, than he or she would be cursed as a werewolf.

I know it sounds absurd and silly, but one must not criticize. One should rise above the mockery and see the phobia for what it is and try to correct it. The wolf spider was given its name because of the class the spider belongs to, Lycosidae, which comes from a Greek word meaning "wolf," and not because of some concocted curse. At least that's what I believe and told Shaun on numerous occasions without success.

Despite his older brother's teasing, Shaun grew to be a responsible, fully functioning, law abiding citizen up until five months ago when he was bitten on the hand by a wolf spider. Now, all spiders have venom, but this particular spider's venom does not pose a threat to humans and it is not hallucinogenic. In the days that followed the bite, Shaun noticed several changes happening to him. He claims to have had an increase in appetite, that hair was starting to grow longer and thicker all over his body, and he could smell things deeper than he ever could before.

These are all things that could be classified as a trick of the mind.

However, I really didn't understand what he meant by "smelling deeper." I just nodded my head and let him know I was listening without judging. In that same session he described, in great detail, his first kill.

How, on the first full moon after being bitten, he caught the intoxicating scent of a deer. The thrill of the hunt called to him and awoke something primal within. As he approached, the doe was alerted to his presence from a snapping twig. She bolted off, her prints showing a terrified gait. He pursued her through the everglades, the scent of her fear urging him on. The doe's neck was covered in a white, slimy foam from its slobber as he chased her further and deeper into the marsh. She slipped in a puddle of murky water and he capitalized on the opportunity with a leap. He knocked her to the ground and sank his teeth into her neck, simultaneously snapping the bone with his bare hands. He gorged on the tender venison, then with his belly full, howled in delight.

How a man, crouched on all fours, can match the speed of a deer, I'll never know. Of course I was skeptical, but I did not show this to him, and thus he began to trust in me and told me of the human victims during the following cycles. Unfortunately, he did not know their names. These were complete strangers who mistakenly crossed his path.

Over the next few days he allowed me to conduct experiments that ultimately proved he was criminally insane. I locked him in a room with a couple of obstacles and the lights out. He bumped and stumbled around as you and I would in the dark. He had no heightened senses, no super strength, and no superior healing.

He assured me that if there was a full moon, the results would be entirely different. So in the name of science, I agreed to reevaluate him and hold off turning in my report.

I was curious. Shaun obviously believed he was a werewolf so strongly that I wondered if his mind could manifest the traits of the wolf during the full moon. I could not simply write it off, as the details he gave were just too accurate. Even the world's greatest writers could not dream of this level of minute particulars.

No. Shaun's mind witnessed these feats one way or another. And a paper this pertinent would secure my place in the annals of history. It would be my crowning achievement.

He has been moved to a padded cell with a live video feed to my office. You should be able to witness the events for yourself and submit the tape as evidence. I will be locking myself in there with him in the hopes that I will be able to talk to him—or hypnotize him, if need be—out of the supposed transformation should it occur.

The staff is aware of the situation and will be monitoring us. Hopefully, they will put their personal opinions of me aside and do their job for a change.

The sun is going down.

Time to put the irrational mind to the test and hope there is a tomorrow.

Chase's gaze left the letter and fixated on the television monitor in the corner of the room. "This is too weird," he said. He turned around and made sure the door was closed. *I probably should just wait for homicide . . . but this could be my chance to shine.*

He pulled the high-back leather chair behind the desk over to the monitor, sat, and hit rewind on the digital feed. In reverse the image was distorted but he could see Julia administering CPR while the orderlies beat Shaun down, then them leaving the room and a struggle between the doctor and his patient, then calm.

Chase hit play.

Both the doctor and Shaun sat crossed-legged on the floor. Shaun's lips moved and the doctor responded. Suddenly, Shaun stood and walked to the window.

Wish this thing had audio. Make my job easier. What's he looking at? There's no moon out there.

Shaun turned around; his mouth twisted in what Chase could only assume was a snarl. The doctor stood, his lips moved. Shaun leapt. The doctor dropped his notepad and threw a wild right. Shaun blocked it and grappled the doctor to the floor. The two struggled for the upper hand. With a knee to the groin, Shaun fell off the doctor. He quickly got to his feet and ran to the door. The doctor pounded on the steel door with both fists and it appeared he was screaming for help, but no one came.

With his back turned to his assailant, Shaun pounced on him and bit into his shoulder. The doctor spun around and slammed Shaun into the wall, but the padding rendered the blow ineffective. Shaun braced his feet against the wall, kicked off, and sent them back to the ground. The doctor's head slammed into the floor. Shaun grabbed him by the shoulders and flipped him over. He leaned in close and clamped his mouth around the doctor's throat, and with a pull, the man's flesh ripped away. Arteries stretched and snapped. A delightful look adorned Shaun's face as he chewed his prize. Blood pooled around the doctor as his arms and legs ceased moving.

The door burst open and Lamont and Franklin, Chase assumed, entered the room. They immediately tackled Shaun to the floor; Julia came dashing in with the straitjacket.

Chase stopped the video and hit rewind.

Had they been at the door like they were supposed to, they would have been able to save him.

He looked to the letter again and knew Shaun was too dangerous to allow to live. The court would appoint some scumbag defense attorney looking to make a name for himself and push for an insanity plea, and undoubtedly win.

The door to the office opened and Lamont stepped inside followed by another black man. Chase shook with a start.

"Figured you were still here," said Lamont. "This is Franklin."

Without a word, Chase offered the doctor's final thoughts to Lamont. The man looked at him, brow wrinkled in bewilderment.

Chase crossed his arms in front of his chest. "Read it."

"What is it, man?" Franklin asked as he looked over Lamont's shoulder.

"It would seem you were all made aware of the doctor's intentions."

"Look . . . we, ah . . ."

"Save it. Let me tell you how this is going to go down. You'll be arrested for involuntary manslaughter. Best case scenario, you lose your jobs. Worst case scenario, you face jail time. However, this doesn't have to leave this room. What happened here cannot happen again. Is there any way you can get Julia over here?"

"Yeah, I can page her on the intercom."

"Do it. We all need to get our story straight before the homicide detective arrives."

Lamont picked up the phone on the desk and dialed one-five-zero, then his voice came over the intercom, "Julia please come to Ebby's office."

It was only a minute or two before she appeared in the doorway. "What is it?"

"I know the truth, but I'm willing to work out a deal. I don't ever want that lunatic on my streets again, so I propose we all tell the detective, when he arrives, the same story. We destroy the letter implementing all of you and I put a bullet in that man's chest. We all say it was self defense and we're all in the clear. Well?"

The three coworkers looked to each other, their faces showing nothing but confusion and mistrust.

Lamont broke the silence. "Is this some kind of entrapment?"

"No. It's on the up and up, but we have to decide now."

"Why are you willing to put your neck out for us?"

Lamont's eyes held suspicion and Chase couldn't blame him. What he was proposing was unorthodox to say the least. "Several years ago my niece was raped and murdered by a man who beat the system claiming God told him to punish the wicked. The psychiatrist assigned to him faced a jury panel and with great conviction convinced them that S.O.B. was rehabilitated. That level of insanity cannot be fixed. Much like how a pedophile cannot be cured. There's just something wired wrong in their brains. Believe me, I'll be taking just as much of a risk as you guys. We'll be in this together."

Lamont turned to his coworkers. "What do you think?"

"I don't want to be here with him. There's two more nights for the full moon," Julia said and Lamont put his hand on her shoulder. She turned into his embrace and he wrapped his arms around her.

"Franklin, you cool?"

"I've got four kids to feed. I can't lose this job. I don't even want to think about what would happen to them if I went to jail."

"Then it's settled?" Chase asked.

"Yeah, man."

"How are we going to claim self defense when he's in a straitjacket, though?" Julia asked.

"We just need to undo it enough. Besides, there's a tape with him killing the doctor fully secured."

She nodded in understanding.

"Speaking of tapes, is there a video feed in Shaun's new room?"

"No," Franklin said. "That was his original cell, so it will make perfect sense as to why we moved him there."

"All right." Chase clapped his hands together. Never would he have imagined himself getting excited over killing a perp, but too many times he'd seen criminals walk and he looked forward to making sure it didn't happen this time. The doctor had asked for help in case he failed and Chase planned to honor that request.

"Let's do this," Lamont said as he let Julia go.

As a group they exited the office and went to Shaun's padded cell. Franklin unlocked the door. Chase stepped in, hand on the butt of his pistol. The drugs were obviously wearing off as Shaun was sitting up. As Chase stepped closer, a low growl warned him not to take another step.

He withdrew his gun and took aim.

A buzzer rang in the hallways.

"The front door," Julia said, a hint of panic in her voice.

"Hurry up," Lamont ordered. "Take the shot."

We'll see if you're a werewolf the old-fashioned way. With a bullet not made of silver. I'll be watching you. Chase fired. A crimson flower blossomed over Shaun's heart and his body slumped over.

"Julia, let the detective in. Lamont, loosen those bindings. And no one volunteer any information."

"Do you think he'll stay dead?" Franklin asked.

Chase holstered his weapon. "We'll find out tonight." He stepped out of the padded room and went to greet the detective. He walked down the hall and as he turned down another corridor, a scream echoed off the sterile walls.

Lamont! He ran back to the padded cell to find the black man on his back, eyes wide with terror, and Shaun nowhere to be seen. He drew his weapon and stepped into the room.

"Lamont are you—" Chase swallowed hard when he saw the man's throat torn out. *That cunning son-of-a . . . he played possum*, he thought, eying the straitjacket lying on the floor.

The sound of a nearby door slamming caused him to suddenly turn. He stared down the hallway and saw small droplets of blood on the floor. *Was my aim off? Did I miss his heart or is he really a werewolf?*

"What's going on here?"

Chase turned to see the detective, dressed in a navy-blue suit and flashing his badge.

"We have a suspect on the loose," he answered.

"Then we need to secure the building," said the detective.

"On it!" Chase ran down the hallway where he had heard the door slam and came to a stairwell. He checked to see if it was clear through the small window, then kicked the door open. With his gun held out in front of him, he entered the stairwell and heard the thundering of footsteps on the metallic stairs.

"Don't do this, Shaun," he said, aiming his gun down between the rails.

Shaun continued to make his way down the stairs. Chase knew he wouldn't be able to catch him and after seeing what he had, he wasn't sure he wanted to.

In turning around the bend, Shaun's head became exposed and Chase took note. He aimed his gun for the next, and final bend and when Shaun came in range, he fired. The bullet struck its mark. A splash of crimson painted the wall behind him as Shaun's body slumped to the floor.

Chase hustled down the stairwell, all the while praying to a God he never acknowledged, but feared he may have been mistaken. For if he was to believe in the existence of monsters, than who was he to deny the existence of an omnipotent being?

When he reached Shaun's body, a door on an upper floor to the stairwell opened.

"Everyone all right?"

"Suspect's subdued," Chase replied to who he hoped was the detective.

"I'm coming down."

"Hurry."

Chase looked down at Shaun's body, unable to see his face in his slouched position. He put his boot to his chest and forced him over. Glossed-over eyes stared back at him. The first bullet was higher into Shaun's shoulder than Chase had suspected.

What a relief, he thought.

"Good work, officer," said the detective as he approached.

"Thank you," he said. "Let's hope he stays down this time."

THE WOLF MAIDEN

IN THE SHADOWS of the Apalachicola forest, a lone female wolf stalked the Everglades. Her tail was straight and parallel to the ground as she searched for food to build her strength, the future of her unborn pups dependent only on her since losing her mate to a passing car. She needed to feed and feed well to produce enough milk.

She failed to find fish or an otter in the sawgrass marsh and now had her sights set on a deer. A buck and two does grazed under a hardwood hammock. Even with her extra weight she was certain she could take one of them down, but she would need to get closer.

Mindful of her steps, and with the skill of a veteran, she inched her way toward the unsuspecting prey. When she was within reach, she leapt out of the underbrush and latched onto one of the doe's hindquarters. The other two deer bolted. Try as it might, the doe could not escape the wolf's powerful jaws.

The wolf wrestled the doe to the ground, clawing at its midsection and spilling the doe's intestines. She released her bite and quickly clamped her jaws onto the doe's neck; with a twist and a pull, the deer's neck snapped.

She ate her full of the meat and dragged the rest of the carcass closer to her den so as not to leave her newborn pups for any longer than absolutely necessary when they were born. Intuitively, she dragged some fallen canopy leaves over to the deer and covered her kill from the sight of hovering vultures, then entered her den for the night. With her belly full, she was ready to usher her pups into the world. She lay down and curled herself into a ball, then drifted off to sleep.

Sometime in the night she awoke to excruciating pain in her abdomen and wetness in her fur. A deep, greenish black fluid decorated her snow-white coat. Something was wrong; she could sense it.

Relaxing her muscles the best she could, she braced herself to deliver her litter. Her breathing heavy, she licked her vulva and pushed the first pup out then immediately went to work on the amniotic sack, licking and tearing the membrane so that her pup may breathe.

Dark fluid splashed as the membrane broke. She licked her newborn pup to stimulate its breathing . . . but it didn't respond. She listened for a heartbeat, but failed to find one.

Saddened, she pushed again, readying herself for another pup to come out.

This was to be her first litter, but instinct told her it should not have been this difficult. There was no movement inside her to help the birthing process.

She pushed harder.

Another pup emerged followed by two more. She tore the amniotic sack off one and quickly went to work on the next. She eyed each pup, searching for any sign of life. The two pups just lay there with no movement at all. The sight of the lost opportunity ached to her very core. All she wanted was a family. Though she was exhausted, she could not bear to see her pups, nor did she have the heart to discard them from her den. This would have been their home and now it would be their tomb.

Defeated, she stood up and exited her den, alone again. Tilting her head up toward the full moon she howled her song of tragedy and despair. She waited for a reply from her brethren, but none came.

With nothing left for her in the Everglades, she moved on, trekking through the underbrush and heading toward the hard earth where her mate had been taken away. Though she had longed for the birth of her pups, now she would have loved to still be carrying the extra weight. The night was alive with an orchestra of insects, the hoot of an owl, and the frolicking of woodland creatures, and yet she felt alone.

What did she have to live for?

Four pups stillborn. Was there something wrong with her?

As the night dragged on she reached civilization. The hard earth smelled of a mix of burnt rubber and decay. Mutilated corpses lay scattered across the tarmac, victims of an encroaching population.

With a nasal sigh she pressed forward, crossing the hard earth in search of anything to keep her company. The houses were few and far between with no movement around them in the midnight hours.

A shout followed by a scream broke the silence. Curious, she darted to the right. Another shout, this one closer, confirmed she was heading in the right direction. A light emanated from a window of a nearby house and she approached it with stealth.

Rearing up on her hind legs, she peeked in.

"Are you happy now? You woke the baby."

"Ignore her, she'll go back to sleep."

"And you'll wake her when you start in on me again. You're only lowering your voice now 'cause you feel guilty."

"Woman . . . shut up! Where are you going?"

"To check on her."

"I said ignore her. If you keep going in there when she cries, we'll never get a full night's sleep."

"I can't do that. She'll cry herself hoarse."

The man got out of his recliner and stormed toward the woman. He grabbed her arm, spun her around and slapped her so hard she fell to the floor.

"You will do it!"

The wolf dropped to all fours and walked toward where she heard the crying. The window was open, allowing in the cool night air. She backed up a few steps then leapt inside. Carefully, she approached a white bassinet in the center of the room.

Inside the bassinet lay a little baby girl. Her eyes shut tight, tears streaming down her face, her cheeks red. Her mouth was wide as she cried.

The wolf heard the woman in the other room get to her feet. The wolf gently placed her right front paw on the bassinet and rocked it. After five rocks, the crying ceased.

"I told you she would stop. Now let's go to bed."

The footsteps grew faint as they walked away from the baby's room. With a sigh of relief, the wolf peered into the bassinet and found herself staring into the baby's bright blue eyes. The baby cooed and blew a bubble with its saliva. The wolf's loneliness lifted.

She finally tasted motherhood and she wanted more. Desired it. Craved it.

As she continued to rock, the baby drifted off to sleep. Not wanting to leave this angel with that fearsome man, the wolf lay beside the bassinet and guarded her until the sound of footsteps woke her. The baby stirred and she wanted to rock her again, but the footsteps drew closer. She ducked out the window and listened.

"Momma's here. You hungry?"

The woman lifted the baby from the bassinet, cradled her in her arms, and exposed her breast. How the wolf longed to feel the soft suction against her nipples. To be needed like only a mother could be.

Once the baby had her fill, she was placed back in the bassinet and left alone once more. The wolf jumped through the open window and reclaimed her spot on the floor beside the bassinet.

When dawn finally came, the footsteps returned. The wolf took one last look at the sleeping baby, then bolted for the open window. As the door to the baby's room opened, she ducked down in a nearby bush and watched.

The baby's mother walked to the bassinet, checked on her, then walked back out of the room. The man paced by one of the other windows. The wolf could not help herself and a low, guttural growl escaped, but it seemed to go unheard.

"Is my breakfast ready yet?"

"In a minute. I was just checking on the baby."

"You have all day to do that. I on the other hand have to be at work in an hour to support your sorry ass."

"Isn't your daughter worth a few minutes?"

"Don't give me that crap. She's not fussin' so why disturb her?"

"You'd think you'd be just a little concerned considering how quiet she's been. She could have died in the night for all you know."

"Don't you dare talk like that. You want another slap?"

With the man's voice growing louder with his rising anger, the baby woke screaming.

"See what you did? Now your breakfast will have to wait."

"I'll get her. You watch my eggs. And don't you dare overcook that bacon. You know I like it fatty."

"You be careful picking her up."

"Woman, don't tell me what to do. I know how to handle my own kid."

The wolf pulled back its ears, straightened its tail and crouched, ready to pounce at one false move. She watched intently as the man picked up the baby and carried her out of the room. Time seemed to slow as the baby passed out of sight between windows. She was still crying at the same pitch, so it was safe to assume the man was not causing any more distress—nor bringing any comfort.

Returning to the room, the man handed the baby over to her mother and sat down at the table. She placed a plate before him, then gently bounced the baby in her arms. The crying stopped and the wolf was relieved.

The wolf longingly watched the little angel, wishing it was she who consoled it. How she wished she could have carried the child off last night and raise her as her own, but the wild was no place for a human baby. Her instinct told her that much. For now she would settle for being a silent guardian.

Once the man was finished eating, he left the house without kissing his baby or the woman goodbye.

Watching the broken family, it was easy to tell the woman cared for the child, and the wolf could not understand how the woman could take such a chance of the man attacking the defenseless infant. Regardless, she was there now. She had purpose. A reason to live and nothing would take that away from her.

She curled herself into a ball under the azalea bush to rest up for the coming night.

The sound of a car door slamming awoke her. Night had fallen, but in the darkness she could see the man clearly. She watched him storm up to the front door and slam it shut behind him. The baby began to scream.

As she approached the window, she heard the man already ripping in to the woman.

"Where's my dinner?"

"Did you have to slam the door? Look what you did."

"Shut up before I slam you. Is it too much to ask for my dinner after coming home from a bad day at work?"

"There's two minutes left on the timer, which you didn't know before you slammed that friggin' door!"

"Don't you raise your voice with me. And shut that baby up!"

"How dare you?"

The woman reached for the baby, but before she could pick her up from the highchair, the man shoved the woman into the stove. The woman's back hit the edge; her arms reached back to steady herself, but she couldn't see where to direct them and ended up putting her hand into the uncovered saucepan. She screamed as she yanked her hand out. The pan slid off the stove and spilled boiling contents onto the floor.

The baby's screams intensified.

"Clean that up!"

The rage in the woman's eyes was evident. With disregard, she grabbed the pan's handle with her uninjured hand and swung it upward. The man leaned back and the hot iron passed by inches from his face.

"Bitch!"

He backhanded the woman and she slipped in the mess on the floor. The back of her head hit the edge of the counter and the wolf heard the familiar sound of bone snapping. The woman's body fell to the floor.

"Hey, get up! Stop fooling around. Michelle?"

The man knelt beside the woman and appeared to have realized what he had done.

Seeing the man coldly eye his screaming daughter, the wolf leapt through the glass and landed inside the room. Glass stuck in her hide, blood matted her fur, but with only one thing on her mind she pushed the pain aside.

"Grrrrr."

"Where the hell did you come from?"

She maneuvered toward the baby, trying to put herself between her and the madman.

"You're not getting my daughter."

The man turned and pulled a knife out of a wooden block on the counter, but the wolf dashed forward and clamped her jaws onto his wrist as he turned back around. He screamed and grabbed the knife out of his hand with the other while she pulled and ripped at his flesh. Before he could cut into her hide with his uninjured hand, she released her grip and jumped back, mindful of the baby.

"Is that all you got?"

She crouched, ready to attack, snarling as her fur bristled. She was ready to protect the baby with her own life, ready to die a mother.

The man lunged forward with the knife out before him. She jumped to the left and clamped her barred teeth into his hand. He screamed and dropped the knife. She released her bite and stood upright, slamming her front paws into his chest and knocking him over the woman's body.

Wasting no time, the wolf lunged for the man's throat. Blood filled her mouth as her long, pointed cuspids broke through skin and penetrated arteries. The man choked on the flowing blood before the wolf leaned back, ripping out his throat. The body convulsed, then lay still.

The wolf turned toward the screaming baby. She wanted to tell the child it was all right, that she was safe now; wanted to pick her up and lie down and lay the baby on her paws—be her mother. But she was ill equipped.

A sudden burst of heat radiated from within the wolf's chest. Her fur shimmered a hot blinding light. Her ears tucked back and her tail recoiled between her legs. The light filled her vision, then faded.

"What happened?" she asked, quickly putting her hand to her mouth as she could not believe she had spoken. As she did, she saw bare skin and five fingers rather than a furred paw.

She grabbed the metallic toaster off the counter and studied her facial features. She looked identical to the baby's mother except for her golden-yellow eyes.

"It can't be," she said, looking down at the floor where the baby's mother had been moments before. *Our desire to be the best mother possible united us in spirit*, she thought. *It's the only explanation outside of a higher power.* She looked to the heavens and mouthed "Thank you," just in case.

The baby stopped screaming and looked at her with curious wonderment. She reached for the child as the baby extended its arms toward her.

She picked her up and cradled her to her naked bosom and it felt like heaven.

"No need to worry any more. Mamma's here."

THE GUARDIAN

Crouched behind one of the few intact tombstones of Jefferson County's cemetery, Adam Corne followed the movement of his prey. It stopped and looked toward the crescent moon. He had learned the hard way which legends were true, and the cycle of the moon had no bearing on the wolf. With the creature in his sights, he fired. The bullet penetrated its hide, but slightly off target. It howled in pain and collapsed to the ground.

Gotta be fast, he thought. *Can't believe I missed the heart. A mistake like that could cost me my life.*

He reloaded his shotgun as he ran toward the fallen beast. From this distance he saw the transformation was reversing, but the werewolf was still alive. An oversight he aimed to rectify.

By the time he reached his prey it was in its human disguise. The bullet hole in the center of her cleavage was no longer bleeding, the healing flesh pushing the silver bullet out of the wound.

My first female. I'd think her beautiful if I didn't know she was a monster. No . . . snap out of it. She's already healing.

"You're making a mistake." The woman coughed blood onto her bare breasts.

She's stalling. He aimed his double-barrel shotgun at her heart. "The only mistake I made was not adjusting for the wind." He pulled the trigger, leaving a crater in her chest.

The moonlight refracted off the mushroomed backside of the silver bullet wedged in her heart. He pulled two more silver bullets out of his pocket, reloaded and waited for a moment with unblinking eyes.

It's done. He looked around. *Not the strangest place I've found your kind in.*

Since the loss of his daughter, Adam had hunted the supernatural beasts. There was nowhere he wasn't willing to travel. From the dilapidated church in New Mexico and the abandoned coalmine in Texas to this Wisconsin cemetery, no place was safe for the creatures.

They'll all pay.

A twig snapped in the distance and he whirled around, shotgun at the ready.

Another one? "Who's out there?"

No reply.

He waited for a moment; his eyes scanned the forest's edge. There was no sign of a threat, but there was the faint scent of sulfur in the air. *It's nothing. Just a woodland animal is all.*

Lowering the shotgun, he left the woman's carcass to rot, and walked back to his van. His wife had always pestered him to sell the customized Chevy, afraid it made "hooking up" too easy. As if he'd ever cheat on his beloved. Now with it being the only thing he had left in this world, he was grateful he never gave in. It was his home away from home.

I'm sorry, honey. I'd give anything to hear your nagging voice once more. I would. Maybe I should go see you, but it breaks my heart every time.

Once inside, he caught sight of himself in the rearview mirror. He tilted it upward, disgusted by the dark circles under his eyes, his chubby cheeks, and scruffy beard.

No time to keep up appearances.

He opened his glove compartment and pulled out his journal and pen. He struck a check mark through the Wisconsin section and flipped through the pages.

If there aren't any strong leads, I'll go see Betty. That's what I'll do.

He kept all his notes on werewolves inside the leather-bound book. The free Internet and old newspapers stashed away at local libraries provided him with valuable information like the names of people who claimed to have seen a werewolf, with dates and times of recorded sightings and their locations. The book was divided into forty-eight sections, one for each state in the mainland.

He thumbed through the information and focused on one section. *Looks like Georgia wins out. Next time, Betty.*

In the last ten years Talbot County had three sightings and numerous reports of slaughtered sheep from local farmers. Though he knew the sheep could rationally be explained by roaming wolves, there was a recent report of a farmer shooting such a creature in the hand. That alone wasn't enough, but added with another from a medical examiner of a man who was found naked and unconscious on the side of the road with a missing hand picked up by a Good Samaritan, and Adam had enough to warrant an investigation. The report stated the man brought the John Doe to the ER and that he later disappeared after the wound was cauterized and put in a recovery room.

Could be a waste of time. Even if it is a werewolf, it could be long gone by now. Still . . .

The engine roared to life. He put the gear in reverse and backed down the gravel road that led to the cemetery. Once there was room for him to turn around, he made a three-point turn and headed for the interstate.

As he made his way toward Georgia, sleep beckoned him. He needed a distraction. The van was the only vehicle on the road at 2:00 A.M., reminding him of where he should be right now—bed. The window was down and the radio blasted, but despite his efforts, the yawns came on more frequently.

I'd kill for a cigarette right now. Guess I'll have to pull over. I'll never make it.

He drove for a little longer, hoping for a rest area. He hadn't come across a sign indicating one and was about to pull over when he saw the side road leading to a brick building.

My lucky day. Either the sign's down or I briefly nodded off.

Happy he made it, he parked the van close to the building under the lights. He got out to use the facilities and upon seeing the vending machines in front of the building, his stomach growled.

"All right," he said, "I suppose we can have a snack before bed."

The vending machines offered coffee, soda, and a wide variety of junk food. Since making the choice to live on the road his diet consisted of high fructose corn syrup, ungodly amounts of sodium, and carcinogens. The only thing he cared about these days was revenge. With his wife in a fear-induced catatonic state, he had no one to impress and relied on the saturated fats and sugars to push his body to the limits. Time was of the essence and took priority. If his body broke down afterward because of the crappy diet, so be it. Too many trails had gone cold on him and he'd do whatever it took to slay the beast that stole his wife from him.

After relieving himself he grabbed some cream-filled pastries and a bottle of water, then locked himself inside the van. He ate. With his hunger appeased, he crawled under the blanket on the bed in the back and closed his eyes.

I should at least call her. See if there's any change.

Feeling guilty, he fished out his cell phone and selected the nursing home she'd been transferred to.

An attendant answered on the third ring. "Forest Hills Nursing Facility, how may I help you?"

"Hello. I'm calling to check on my wife, Betty Corne. Has there been any change?"

"No, sir. I'm afraid there's been no change."

"She's still just sitting there staring out into nothing?"

"Yes, sir. All we can do is keep her comfortable."

"Does the doctor have anything new to say?"

"No. Without knowing the catalyst that put your wife into such a shock, there's little he can do."

"All right. Thank you for your time."

"Sir, if I may. If you were here every day by her side, her chances would be much better."

"Well, I thank you for your candor, but I'm doing exactly what she needs. Good night."

He hung up the phone and tossed it to the edge of the bed, then laid his head on his pillow. The doctor had thought if he could recreate the fear that put her into shock it may snap her out of it. But after every kill, the beasts transformed, and capturing a live one was too great a risk for him, his wife, and the nursing staff.

Is the world even ready for the truth? Look how Betty reacted.

His thoughts lingered on the night that changed his life. It seemed like forever ago when he was just a civil engineer working for the State of New Jersey and taking his family on a summer camping trip. When he was a boy his grandfather had built the log cabin in Pennsylvania about a half hour's drive from the state line. He had visited that cabin at least twice a year each year of his life and had nothing but fond memories. Now it was the source of nightmares.

Betty and him were sitting on the floor by the fire, playing a game of Monopoly, when a scratch on the outside wall caused them to jump.

"What was that?" his wife asked.

"I don't know. Probably just an animal looking for some garbage."

They returned their attention to the game and as Betty rolled the die, another scratch startled them, this one going across the full length of the wall.

"I'll check it out."

"Daddy, don't go," Julia, their daughter, said.

"I'll be just a minute."

When he reached the door, it buckled off its hinges and crashed on him, pinning him from the waist down. On top of the door was the largest wolf he'd ever seen. It stepped closer then pressed its massive paws down on his chest, forcing his breath from his body. It lowered its head toward him; gooey saliva dripped from its fangs and splashed on his cheek. The beast was black as midnight save for the smoky-gray mane. He stared into its yellow eyes and saw nothing but hatred. The beast broke eye contact, raised its head and roared.

His wife moaned.

Adam didn't care about himself; he had already made peace with the fact he was going to die right here in this compromising position, but he needed to buy his girls time. He looked to his beloved wife and daughter. Betty stood there frozen with terror, her curly black hair now streaked with white. Julia had her by the arm, tugging on her and begging her to run with her.

"Run, sweetheart, run!" Adam screamed.

"I'm not leaving."

"You have to!"

His daughter obeyed and left her mother's side. She ran toward the back door and the beast gave chase. He tried to grab the beast's paw, but it proved too quick and his fingers pinched nothing but air. The monster ran passed his wife as if she wasn't even there.

"Leave her alone!"

With a grunt, he pushed the door off him, his legs racked with pain, but he muscled through it. Julia needed him to be strong. He grabbed the shotgun from over the mantle and followed the creature. Outside, his daughter's screams and the beast's snarls echoed in the night.

"Hold on, honey, I'm coming!"

He ran in the direction of the scream, but it was difficult to pinpoint her exact location. His heart thundered in his chest; his pulse raced.

Please, God, not my little girl. Why did it leave me and Betty alone?

He stopped for a moment. This deep into the woods everything looked the same. He listened. Everything was quiet. Too quiet.

"Julia! Julia!"

The silence was broken by the sound of teeth grinding on bone and wet, slurping sounds.

Adam shoved the memory back, not wanting to see the carnage that had befallen his little girl. Even months later, the image of his child disemboweled and partially eaten haunted him; he suspected it would until he breathed his last. He had failed to protect those most precious to him and the one responsible for slaughtering his daughter and sending his wife into limbo was still out there.

How many families has it destroyed? All because you let it get away.

He didn't understand why the beast left him and his wife alive to witness the brutality, and he secretly wished it had spared him this misery, this guilt, and doubt. One thing was for certain: he looked forward to torturing the information out of the animal. The trick would be to have enough silver on hand to prolong its agony, for as long as silver remained in the beasts' flesh they remained as their human counterpart.

Eventually his body gave in to fatigue and he drifted off to sleep thinking of happier times in the hopes of eluding the nightmares that plagued him.

His sleep was restless, but free of torment. When dawn broke, he climbed back into the driver's seat and carried on his way. He stopped only to grab a quick bite and to relieve himself.

He drove all day and well into the night before he reached the Georgia State line.

It's just a matter of driving through Harris and then I'll be in Talbot. Might as well keep going, he thought, then polished off his can of Red Bull.

His eyelids grew heavy as he continued to drive and in the midst of a yawn he caught sight of an object in his peripheral crossing the road in midair. The sight of the charred, humanoid figure floating in the air on large bat-like wings sent a jolt through his gut. Veins of orange pulsed across its naked body as if its blood was molten lava. Embers danced from the corners of the thing's eyes. Mesmerized by the mysterious creature, Adam's reaction time was off and the van drove straight into it. The smell of brimstone filled his nostrils as the body crashed into the windshield.

That smell . . . just like at the cemetery. I'm losing control.

The van swerved to the right and fell into the embankment. Adam's head slammed into the steering wheel and blood flowed from his busted forehead. Sparkles of light danced in his vision as unconsciousness threatened to take him. The creature's wings flapped feverishly as it tried to dislodge itself from the glass.

A snarl snapped Adam to attention, and in a blink of an eye a hairy beast lunged from the nearby woods and tackled the creature off the hood of the van. A severed leg dropped to the floor and turned to ash on impact.

He grabbed his shotgun and stepped out of the vehicle.

I should have known if werewolves existed, then other weird creatures did, too. What the heck am I up against?

An all too familiar sound broke the silence: the snarls and grunts of the beast as it tore into its prey. As he walked around the front of the van he carefully eyed the werewolf as its claws slashed and tore into the winged creature.

It's not the one I'm looking for, he thought as he raised the shotgun.

The winged creature's struggle ceased; its body turned to ash. Adam aimed the shotgun and fired. The wolf leapt to the side and the bullet lodged itself in the beast's hindquarter. Its body toppled over. He took two steps closer, gun leveled on the beast.

The brown fur receded and the top layer of skin bubbled and melted away, leaving a naked man sprawled across the pavement. Adam hesitated. The man's arm shielded his chest and with one bullet in the chamber, he couldn't afford the risk of missing.

Can't be certain I'd get penetration through the arm as well. And if I didn't, I don't think there's time enough to reload?

The man extended his other arm out toward the barrel of the gun. "Please."

I just need a clear shot, he thought. He could already see the bullet rising out of the man's thigh. *I'll wait until the transformation begins again, then pump another bullet in him to stop it. Hopefully, that'll buy me time enough to reload.*

"Why are you doing this?" the man asked.

What? How dare you. Before he could lay into the man for his audacity, he was grabbed by the shoulders and lifted into the air. *Another one?*

Smoke pierced his nostrils and his flesh roared with pain from the creature's fiery touch. He pointed his shotgun at the thing and fired. The creature bellowed as the bullet passed through its wing, but it showed no sign of slowing down.

A growl came followed by a deafening screech. Adam was released from the creature's grip. He plummeted to the ground and landed on his feet, but fell to his backside as his ankle twisted on impact. The winged creature was taken down by the werewolf he had shot.

I don't understand, he thought as he watched the werewolf rip into the charred flesh of the creature and eviscerate it. As the organs were hurled into the air, severed from the creature, they turned to ash and soon there was nothing left of the winged creature.

Crap!

He fumbled in his pocket for bullets as the werewolf turned and looked his way. The beast leaped into the air and snatched the shotgun with one of its clawed hands and shoved Adam back against the pavement with the other.

Déjà vu. He noticed, unlike the hand holding the gun, the one holding him down had no fur and the skin was black as if dead or necrotic. *That's a regenerated hand for sure. He's the one from the report, but why has he remained in this location? He's taken an awful risk.*

The beast stood, relieving the pressure on Adam's chest. With two hands on the shotgun, it broke it in half and tossed it aside. It looked to the heavens as it transformed back into a man.

Instead of killing me, it just takes away my gun. Doesn't it know I'll be back with a new one? He's toying with me, playing with his food. Well, I'll show him!

The man stood naked before him. He averted his eyes, uncomfortable with the proximity. His ankle already felt swollen and if he thought it could take his weight, he'd kick the crap out of this fool for not killing him when he had the chance.

"Why did you try to kill me?"

"Are you serious?" Adam asked, and the stern look he got in reply relayed that he was. "You're a monster. That's why."

"And what do you think that was that attacked you?"

"Another monster, just like you."

"You're an ignorant man. Those things are nothing like me. They are fallen angels. Demons. Just because I'm different from you doesn't make me a monster. I'm still human."

"That's just a front. I know exactly what you are and what you're capable of. Better just kill me now, 'cause I'll kill you the first chance I get."

The man's wrinkled brow relaxed as if he suddenly understood *all* of Adam's pain. "What have you witnessed?"

"The brutal death of my daughter at the hands of one of you. Monster!"

The man sighed. "You don't understand. Long ago, when Lucifer declared war on Heaven, angels from both sides fell to Earth in their struggle. The Dark Prince's minions quickly seized their opportunity and cut the wings off those who fought for His glory. Many angels lost their lives."

"Wait a minute," Adam said. "I thought God was all powerful, how could He let his angels be killed?"

Joel sighed. "Just because I believe in Him with absolute certainty, doesn't mean I have insight into how He thinks. Now, may I continue?"

Adam nodded and gave his full attention.

"When the Archangel Ariel fell, a female wolf stepped out of the forest to protect him. She fought valiantly without care for her own safety and when Ariel awoke, he healed the wolf's wounds and granted her immortality as a thank you.

"Seeing her resolve and ferociousness, when all was said and done and peace restored in Heaven, God asked her to guard the gate of Hell to keep its prisoners in place. She agreed.

"Lucifer feared her power and did the only thing he could: he gave her the ability to shape-shift into a woman, a creature whom he believed he could corrupt. She took on a human name, Elena, and when needed, she transformed into an even more powerful being. One possessing man and wolf's best traits. Lucifer took every opportunity to tempt Elena and failed each time, so he created more doorways than she could ever manage to protect."

"That's a beautiful fairytale, but how stupid do you think I am?"

"Then explain to me the hell spawn that *I* saved you from."

"Why did you save me?"

"Quite frankly, I have no idea. I'm sorry for your loss, I really am. Did you kill the rogue?"

"Not yet. But I've killed others that I've come upon."

"How many?"

"Three."

"Where?"

"Texas, New Mexico, and Wisconsin."

The man turned away from him, shaking his head. The moonlight refracted off his backside and Adam had to look away.

"I have some clothes in my van. Either kill me or get dressed."

The man narrowed his eyes. "If I wanted you dead, you'd be dead. I am a sworn protector, much like my brethren you maliciously killed. There are evil humans in the world, but we don't go around killing all of you, now, do we?"

Adam lowered his head. The words weighed heavy upon him. *He's right. That woman told me I was making a mistake and yet I didn't ask for an explanation. And I did smell sulfur. No . . . could it be?*

"Each one of us guards a doorway to Hell. There are four doorways presently unguarded now."

Adam immediately took offense, his guilt apparent. "I told you I only killed three."

"You're not accounting for the rogue. He obviously abandoned his post. Most likely tempted by the demons."

"Werewolves keep demons in line?"

"We stop demons from dragging the souls of the pure to the bowels of Hell. Some people believe Lucifer's power grows with every soul that winds up in Hell, but they're wrong. Only good souls that are trapped in Hell increase his power. They're unjustly locked away in the pit."

"Are they killed or kept alive?"

"I honestly don't know. There may be a chance of rescuing them before their souls are ripped from their fleshy binds."

How many innocents have they laid claim to because of me? "How many portals are there?"

"Nine. One for each circle of Hell."

"I assume it's too much to ask that they're all here in America."

"Yes it is. And now only one is left guarded."

I can't believe this. I thought I could handle anything. Yet, here I am trembling. No. I've hunted werewolves. I can hunt demons, too. "I want to help."

"You've done enough."

Adam fought the pain and stood. He balanced his weight as best he could to his left ankle. "I need to make this right. I can handle it."

"Let me tell you what you can handle: nothing."

"But I've—"

"What, killed werewolves? If my brethren hadn't been honoring their vow, never, and I mean never, could a mortal take them down."

"I almost had you. If that creature hadn't stopped me, you'd be dead."

"Your arrogance amazes me. You are no match for the wandering souls never mind the demons of Hell."

"Then make me like you." *Did I just say that?* "Is that even possible?"

The man scratched his chin, and then said, "It's possible. In his arrogance not only did Lucifer give her the ability to transform, but also a means to create an army for him. Through a bite, the power can be transferred, but the Dark Prince would never create a being more powerful than himself. Because of him, silver is deadly to us. A material known for its purity and abundance. Only Elena is immune, and truly immortal.

"It has been decades since we've needed to increase our numbers. The question is: are you worthy? We cannot afford another rogue. The world is not ready to handle the truth."

"Tell me about it. I learned that one the hard way, too."

"What exactly happened to your family?"

Adam filled him in, no longer concerned with the man's nakedness.

"That's terrible. And he was black with a gray mane?"

"Do you know him?"

"Yeah. Merik, one of our oldest."

"He cracked, then?"

"It would seem so. Again, I'm sorry. Your wife's reaction definitely proves my theory correct. It's one thing to see it on television, but quite another face-to-face."

"Please, give me the strength to hunt him down and to take his place."

"Wait," said the man as he sniffed the air. "Stupid!"

"Hey! Where are you going?" Adam asked. As the man ran off, he could see his muscles bubbling under his skin. *He's transforming, but why?*

Adam hobbled after him, shifting his weight with each step. He worked through the pain and moved as quickly as his bum ankle would allow him. It was difficult to keep up with the wolf, but the snarls and broken branches kept him in the right direction. Soon he came upon a crumbled stonewall and stopped.

It's like something out of medieval times, he thought as he stared at the remnants of an old village. The buildings were made of stone, ancient and blackened by a fire long extinguished. The roofs were partially covered with thatch, the holes either created by the fire, wind, or animals.

Sulfur. He turned his head side to side, but there was no sign of a demon or the werewolf.

"Where are you?" he asked as he climbed over the fallen stones.

A rustle in the nearby bush caused him to quickly turn to the right. The beast snarled as it leaped out from the underbrush. Its jaws clamped down on Adam's left hand. He screamed as the fangs went straight through his palm.

"ARGHH!" Adam shouted.

The bite released and he inspected the four holes. Blood ran down around his wrist, trailed his forearm and dripped to the ground from his elbow.

"You could have given me a warning," he growled as beast changed to a man.

"Just wanted to prove my point."

Oh whatever. He had to bite back tears. "I don't feel any different. Except for the throbbing pain."

"Give it time. Slowly you'll notice your senses heightening. Your skin will itch and no amount of scratching will relieve it. The first time you change it will be out of your control, but once you change back to a man, you will be able to change at will."

"Okay, that'll give me time to get the van fixed up. Tell me why you ran off?"

"Another demon tried escaping."

"Did you kill it?" he asked, then ripped his shirt to use as a bandage.

"Sorry to say, you can't kill a demon. Only send it back to Hell."

Adam wrapped his hand. "But I saw you rip the other two apart and they turned to ash. If you can kill an angel, then you can kill a demon. Aren't they supposedly of the same species?"

"Impressive. Are you a scholar?" he asked.

"No," Adam said.

"When the demons breach our world, they are not whole and so cannot truly be killed. A part of them is left in Hell for safekeeping. Think of what you've seen today as a shadow of their true selves. And total dismemberment is the only way to send them back. That's why we make the perfect guardians."

"I suppose. So what is this place?"

"It used to be my home. Unfortunately, man cannot live near the gateways. They're susceptible to influence. Here, the town leader set fire to each house in the middle of the night. My father got me out of the house in time, but he went back in to get my mother and neither of them came out.

"At the time, there was no guardian here. Some of the survivors tried to rebuild, but . . . when a guardian finally came, I was a man. Like you, I witnessed her push back a demon. She noticed my lack of fear in her presence and she explained what I have to you. I, too, volunteered to help and chose to stay here. It's my home again.

"The church in New Mexico has been deserted since a priest raped, tortured, and murdered the nuns in the nunnery. He was weak and fell to their influence. At the mine in Texas, a worker, consumed by greed, blasted the mine's entrance, sealing himself inside. A rescue crew found him eating his coworkers and the mine was closed. As for the cemetery in Wisconsin, well, people are simply scared to go there as they believe it to be haunted.

"Speaking of which, you should go back there. Perhaps make that your new home."

"I cannot do that until I've found and killed Merik. You were going to tell me where I could find him."

"No, I wasn't. I have no idea where he is. Vengeance should not be your priority right now."

"Look . . . . I don't even know your name."

"Joel. Joel Walsh."

"Okay, Joel, as I was about to say, Merik is out there destroying lives. As far as I'm concerned he's just as much of a threat as the demons."

"No, he's not. Yes, it's tragic that people are dying, but they're getting to go where they belong. There is more to life than this." Joel waved his hands in the air, gesturing to their surroundings. "The hereafter is what is important and there are innocent lives being denied that. Nothing is more important than reestablishing the guardians."

Adam processed Joel's words. Though he didn't want to admit it, he was right. "I'm assuming you meant this was the only portal left guarded, correct?"

"Yes."

"And if I killed three of the four here in the US, then that means Merik . . ."

"Merik was charged with protecting the portal in Great Britain. London. If he's here, he is far away from his duties and you have to come to terms with the fact that you may never find him."

No.

"Vengeance will not bring your daughter back."

"Fine! Then tell me why I should go to Wisconsin."

"Because with the cemetery there, we run the risk of the dead reanimating."

"Come again." Adam made peace with werewolves and demons, but zombies? The idea tingled the hairs on the back of his neck.

"Demons aren't the only things that try to escape Hell. The souls of the wicked attempt to break out as well. Fortunately, on their own they can't harm the living, but should they possess a corpse they become corporal."

"Are we talking flesh-eating ghouls like *Night of the Living Dead* here, or just some newly released inmates looking for a good time, who'll most likely scare the crap out of the populace?"

"Definitely the latter, though some may try to bring an innocent back to bargain with. But evil spirits in this world are rare. They have to get past the demons before crossing through the portal. And much like any prison system, the inmates are kept under scrutinizing eyes."

Adam breathed heavily through his nose, making a whooshing sound as he sighed.

"I understand your guilt, but there's no time for it. We need to get you back on the road."

"Why don't you come with me?"

"I can't leave my post. This is something you'll have to do on your own."

"How will I know who is worthy of becoming a guardian?"

"Use your instincts and hope for the best."

Adam caught a faint call for help. It was distant, but distinct. He turned his head to face the direction he heard it from.

"Ignore it," Joel said, surprising him.

"Why?"

"It's the tortured screams of the wicked coming from the portal. Your hearing is improving."

"Now that you mention it" —he flexed his ankle— "the pain's gone. Can you show me the portal? I'd like to know exactly what I'm dealing with."

"Sorry, but they're not visible. In order to know their exact location you'd either have to see a demon pass through one or use your keen sense of smell, which you don't have yet. I can take you to the spot, though. It's in that house." He pointed toward the house off to the left.

"What are we waiting for?" Adam walked over to the house and entered through a hole in the wall.

"Careful," Joel said, "you're getting too close."

"You're worrying too much. I know what—"

The world disappeared in a wall of fire. Heat like he had never known enveloped him; sweat formed and evaporated. Screams blasted him from every direction. His hands shot upward to cover his ears, but nothing could block the deafening sounds. He dropped to his knees; a trickle of blood ran from his nose. Something grabbed him from behind. He screamed, but was unable to defend himself, afraid that if he removed his hands his head would explode. He was pulled backward out of the pit.

"I tried to tell you. If you're serious about becoming a guardian you're going to have to keep your arrogance in check."

His heart pounded so hard and loud it thumped in his ears. "I'm-I'm sorry. I promise I'll do b-better."

"With your senses all out of whack you need to be more careful. Your body will be going through spikes as it learns to control them."

"I thought I was a goner. It felt as though my brain was pushing on the inside of my skull."

"Now that you've seen Hell, I think it's time you got going."

"Yeah, I agree. Though I'm sure the pit is my final destination, I know I deserve it, and I'm ready to give myself to protect the innocent."

"Glad to hear it. Let's get your van out of that ditch."

They walked back to the road and their combined strength was enough to push the van back onto the pavement. After a full inspection, Adam surmised the damage wasn't too bad. The radiator was intact and the tires remained fully inflated. He could drive with a broken windshield and a dented fender.

"Thank you for everything, Joel. Again, I'm sorry."

"Just make it right."

"I will. Goodbye."

Adam started the van and drove away. Joel remained at the edge of the road waving and watching. Slowly he drifted from sight. Considering he had been awake all night and hadn't had a single cup of coffee, Adam felt invigorated anyway. His reflexes were sharp as adrenaline pumped through his system.

I feel so alive.

He drove through the day and into the night, making even fewer stops than usual. His lack of an appetite disturbed him, but he blamed the changes his body was undergoing. Without eating there was no need to relieve himself so he kept trudging.

Oh! A sharp, stabbing pain hit him in the chest. His right hand instinctively left the steering wheel and pressed against the source. He looked down at his hand and saw the skin bubbling. *What the—*

He pulled the van over and ran into the wooded area. Nothing but darkness. He had seen this phenomenon enough to know the change was upon him and he'd be damned if he was going to risk losing his home during it. He ran as deep as he could before the pain crippled him. He feared a passerby or two would witness the change if he remained too close to the interstate. He went to work taking off his clothes. With few possessions in this world he couldn't afford them ripping to shreds.

On his knees, his body ignited in pain. Muscles bulged and rippled, skin stretched, bones twisted in impossible directions. Claws made from the sharpest bone lengthened as they sliced through flesh. His teeth fell from their roots as they gave way to powerful canines; he spit them out into his hairy hands.

The pain subsided and the transformation was complete.

With the eyes of the wolf he looked to the sky to see the new moon and howled a song of gratitude to the Lord above. He was given the means for redemption, to right the wrongs he had committed and if he was cunning enough, he'd have lifetimes to achieve it.

The woods were alive with life. He heard the distant breathing of a doe, the heartbeat of a squirrel nestled in the hollowed out trunk twenty yards away. Could smell the markings of a local wolf pack, the asphalt he left behind, and the water from a lake a half a mile away.

The call of the wild beckoned him and he answered. He charged into the night eager to put his new powers to the test.

* * * *

When dawn broke, Adam awoke at the edge of the lake, naked and cold. He looked over his body and noticed his muscles were more defined and fuller than before the change. The beginnings of a beer belly were gone and the stomach muscles were perfectly outlined.

This is amazing. I feel twenty again. Now . . . let's see if I can bring it on.

He cleared his mind of all other thoughts and concentrated on the change. He thought about the thrill of running wild and the wind kissing his fur; the power of the beast and its ferociousness.

Wolf out.

Nothing.

Aahwoo!

His thoughts turned to the demons breaking through to our world and taking that which did not belong to them. He thought about his daughter's body mangled and partially eaten.

The wolf called out to him.

The change came fast. His bones cracked and popped as they reshaped themselves. His teeth fell out, filling his mouth with blood as one-by-one, sharp canine teeth took their place while his jaw extended. A tidal wave rippled across his flesh, blanketing his body in fur. He sniffed the air in search of his clothes; he caught their scent and darted off. Within minutes he found his discarded clothing and concentrated on reversing the transformation. Calm and relaxed, the fur dropped away and his bones realigned themselves in order for him to stand upright. He got dressed and made his way toward the van.

Please let it be there. And please let it be in one piece.

The van was just where he left it and in the same condition. Once inside he checked his map. The cemetery was just sixty miles away, but he was suddenly hungry and decided to stop in town for a bite.

He pulled into a local diner; a classic joint disguised as a train car with '50s décor and gas pumps out front.

Two birds with one stone, he thought and shut off the van.

As he walked into the establishment, the patrons stopped their conversations and glanced his way. *Not one of us. Just like in* Invasion of the Body Snatchers. He half-laughed. Though the notion unnerved him, he ignored their piercing stares and sat himself in one of the booths as the sign at the door instructed.

Chatter filled the diner as the conversations continued. At first every voice bled into each other, an unintelligible cacophony, but with a little concentration he managed to single each one out and listen to the variety of topics. He learned Jackie Frink was loose with her morals; Thomas Porter was going to take the blue ribbon in the chili cook off; Daisy May had landed a boyfriend and that Patrick Torres was reported missing last night.

It didn't take them long to figure out this portal was unguarded, did it? He drowned out all other conversations and listened intently.

"Are you ready to order?"

Poor timing. "No, give me another minute, please."

"Okay, hun."

The middle-aged waitress walked away and Adam was able to return his attention to the conversation about the young boy.

"I seriously doubt he ran away. That boy has a good head on his shoulders. Too many doors were opening for him."

"I know it's a real shame. The world needs more teenagers like him."

"Don't I know it? I'd gladly trade both my boys for one like Patrick."

Adam sat there contemplating on whether he should eat or head out and see if it was too late to save the boy. He knew the chances were slim, but it was his fault.

I may be starving here, but it won't kill me.

He stood and walked out. He believed he could make better time in wolf form cutting through the woods so he left his van parked where it was. As a hunter he hated the fact the beasts chose such rural locations, the vast woods where he would have to search for them, but now that the roles were reversed, he was happy to have the cover. After undressing, he tucked his clothes into a pile of fallen foliage and thought about the pain of losing his daughter. The transformation was immediate. And painless.

As he charged through the woods, zigzagging around the ancient trees, the tiny woodland creatures foraging sought higher ground, the birds in the tree canopies scattered into the air, and deer bolted off into the opposite direction.

That's right, make way for the new king, he thought.

There was a faint odor of brimstone in the air and Adam used it as a guide to maneuver through the dense forest. In no time, he found the wrought iron fence that surrounded the perimeter of the cemetery. In the daytime he could see the vines overtaking the metal, the weeds creeping across the walkways, and the crumbling tombstones.

It's a shame no one takes care of this place anymore. Seems you've all been forgotten. Perhaps as guardian I can bring this place back up to par. Wait . . .

He looked around and saw no sign of the woman he murdered.

Someone's been here. Maybe the demons dragged her carcass to Hell to show the others the portal is unguarded. Well, they're in for a surprise.

He sniffed the air.

Over there.

As he stepped to his right a hand burst through the earth and latched onto his front paw.

What the—

Another hand grabbed hold of him, and then a rotting head broke through the ground. Dirt fell off the sickly-green flesh; maggots writhed inside the rotting skin.

There's no time for this.

Adam stared into the dead gaze of the rotting corpse and without wasting any more time; he clamped his powerful jaws onto the head and severed it in a single bite. The hands released their hold and flailed wildly before going limp on the ground. He crushed the head in his maw and spit out the rotten meat, then continued on his way.

The scent emanated from a mausoleum. He leaped over three tombstones that stood between him and his destination. The gate dangled off its upper hinge; he ripped it off the rest of the way as he knew he wouldn't fit through the opening it created. Inside, the smell of death overwhelmed him. He looked from left to the right, but saw no obvious sign of the portal only the massive concrete coffin in the center of the crypt.

Remember, you simply walked through the last portal without knowing it. Leave no corner unexplored.

As he walked around, a grinding sound broke the silence as stone rubbed against stone.

Now what?

His eyes fixated on the darkness of the crack forming as the lid moved across the coffin, but he could see nothing until a skeletal hand grabbed the edge. With its new leverage, the lid moved quicker and spilled off the top. A loud thud echoed throughout the chamber when it hit the floor.

The decomposed body sat up. Only patches of dried skin and shrunken muscle remained on the old bones. The hair, long and gray, barely clung to the barren skull. The eye sockets were vacant save for an abandoned spider web, and a thin layer of cobwebs covered the corpse's brown suit. It reached out for Adam and he swatted the hand away, severing it at the wrist.

Decapitating worked before, he thought, *or did I merely release the soul that possessed the body?*

The creature swung a leg over the top of the cement coffin and Adam leaped and pounced on the zombie. The momentum knocked the creature out of the coffin and instead of slamming the zombie against the concrete floor, the zombie was pinned to blackish-red rock.

Brimstone! We passed through the portal.

A screech filled the air and Adam took his attention off the creature under his paws and looked around. A demon fast approached, this one different than the two he had seen in Georgia. Its skin was blackened like the others, but it had four additional arms protruding from its sides and what appeared to be liquid lava for hair. The sight of its sunken and shriveled breasts repulsed him. He had thought all angels and demons were male, then realized demons were masters of deceit and the form before him was most likely a ruse. Then he remembered what Joel had said.

If each portal leads to a different circle of Hell, then it's quite possible each circle has different inhabitants.

He stood and grabbed hold of the zombie by the midsection then lifted it over his head and tossed it at the female demon. She stopped her advancement and caught the zombie with her lowest set of arms. The other four immediately went to work on pulling the creature apart, stripping the soul of its newfound flesh. Bones lay at her feet as the escaped soul was ripped from the carcass and dragged back into the bowels of Hell.

Guess she figures my being here isn't a threat. Big mistake.

Without a clue as to where the boy might have been taken, he figured the direction the demon was headed was as good as any, so he followed it at a safe distance. As he walked in the blistering heat, his mouth hung open and his tongue dangled off to the side.

I can't believe it. I'm panting. So thirsty…

The deeper he went, the narrower the path became and the hotter the temperature. His paws burned and healed. The pain was a constant distraction. Molten lava threatened to swallow the path at any moment, but he pressed on without fear until he came to a fork in the road.

Great. Which way?

He stopped and peered down each path. He listened for a sound. His pointed ear lobe tingled as he strained.

"Get away from me!"

The voice came from the left passage and he bolted toward the voice.

Patrick?

"I don't belong here. I've done nothing wrong."

The voice was louder. He was getting close.

Hang on, kid. I'm coming.

Adam turned with the bend in the path and saw a teenage boy running toward him, a winged demon hovering above him, taunting him.

"Oh no!" the boy said as he skidded to a halt.

The demon bellowed and flew past the boy, its sights locked on Adam. It descended toward him, its talons extended, ready to tear into his hide. He roared and leapt into the air ready to meet the threat head on.

Their bodies collided and the werewolf's strength proved to be too much. All of his weight crashed down on the winged beast as its body slammed against the rock. Instantly his claws and teeth tore into the demon's body; its flesh tasted burnt and bitter, but his attack was relentless. Arms and legs were severed at their joints followed by the creature's head. The werewolf walked away from the quivering mass of limbs and slowly approached the boy.

"Stay away from me!"

Adam reversed the transformation and stood before him.

"Dude," the boy said as he raised his arm to eye level.

Adam knew exactly what was wrong. He remembered how uncomfortable Joel's nakedness had made him. "No time for modesty. We have to get you out of here."

"I'm not going anywhere with you. You're a monster."

"But I just . . . ungrateful . . . never mind." Adam pointed behind the boy. "Just run that way as fast as you can, Patrick, and bear to the right when—"

"How did you know my name?"

"Lucky guess. Just know that I'm a friend and I came here to help. You don't belong here."

"This is Hell, isn't it?"

"Yes. I just need to check something," he said, extending his right hand toward Patrick's neck.

Patrick pulled back.

"I just want to check for a pulse. Make sure you're alive."

"All right." He leaned forward.

Adam felt an erratic thumping under the kid's sweaty flesh. *So they don't kill their victims . . . at least not right away. There's still hope for anyone else they've taken.*

"Could you please tell me what's going on?"

"There's no time for explanations. There are others—"

His ears tingled as he heard a wet movement behind him. He turned around and saw the demon's limbs reaching toward each other. Veins snaked their way toward each other from the wounds and when latched on, they reconnected and dragged the severed limb back into place.

In Hell, they're indestructible. He turned to Patrick. "Run!"

Before the creature's regeneration was complete, Adam transformed into the wolf and pounced. He severed each limb once more and tossed the body parts in different directions.

That should take you awhile to put yourself back together.
"AHH!"
I'm coming, Patrick.
He ran on all fours. The boy hadn't gotten far before he was attacked by two more demons. He was crouched into a ball as the demons circled above him. They swooped down and scratched at his back, but did not try to lift him up and carry him away. Patrick screamed each time a talon tore at his back and shoulders.

These creatures are so arrogant. They toy with their prey a little too much.

Adam dug down and put on the speed. As he ran by he swiped a claw at one of the demons, severing it in half at the waist. The torso still hovered in the air as its legs fell to the ground.

The creatures screeched, no doubt calling for help, as Adam circled back. He jumped and swiped at the flying torso and the creature's head and chest joined the rest of its body on the ground. The other latched onto his shoulders and lifted him in the air. The wolf grabbed the legs and yanked with all its might. A pop echoed in his ear as the legs were pulled from their sockets.

The winged creature bellowed in pain and remained hovering above. Adam landed on his feet, dropped the legs, and jumped straight into the air. He drove his claws into the chest muscles of the demon and pulled it to the ground. Once it was dismembered, he barked at Patrick. The boy's shaky form turned in his direction. He signaled for the boy to follow with a nod of the head. He stood and obeyed.

Using the boy's own scent, which was rubbed into the rock floor when the demon dragged him, he escorted Patrick back to the portal. He hung back and waved the boy on. Once he passed through, Adam took a look back.

If they didn't kill him there could be others that need saving.

He passed through the portal, believing the boy's safety was more important than going back for potential survivors. He found Patrick waiting for him just outside the crypt.

I'm surprised he stuck around. Kid's got guts.

"I want to know what's going on, and I want to know now."

Like I thought: guts.

The transformation reversed and Patrick immediately let loose his questions.

"What was that place? Are you a werewolf? Is the world ending? How is all this possible?"

"Easy, kid. I'll answer your questions one at a time and to the best of my ability, but I don't think this is a safe place to do so."

"No place is safe. That thing snatched me from my bedroom. It came right in through my window."

"Fine, you have a point. That demon took you to Hell because you have a pure soul."

"Well that goes against every belief."

"I know. Let me explain."

Adam told the boy everything Joel had shared with him and his own role in the events.

"I want to help."

The boy's words shocked him. That was not the response Adam was expecting. He was bracing himself for the mockery, the finger pointing, and the shame.

"You have your whole life ahead of you. You can be anything you want."

"Good. 'Cause I want to be a guardian. There is no way I will sit around and watch this crap happen to my friends and family. This is the most important thing I could do."

He is pure and headstrong. My instincts tell me I can trust him, but am I condemning him to failure?

"I see the doubt in your eyes," Patrick said. "You don't think I'm strong enough, do you? Well, I broke free from that thing's grasp all on my own, and I was running back to the portal well before you showed up."

"True. But you're going to need more than physical strength to combat this evil. They will try to recruit you. Corrupt you."

"I understand, and I won't let them. I have too many loved ones here."

"And are you prepared to watch those loved ones grow old and die while you stay young and hidden in the shadows?"

Patrick lowered his head as he gave careful consideration to the notion.

"Better that than to live with the guilt of them being condemned for all eternity and knowing I could have done something," he finally said.

Couldn't have said it better myself. "Prepare yourself."

Adam transformed into the wolf and towered over the boy.

"I'm not afraid," Patrick said as the wolf's maw lowered toward him and clamped its teeth onto his shoulder.

He winced and turned his head the other way as the teeth penetrated skin and into the muscle. The wolf released the bite. Its long tongue reached the left edge of its jaw and circled the jaw line.

The blood . . .

It continued to clean the blood from its fur.

It likes it too much . . .

A low, guttural growl surprised Adam and Patrick.

No. You mustn't . . .

Patrick stepped back and the wolf stepped forward.

"This isn't funny," Patrick said.

I agree. Why does it feel like we are of two minds on this?

The wolf's lip trembled as it growled again. It stared at Patrick intently and Adam could sense its murderous thoughts.

Adam concentrated on reversing the transformation. He thought of happy times with his beloved wife and daughter; the nights he and Betty read Julia to sleep; bath time in the kitchen sink when she was so small and still had those baby-blue eyes. In that kindergarten play, Julia was the best tree in the forest.

It's working. The beast's blood lust subsided and the transformation reversed.

"Sorry about that," Adam said, standing there in the buff.

"What happened?"

"Guess I'm going to have to be more careful. The taste of blood almost put the beast in a frenzied state."

"Oh," Patrick said with a look of doubt.

"Don't worry. You shouldn't have the need to bestow someone else with this gift. I'm new to this myself. Joel showed no sign of losing control so it's safe to assume better control comes with experience."

"I hope you're right. There's no going back now."

"No . . . there isn't."

"What now?"

"Have there been any other missing persons reports lately that you know of?"

"No."

"Then I suggest we stay together and not chance going back in for more survivors. Do you have any idea where it was taking you?"

"None. It didn't say a thing."

"They are of few words, that's for sure. Once you've undergone the change, I'll move on to Texas and either take my post there or find someone worthy like you."

"You can't stay there without going to New Mexico. That portal cannot remain unguarded."

"I know. I agree. Maybe you should go back to town. People there are worried. This way, no one comes out into these woods looking for you."

"Good idea. You'll be okay by yourself?"

"Yeah."

"What about—"

Both Patrick and Adam looked downward at his nakedness and smiled.

"I should be able to find my clothes while you're gone. Then I'll come right back here."

"You don't think they'll try to break through while you're gone?"

"Not during the day . . . no."

"All right then, I'll be back as soon as I can."

"Good luck," Adam said. As Patrick ran toward home, Adam could already sense the change in the boy. He was running faster than any mortal man. *It was the right decision*, he thought.

Adam set out to find his clothes and to finally have the meal he was so looking forward to.

* * * *

"How did you make out?" Adam asked as Patrick appeared from the woods, pushing a tree branch aside. He carried a lantern and a backpack.

"I had to sneak away from my parents. They wouldn't let me out of their sight. I brought food and a change of clothes."

Smart kid. "Your parents' reaction is understandable. What did you tell them?"

"Half-truth. That some stranger took me from my room and dragged me into the woods."

"What about the cops? You didn't—"

"Relax. I know what you're thinking and they're not going to search these woods. I pointed them in the completely opposite direction. And I mentioned he was planning on moving on. They put all their men on searching the area."

"And why, exactly, did he take you?"

"I said he was a pedophile and that I escaped before he could touch me. Brilliant, right?"

"Not exactly. They'll never stop searching for a predator like that. Especially in this backwoods town."

Patrick's eyes grew wide. "Hey!"

"No offense."

"It's all right. Maybe you're right, though."

"I think you laid it on a little thick, but it's too late to worry about that now. How are you feeling?"

"Strong. I've never been the physical type. It's quite amazing really."

"Don't let it go to your head."

"No worries there. When will you be heading out?"

Adam put a hand on Patrick's shoulder. "I'm not leaving until you're confident enough."

"I feel pretty good. I'm torn, though."

"On what?"

"What if there are more people in that portal? You saved me, we can save them."

"I know how you feel . . . but we can't risk it. There's a good chance we can't save any of them. We have to accept that it's too late for them and we need to do everything we can to stop it from happening again."

Patrick hung his head.

"Promise me you won't go back when I leave."

The young man looked him in the eye. "I promise."

"Good. Now, no more talk of this. Let's talk about something else."

As the night progressed, Adam and Patrick's conversation ran the gamut from girls to sports and the powers of the wolf. Outside of the riveting campfire conversation the night was uneventful. The demons stayed in their prison and Patrick's transformation had yet to happen. The two managed to get a couple hours of sleep before daybreak and Adam awoke to the smell of bacon cooking on a griddle.

"Mornin'."

"What's this?" Adam asked as he sat up.

"Breakfast."

"Aren't you a regular Betty Crocker."

"I can toss yours aside if you want."

"No . . . no . . . I'm sorry," Adam said with a smile, realizing Patrick was teasing.

"The water's ready for coffee. Hope instant is all right."

Adam stood and stepped toward the kettle dangling over the campfire. "Better than nothing, right?"

"Absolutely."

"How do take yours?"

"One cream, two sugars."

The mugs were already placed out along with some small containers of liquid creamer and sugar packs. *Impressive*, Adam thought. *Kid's thought of everything.* "Where did you get this stuff? Did you steal it?"

"You can't steal what's free."

"True. Here you go." Adam offered the cup of coffee to Patrick and as he reached for it, Patrick's hand trembled. The hand smacked against the cup and knocked it out of Adam's grasp.

Realizing what was happening, Adam put down his mug and drove Patrick's seizing body to the ground, pinning him under his weight. There was no way to know if this was a simple seizure before the final transformation or if this was the real deal. All Adam could do was wait it out.

He suddenly felt hair tickle his palm. *This is it.*

Adam pulled his head away from Patrick's elongating maw. Being this close to the large canine teeth growing from his gums unnerved him, but he kept the pressure on the expanding arms.

The power is incredible.

When the transformation completed, a low growl emanated in Patrick's throat. Adam put all his strength into leaping off the beast. He thought about transforming himself as Patrick stood. The beast looked at him, then to his own clawed hands.

"Patrick?"

The beast looked at him, the wildness in its eyes replaced by ration and understanding.

"It's done, Patrick. Now try to reverse it. Think of happy things. Calm yourself."

The werewolf lowered its arms to its side and stood there, eyes closed. Before Adam could blink, the beast's hair fell to the ground, its muzzle receded and Patrick stood naked before him. The boy's hands shot downward to cover his unmentionables and a pinkish hue radiated in his cheeks.

Adam smiled and said, "Welcome to my world."

* * * *

Adam stuck around Jefferson County for the next two days. He had to make sure Patrick would be all right on his own and with no demon activity, he assumed Hell's prisoners caught on to the fact this was once again a stationed portal. The two exchanged cell phone numbers, said their goodbyes, and parted ways. Though he was racked with guilt for abandoning him, there was no other way. Their existence was one of solitary now.

As he planted himself in the driver's seat of his van he thought of his wife. He pulled the visor down and stared at the picture clipped behind it. There, cheek to cheek, his two leading ladies smiled back at him.

My beautiful angels. Man, I miss you both.

His daughter had her mother's dimples and looked so cute in her pigtails and that one missing front tooth. He dragged his index finger over her face. *You would have been a heartbreaker. I can't help but wonder what you would have grown up to be? I know you wanted to be a princess, and I'd like to think you are one in Heaven's Kingdom. Are you watching over my little girl, Lord?*

A tear ran down his face. He let it fall away and inserted the key in the ignition. The engine roared to life. He changed gears, then headed toward the interstate. His thoughts lingered on his wife and what the doctor had said to him.

Could it work? he thought. *Could I essentially scare her back into her right mind? Now that I know You exist, maybe You can make us whole again, Lord. That's not how it works though, is it?*

A whoosh of air escaped as he sighed heavily through his nose. The idea of revealing to Betty he had become what he had spent so much time and energy fighting frightened him. Fear of losing her over it tormented him. He didn't think his heart could handle the rejection, not from the one person in this world he deemed worthy of loving.

Still . . . even if she ends up hating me, it would be what's best for her. I think I'd rather have her hating me than wasting away in that facility.

He stopped at a red light and looked to the highway sign. An arrow pointed left for west and another pointed upward for the north interchange.

Texas or New Jersey? Left or straight?

The light changed to green and Adam drove straight ahead. *I have to try*, he thought. *It'll be a constant distraction otherwise.*

With the endurance of the wolf, he drove the twelve-hour trek with ease, and made only three stops. One was to shave and get a haircut; he didn't want Betty to see he had let himself go. When he arrived at Forest Hills there was only a half hour left for visiting time. He thought about waiting until morning, but then decided he'd have an easier go of it with the smaller night crew.

He parked the van and headed toward the lobby. The receptionist had her nose buried in a romance novel; the finely chiseled man on its cover gave him a brief sensation of inadequacy. The feeling passed and he cleared his throat to get her attention.

"May I help you?" she asked, not bothering to lift her gaze from the pages.

"I'd like to see my wife, Betty Corne."

"Visiting hours are almost up. Couldn't you have come earlier?"

"Perhaps," he said coldly, "but I'm here now."

The young woman flipped the book upside down and placed it on her desk. "Let me see if she's up for visitors."

"She's catatonic. I don't think she'll mind." He placed his palms on the desk, widened his eyes, pursed his lips, and tilted his head slightly to the right. "I just want to say goodnight and let her know I'll be back in the morning. Can I do that?"

The woman looked deep into his eyes, released a nasal sigh, and said, "All right. Go on up."

Gotta love the look. It never fails. "Thank you."

The elevator doors opened as soon as he pressed the up arrow. He stepped in and pressed the third floor button. As the doors closed he stared through the large windows in the lobby and caught the rustle of the nearby bushes.

Could be anything at this time of night, he reasoned and gave it no further thought. When the elevator stopped and its doors opened, a nurse greeted him.

"Nice of you to visit, even given the time. I'm sure she'll be happy to see you."

"Any change?"

"No. Go on in. I'll turn her bed down last to give you a few extra minutes."

"Thank you," he said, then walked down the hall. Betty's room was the fifth off the elevator.

When he entered the room, she was sitting in her wheelchair, staring out the window. There was no awareness of his presence and he felt his heart tighten as if a clawed hand had reached into his chest and squeezed. *Oh, Betty.*

He peeked out the door toward the nurses' station, then back the way he came and saw no one. He closed the door and slid the chair in front of it. The risk was too great to transform without a lock on the door.

"Honey, it's me," he whispered as he approached her. His hand shot toward his mouth to stifle a gasp as he caught sight of the drool threatening to run from the corner of her mouth. Her eyes were wide, but vacant.

Please let this work, he thought as he undressed. "Don't be afraid, Betty. I would never hurt you. The doctor thinks that if the shock that put you in this state could be recreated, you might snap out of it. I do this because I love you with every fiber of my being."

With his clothes piled on the floor he initiated the change. He concentrated on the image of his daughter in pieces in the woods; the one thing he had never wanted to see again was the one thing that brought on the necessary rage. As his body twisted, contorted, and reformed, his eyes were locked on his wife. Her body still refused to move, not a single flinch and there was no visible signs of comprehension until a single tear streamed down the left side of her face.

Betty? I'm sorry.

Glass shattered and a large figure tackled Adam to the ground. He was hoisted into the air and thrown against the nearby wall. Bones cracked on impact, his leg folded underneath him and twisted backward. He looked to see the freight-line truck that had taken him down with ease.

YOU!

Standing before Betty was the beast that put Adam's life on this downward spiral. There was no mistaking that black fur and ring of gray around its neck. It pounced on him, its claws slicing wildly and tearing into his flesh. He struck outward with a few of his own blows, but they were swatted away with ease. Pain surged through his body as muscle and flesh parted to the razor sharp claws of the beast.

Just as Adam felt unconsciousness beckoning him, the barrage stopped and the beast backed away. In the blink of an eye, the beast was a strapping, finely-chiseled man with dark features.

"You were doing so well. Why'd you have to switch sides? The master had high hopes for you. You were successful where so many of his children were not. But all good things must come to an end, and my master wants you out of the way."

Adam wasn't about to transform and enter idle chit-chat with this monster. He needed to heal so he could slay him. Already he could feel his flesh mending itself. *Just a little longer and it's round two.*

"Suppose you're wondering why you? Well, sorry to say, it's as simple as wrong place, wrong time. If you gave into temptation you'd discover children are the sweetest meat. And I must say . . . your daughter tasted oh so sweet. So innocent."

Shut up!

"Are you going to lay there beaten and broken, or are you going to stop me?" Merik transformed again, not a sign of pain on his face as he changed. He turned toward Betty and raised his clawed hand into the air.

NO!

Adam leaped toward his rival and grabbed a hold of the beast's forearm before it could drag its razor sharp claws through the flesh of Betty's face. The rogue werewolf's free hand arced upward and Adam pulled his head back; the clawed hand harmlessly passed by his face. There was a knock at the door, followed by a jiggle of the handle.

"What's going on in there? Mr. Corne, open the door."

Adam turned away from his enemy for only a second to make sure the chair held steadfast against the door. A sharp, piercing pain radiated at the base of his neck and he howled as a chunk of his flesh was ripped away. He turned back in time to see the creature chew and swallow the missing part of his hide.

Before Adam could retaliate, he was struck with a head butt. He released his hold on the creature's arm and instinctively brought his hand to his face. With his free hand Merik grabbed hold of Adam's groin and lifted him into the air. The door shook in its jamb as whoever was outside desperately tried to get in.

"Get security! Mr. Corne, open this door."

There's too many distractions, I'm losing this fight. Betty . . .

Adam was pulled down and slammed into the rogue wolf's knee. His spine cracked as it folded under the weight. He roared in pain before he was tossed out the open window. His body hit the ground and a soft whimper escaped.

Get up!

Try as he might, his body just would not—could not— obey. Every bone felt as if it was broken, every breath a chore to take.

Come on.

He extended his arm and plunged his claws into the earth and braced himself. As he managed to get his chest up and a knee under him, a massive force drove him back down, crushing his spine once more and reversing the little healing that had taken place in the short span.

A scream in the distance rang in his ear.

Betty? Did you pull out of it?

Teeth clamped down on the back of his neck.

Make it stop, he thought as overwhelming pressure continued to be applied. He could feel the teeth move under his skin. *This is it. I failed. Forgive me, Heavenly Father.*

A cold permeated his mind, followed by numbness. The world spun as his head tumbled away from his body.

His body lay just a few feet away. Blood pumped out and pooled around the shoulders. He felt the metamorphosis reverse in his face, then saw his body undergo the change.

The rogue wolf howled in triumph.

"What is that thing?" someone asked.

"Just shoot it!" another said.

Gunfire echoed in the air and the rogue dashed toward the surrounding woods.

Adam watched as two security guards approached his naked, headless body.

"Poor bastard."

"Yeah. Our first instinct was that he killed his wife."

Betty's dead? No.

"I know, right? He was killed by the same thing."

"Why'd that thing take his clothes though?"

"Beats me."

I'm not dead. He tried to blink at the guards, but they were no longer looking at him and he couldn't be certain if he had anyhow.

"What was it?"

"No clue."

Look out!

"Better call it in before—"

A clawed hand burst through the man's abdomen. Blood and intestines spilled to the ground. Adam watched the beast flank the two jibber-jabbing guards. He wanted to warn them, but without his nervous system, nothing responded. The other guard could only look on in horror as the beast pulled its arm free and his friend's body dropped to its knees, then slumped forward. In a flash, razor sharp claws peeled the skin off the man's face. The body fell backwards and convulsed before remaining still.

I'll see you dead. You took everything from me, Adam thought as the rogue wolf lowered its maw toward him.

The creature sniffed the air around him, then stepped away. Adam felt a tingling sensation in his neck. He didn't understand why he was still alive and had no clue if this was to be his future, his own personal prison. *Trapped inside my body just like Betty. What is that?*

Red tendrils stretched and slithered toward his body.

Could it be? He questioned as the tendrils elongated from his body's neckline. *Yes. Those are my veins.*

Guided by an unnatural force, the veins intertwined and fused together. The world moved in a blur as his head was dragged across the earth and pulled back in place. A few moments more, veins, muscles, ligaments and bones locked and intertwined, and he was whole. He stood. Not as man, but beast. The rogue wolf turned around as if sensing the danger and charged. With Adam's anger reaching its pinnacle, the healing completed in time for him to receive the beast's attack. Grabbing it by the shoulders, he leaned backward and drove his rear paws into its abdomen, his claws slicing into its flesh. Using the creature's own momentum he tossed it to the ground behind him and quickly spun around.

He swiped his claw and raked his nails across its neck. Blood bubbled from the wound as it struggled to breathe.

This is going to get us nowhere. I need my gun, he thought as he looked to his van. As he took a step in its direction, his enemy clamped onto his leg. *I'm getting tired of you biting me.*

He plunged his fingers into the beast's eyes, the soft tissue bursting juices on impact. It released its hold with a yelp. Adam placed one hand on the beast's upper jaw and one on the bottom, then pulled with all his might. Bones cracked and tendons popped as the top of the beast's head separated from his body.

How do you like it?

Adam cradled the severed head like a football and walked toward his van. He knew the more distance between the head and body the more time he had to retrieve the only means of putting this war to an end. He reversed the change as he came up on the driver's side of the van. If he was going to do this, he was going to do it as a father and husband, not a monster.

"You'll be my trophy," he said as he placed the head on the adjacent seat. The severed head's gaze followed his every move and Adam smiled. He reached behind his seat and retrieved his other shotgun. He checked the barrel: it was still loaded. "Be right back."

As he approached Merik's body, the feint sound of sirens reached his ears.

Gotta move fast. Those guards didn't get to call in what they really saw in Betty's room. They'll arrest me on sight. Can't believe I'm going to be blamed for my wife's death. Betty? He looked up toward her window and wondered what state the monster left her in. *Better not to think about it*, he thought.

Merik's body was still in wolf form and Adam couldn't help but wonder if age was a direct link to power. He hoped to find out for himself. He aimed the barrel at the creature's heart and with a little pressure on the trigger, a crater emerged, blood and chunks of hairy flesh erupted on impact. The body's transformation reversed and Adam knew then the job was done. He dashed back to his van and looked into Merik's green, dead eyes.

"May we meet again in Hell," he said, closing the door and starting the engine.

The sirens drew closer.

Texas and New Mexico are out of the question. They'll find me. Can't risk it. I'll have to call Patrick. It'll be up to him, though I'd hate to put that much responsibility on his shoulders. Perhaps Joel will help? I'll need to call him, too.

Swirling red and blue lights rose on the horizon in his rearview mirror.

Time to move. He revved the engine. "What's it like living in London?" he asked Merik as he put the shift into drive. "Fine, don't tell me. Guess I'll just have to find out for myself. I'll take your place as guardian and I will not be tempted. God is already disappointed with me and I will not fail Him again."

The only question is how to get there, by air or sea? By sea, the van can travel with me.

As he pulled out of the parking lot, he noticed several of the nurses on staff staring out the windows. They'd make his van for sure and he'd have to ditch it.

Air it is. Looks like you'll finally be getting your wish, Betty. Give my love to Julia.

DANCE OF THE WOLF

Steve Figura watched from a safe distance as Tony Paiva and his lackeys picked on an underclassman. The jocks shoved the boy around as if he was a hacky-sack. They laughed and giggled like little kids half their age as the boy, one-by-one, dropped his textbooks.

"Jerk-offs," he mumbled. *Just once I wish someone would kick their ass.* But no one ever did anything to help.

Though he knew he was being a hypocrite, he gathered his belongings into his backpack, stood, and walked toward first period. When he had stepped off the bus this morning he thought he'd forgotten his Algebra homework, but it was there, tucked safely in the book.

I can't wait to leave this place behind, he thought.

Graduation day was coming; two more weeks of high school then he'd leave Massachusetts behind and move to live with his father. With their prior planning, everything was in place. By the end of summer he would've had his Florida State driver's license for a year, allowing him in-state tuition rates.

No more cold winters. No more asthma attacks. Nothing but blue skies and sunshine coming my way.

"Hey, Steve!"

Here it comes, he thought.

The one event he had to get through before his life began to turn for the better was prom. Unfortunately, he didn't have a date and that meant he would have to make good on an old promise.

"I talked to your mother last night," Cathy said.

Oh great! "I haven't forgotten, and yes, I'm going to keep my promise. We'll go."

Cathy's face radiated as color filled her cheeks. A smile formed and Steve was taken aback.

"You're braces are off."

"I know, isn't it great? The timing couldn't be any better." A tear ran down the left side of her face. "I was so worried the pictures of the greatest night of our life would be ruined, but now . . . we're going to have a great time, I promise. My mom's picking me up after school to get a dress so you'll be riding home alone, sorry."

She's getting too excited. "Cathy, I don't want you to—"

"I know you don't want to be my boyfriend, and I'm not going to pressure you. Let's just have a good time like two best friends should, okay?"

He smiled. "Okay."

"Walk me to class?"

"Of course."

As they walked toward Mr. Murphy's class, Steve couldn't help but wonder why he had ever made such a stupid promise. He and Cathy grew up together, helped each other through their parents' respective divorces, but not once had he ever thought of her as anything more than a friend. *Best friend* was pushing it, though, and yet here he was making good on a three-year-old promise. Even without the braces, Cathy wasn't what he considered attractive.

Am I this desperate? Why do I even want to go to this stupid thing? I hate these people.

"Penny for your thoughts?" she said, interrupting him.

"I was just wondering why I even want to go to this stupid dance."

She rolled her eyes. "It's not stupid. It's a right of passage. Think of it as a reward for all our hard work. Besides, it's a party, and how many have you attended during your senior year?"

"None."

"Me, too. And everybody who's anybody will be there. The nerds and the jocks, the beautiful and the plain, we're all invited."

"Just because we're all invited doesn't mean it's going to be all kumbaya."

"What's wrong with you today?"

"I don't know. I just wish I could fast forward through these next two weeks."

"I know you want to get to Florida, but I was hoping we could at least enjoy this time together. I kind of took it as a sign you didn't ask any of the girls to go to the prom. As if you wanted to go with me, but were too afraid to ask."

Yeah right! "I've just been busy, and besides, I don't like anyone here."

"Except for me, right?"

"Ri-ght."

"You're such a kidder," she said.

"And what about you? I don't recall seeing you asking any boys out. Did you intentionally *not* have a date?"

"Maybe. Me asking you to promise to take me to the prom if neither of us had a date was my way of testing the waters. You know I like you—really like you—and I have something special to give you prom night."

What do you say to that?

"Don't worry, it's not a bunny boiling kind of crush." She kissed him on the cheek and entered their English classroom.

He stood there for a moment, shocked at Cathy's behavior. Maybe losing the braces had given her newfound confidence?

"What's the matter, never been kissed by a girl before?" Tony asked.

"Well, she may be a girl, but she's still a dog," Louie, Tony's right hand man, said.

"Like I care about your opinion on anything."

"Don't worry, man," Tony said, shoving his shoulder into Steve as he walked through the door, "the ugly ones always put out."

Louie followed like the dog he was. "Yeah, you can't beat a sure thing."

Steve narrowed his eyes at the two as they walked into the room and took their seats.

"Is there a problem, Mr. Figura?" Mr. Murphy asked.

"No, sir."

Steve took his seat and stole a glance at Cathy. She smiled in return.

Is that what she wants to give me? That would only complicate things. Yuck. A shiver ran through him.

Mr. Murphy placed his briefcase on his desk and began the day's lesson, but with only two weeks left of school he was lucky to have the attention of half the class. Steve's eyes were either focused on the clock or the neighboring window, not on the blackboard.

Later, with only ten minutes left of first period, Mr. Murphy said, "For your final assignment" —the class groaned— "I want you each to research and write a term paper on a myth or legend. It is up to you to find one that interests you. I won't force one on you."

I could write a killer paper on Dracula . . . but one of these lame-asses will probably do the same. Maybe werewolves?

"I expect ten pages double-spaced and an appendix detailing your sources. This assignment will constitute fifty percent of your grade. So for most of you, this is an opportunity to improve your overall grade."

Yeah right. Most of them are going to screw this up.

"These will be due on the final day of class. I know most of you still have preparations for prom to make, and final exams in other classes, but two weeks is more than enough time for this assignment. Any questions?"

No one responded.

"All right, then, enjoy the rest of your day."

With that, the bell rang and the class shuffled out. There was only six minutes between periods and Steve wasted no time getting to his next class. Though he knew it made him look geeky, he didn't understand why so few used a backpack.

So many of his classmen preferred to go to their lockers to switch out books between classes and most were late by a few minutes. As long as the teachers didn't complain, Steve knew that kind of behavior would continue. *Just wait till you try that in the real world, boys. Ain't gonna fly.*

The rest of the day was a blur. Steve's mind was preoccupied on which of his favorite myths he was going to research. He loved everything that fell within the realm of horror, from movies to comics, and this was a great opportunity to do a class project he was passionate about. He knew some of his favorite classic monsters were based on some truth like Dracula being inspired by Vlad Tepes and Elizabeth Bathory aiding the belief in vampirism. Though outside of Indian folklore, he didn't know what might've been the initial inspiration for the shape shifter and this intrigued him.

On the bus he sat alone, minding his own business and itching to get on the computer. Tony Paiva stood at the end of the bench with Louie looking over his shoulder.

"Move."

"Go find your own seat," he said, not bothering to look at the two punks.

"We want to sit together," Louie said. "It's easier for you to find another seat."

"That's cute. Bully someone else."

Tony crossed his arms. "If you don't get up now, I'll knock your teeth in."

Steve looked to the back of the bus. Since his was the second stop, it would be a pain to have to step over all the legs stretched out into the aisle and waste valuable time. "I don't think so."

Tony grabbed him by the collar.

"Knock it off!" the bus driver said. "Go find a seat."

"This isn't over," Tony mumbled, walking toward the back.

Louie gave him the bird and followed Tony.

Steve just shook his head. *What a bunch of jerks.*

Fifteen minutes later, the bus pulled up to Clancy Street and Steve got off and walked toward his house. When the bus pulled away, he realized it had lingered longer than usual and when he turned to check, Tony and Louie were running toward him.

No way I'll make it to the house and get the door closed in time, he thought, dropping his backpack. *This is going to hurt.*

He raised his fists, but Tony was showing no signs of stopping. He braced himself for the impact.

Tony lowered his head and took aim at Steve's midsection. Just as he was in range, Steve grabbed hold of Tony's waist and twisted his body, slamming him to the ground. Positioning himself on his knees, Steve managed to land a punch square on Tony's jaw.

As he raised his arm to deliver another blow, Louie grabbed him from behind.

"Coward!"

"Like I'm gonna let you beat him up."

"Hold him still," said Tony as he got to his feet.

Tony curled his right hand into a fist, brought it back and unleashed a punch into Steve's exposed stomach. He tried to hold his breath to help take the blow, but it was too strong. He gasped, and Louie released his hold and he fell to his knees.

"Get up!"

"What are you kids doing? I'm calling the cops!"

Thank you, Mrs. Langler.

"Let's get out of here," Louie said, then turned and ran.

"You got lucky this time." Tony kicked him in the midsection before running off.

At least there won't be any visible bruises, Steve thought.

Never could he have imagined being happy about his next-door neighbor's nosiness. She had a knack for squealing on him whenever the opportunity presented itself. He had been grounded for a month when Mrs. Langler called his mother to let her know he had climbed out of his bedroom window, shimmied down the lattice, and ran off. His mother had known immediately where he was going because he had begged and pleaded to go see *Death Puppet* and she refused.

When he arrived at the theater, twenty minutes before show time, an officer was waiting to take him home.

Though I learned to cover my tracks better, I still haven't seen that movie. And I've heard such good things, too. You old hag.

She watched him through the sheer drapes. He waved to her as he bent down to pick up his backpack. After he fished out his keys from his pants pocket, he walked to the front door. A quick glance over his shoulder told him she was still watching so he smiled and waved one last time before entering his house.

Once inside, he tossed his backpack on the sofa, turned on the television, then headed upstairs to his room. *I look forward to our chat, Mother*, he thought and smiled.

So many times she had complained vehemently for him to pick up after himself, to not waste electricity, and if he saw something that needed doing to get it done. He intentionally ignored those requests and drove her nuts.

He turned on the computer and when it was booted up, he began his research by entering "lycanthropy" in the search field. He found nothing he didn't know already, but then at the bottom of the page, under a hyper-link, he saw the words "lycanthropous flower".

If that's anything like it sounds . . .

He clicked the link and it took him to a website with the picture of a poorly rendered computer image of a werewolf, and the toughest readable font imaginable in yellow against a red background.

Eyes squinted, he struggled to read the information.

That's interesting, he thought.

The lycanthropous flower was found on the Balkan Mountains, which ran through the center of Bulgaria into eastern Serbia, and when worn during a full moon turn its wearer into a werewolf. *That's supposedly the Transylvanian region. How authentic.* He chuckled at the thought. *If only it were true.*

He hovered his mouse over another hyper-link, this one for purchasing. *If only. Wait . . .* The date of the prom had been circled on his calendar, and in the upper right hand corner, the days displayed the lunar cycle. *There's a full moon during prom. Interesting. Could be fun, even if it is a pipe dream. Let's see how much.*

The link opened an online shop in another window. The plant itself was fifteen dollars and thanks to the new flat rate priority postal boxes, shipping was an additional thirteen.

Let's see how much a corsage is going to cost me for Cathy.

He changed his search and scrolled through the various outlets, not finding one under forty bucks.

This is great. I'll be able to save some money on a corsage by making it myself with this flower and put a myth to the test for my report.

Going into his internet history, he brought up the online store selling the lycanthropous flowers and placed his order. Expected delivery was three days.

And Mom won't be able to nag when she sees the credit card report. Especially if I show her those corsages that were pushing the sixty dollar mark.

With a sense of accomplishment, he continued his research on werewolves. He didn't believe the myth to be real, but he was excited nonetheless. He failed to find any documented cases of the myth working, or any of the other means people believed in order to transform into a werewolf.

It's a cover-up, he thought with a smile.

"Steve!"

What's she doing here? He minimized the window on the screen and walked into the hallway.

"There you are, why's the TV on?" Cathy said as she bounded up the stairs. "Are you all right? Mrs. Langler told me what happened."

Of course she did. "Yes. I'm fine. Actually got a good shot in myself."

"Shouldn't have done that. He won't let it slide."

Steve crossed his arms in front of his chest, not believing what he heard. "What was I supposed to do, let him kick the crap out of me?"

"No, but—"

"Look, I already have a mother. One I don't get along with. I don't need another."

A tear threatened to fall. "I'm sorry."

"Me, too. I didn't mean to upset you."

"It's okay. I understand. I'll go."

He let her leave without saying another word. He wondered if he should feel bad, but decided she was the one who barged in and stuck her nose where it didn't belong.

Unfortunately, Cathy had been right. On his way to his locker, Tony caught him by surprise with a punch to his midsection. Winded, he collapsed to his knees and then was struck by a follow up right hook. His head was sent downward to the floor, but he managed to get his arms out to brace himself.

"Now we're even. If you ever disrespect me again . . . you're dead."

Steve looked up and even through his teary eyes he saw Tony's swollen lip.

"Don't even think about telling anyone," Louie said.

"The people on the bus are going to know," he said and received a kick in his midsection. His body rolled over and his back slammed against the linoleum.

"They'll keep their mouth shut, and so will you." Tony spat on him and then walked away without another word.

Steve said nothing as well, afraid of getting hit again. His ribs ached as he strained to stand. *You'll get yours, you coward.*

For the rest of the day, Steve kept to himself. There was swelling in his left cheek, but he managed to keep the bruising to a minimum by applying pressure to the area and with the aid of some Visine he kept in his pockets. *It gets the red out,* he joked.

On the bus, Tony and Louie eyed him as they passed, but he kept his gaze forward, not wanting to make eye contact. Cathy sat beside him and thankfully she too kept quiet. There was an awkward silence between them; Steve wasn't sure if he liked it or not. He had always thought her to be a jibber-jabber, but now something inside told him her voice could make it better. He went to ask her if she had any luck finding a dress, but he stopped short, afraid of confirming his instinct.

No. I cannot afford these feelings. With his hands in his lap, he said nothing for the duration of the ride.

Steve laid low for the next few days. He would never hear the end of it from his mother if she had to take prom and graduation pictures with him having a black eye. The bruise on his cheek was now a faint yellow and soon all traces of his scuffle with Tony would be a memory. He just had to keep it that way, though Tony and his lackeys made it difficult with their teasing from afar, but he ignored them and kept his eyes on the prize.

It better be there, he thought as he stepped off the bus.

"Are you going to tell me what you're waiting on?" Cathy asked as she tried to keep pace with him. "You've been racing to the mailbox every day once we get off the bus."

"It's a surprise, though it's taking longer than I thought it would. I would have sworn the order confirmation said three days."

She looked at him wide-eyed. "Who's it a surprise for?"

"Your look tells me you already know. Have you been talking to Mom again?"

"Maybe. She did tell me about an odd credit card purchase that showed up in her email."

"Not for nothing, but you two talk *way* too much. Getting double-teamed by his mother and—"

"And what?"

"His date . . . it's not something that appeals to a guy."

She wrinkled her brow.

"What?" he asked.

"You almost said it."

"I did not."

She smiled. "Admit it, I'm wearing you down."

"You seriously want to risk a sixteen-year friendship?"

"No, I don't. That's why I've been patient."

"I see."

"As far as your mother goes, what can I say, she wants us together."

"I know," Steve said, rolling his eyes. "She always says we're perfect for each other, how lucky I'd be to have a girl like you, how good you would be for me—I could go on and on, but I think you get the point. I'm tired of her butting into my life."

"She cares about you. You want her to be more like your absent father?"

Steve's nostrils flared. "That's too far."

"I'm sorry … I …"

"Forget it. He didn't leave me because he wanted to. You know that. He left for the same reason I will: there's no future here. I'll be damned if I'm going to work retail for the rest of my life. That's all that's left here. The few engineering jobs that are still here are all taken. It was either leave the state or be a dead-beat dad when the factory closed down 'cause he couldn't afford to pay child support."

"I know. I do, really."

"You should go," he said. He looked at his house. *Excellent. It's here.*

"All right," she said then darted across the street to her house.

He couldn't tell if she was crying or not, nor did he care at the moment. He had expected a sealed envelope with a compressed flower inside, but instead found a package on his doorstep. He picked up the box, unlocked the front door and went in. Once in his room, he opened the box to a pungent odor, one of rotting meat and old garbage. Inside was a potted flower and a note. An offensively white, sticky sap lined the box so he carefully removed the plant and placed it on his desk.

He unfolded the note. It read:

I'm not sure if you have ordered this because of some game or if you're serious about becoming one of us, but it really doesn't matter to me. I've done some checking on you and you're a smart kid worthy of the gift. It would be an honor to run wild with you.

Understand the flower is very powerful, but only during a full moon and at its freshest. If you're simply curious, then wear the flower during the next full moon and its effects will disappear once the flower is removed or dead, but if you wish to be a lycanthrope permanently, ingest the flower and embrace the call. If your will is strong you can overcome the beast's instincts and harness its true power.

Know this: there are many of us scattered across the globe. Perhaps one day we'll claim this world as our own, but for now we remain in the shadows and will not come to your aid if you expose yourself. Whatever your decision, welcome to the pack.

"He actually believes this will work," he said. "Is it possible?" *No, he's teasing. Has to be.*

He picked up the plant and inspected it; the odor was subtler. The flower was white with traces of a vibrant yellow. It was healthy and he would need to keep it as such for a few more days. He placed it on his window sill and left the room to fetch a glass of water for it. He returned and put the flower in the glass.

As the soil absorbed the water, Steve couldn't help but wonder if the man was telling the truth and what would happen to Cathy. Though he was still upset with her for implying he had a terrible father, he couldn't turn his back on their friendship.

Will she be a mindless beast? Will she recognize me? Will I get close enough to remove the flower? Am I wasting this on her?

He turned on the computer and contemplated emailing the man, but he thought better of it. Instead, he searched the Web for a different myth just in case.

How would it look if I turned in a paper detailing the myth that could potentially have killed my fellow classmates? No. I'll be ready for either outcome. And if it is real, I need to know how to use it to my advantage.

The idea of luring the beast to Tony and Louie crossed his mind, and in doing a little digging online he found wolves were attracted to carcasses and pheromones. Neither would help him on prom night.

* * * *

When prom finally came around, Steve's mother walked him across the street to pick up Cathy. She wanted to see Cathy in her dress and take pictures of the two, no matter how much it embarrassed him.

He looked up to the sky and took notice of the full moon. *Fingers crossed*, he thought, then rang the doorbell and the door immediately opened.

"Cathy?" Steve swallowed hard as he looked at the young woman he had failed to see. Her long brown hair was tied back and dangling in a ponytail, curled and full of body. The light purple dress complemented her rosy cheeks and emerald green eyes. The dress was low cut, her bosom tastefully rising over the edge.

"How do I look?"

"You look beautiful," his mother said.

"She was asking me, Mom," Steve said. "And I agree, you look . . . amazing."

Cathy smiled and blushed. As she stepped outside her parents came with her.

"Quickly, you two get together. Put your arm around her so I can take a picture," his mother said.

Steve did as instructed. "Hurry up, Mom."

"Where's my corsage?"

"I forgot it in the car, I'm sorry. We'll just do the pictures without it."

"Okay," she said.

Phew. That was close. I knew she'd ask about it, but I can't chance giving it to her now.

"Why did you put it in the car?" his mother asked.

"I'm sorry, but I've got a lot on my mind here. I made a tiny mistake, there's no harm."

"Come on, no arguing," Cathy said.

"You guys look great together," Cathy's step-mom said.

"Don't be getting any ideas about my daughter," her father said. "You bring her right home after prom."

"Daddy!"

"Don't worry, sir, I will."

Her father smiled and nodded.

"Are we done with the pictures?" Steve asked.

With her hands on her hips, his mother said, "What's wrong with you? Why can't you just grin and bear it for a few minutes. This is a once in a lifetime opportunity."

"He's right, Mrs. Figura," Cathy said, surprising Steve and his mother, "we have to get going. It's first come first served."

"All right," his mother said, sounding defeated. "Have a good time."

Out of character, Steve kissed his mom on the cheek.

Before he could pull away she whispered in his ear, "You look so handsome. Just like your father."

"Thank you," he said, then hugged her. "All right, enough of this. Let's go!"

Steve grabbed Cathy by the hand and pulled her away from their families. The parents waved with one hand and wiped tears away with the other.

"You couldn't rent a limousine?" she asked as he opened the door to his mother's Buick.

He smiled. "Sorry, they were all booked."

She smiled back. "Likely story."

Once she was in he closed the door and walked around to the other side.

"Is that my corsage?" she asked.

"Yes. Let's wait 'til we get to the hotel."

"Okay."

The prom was at the ballroom of the Radisson Hotel in Providence, a forty-five minute drive from Dartmouth.

"Are you excited?" she asked.

"Actually, I am. You do look fantastic."

"Thank you. Are you going to be able to keep your eyes off my cleavage long enough to get us there safely?"

A smile forced his way onto his face. "You noticed?"

"Yeah, but don't worry. I kind of like it. You've never looked at me like that before."

"You never wore girly clothes before."

"If I know you'll give me this kind of attention, I will from now on."

"Deal."

The rest of the ride was spent with trivial chatter. Steve didn't offer much to the conversation as his conscience tortured him. He was unsure if he should go through with his plan. His rational mind told him nothing was going to happen, that the two of them were going to have a great time, but his heart was telling him not to chance it in case something *did* happen.

When they arrived, Steve parked the car and before they even stepped out, Cathy inquired about the corsage.

She's not going to let this go. If it works, will it be instant or delayed?

"Well?" she said.

"Okay, don't get your panties in a bunch."

"No worries there, I'm not wearing any." She giggled.

Steve felt his jaw go slack.

"Speechless, huh? Come on, and don't stick me with that pin."

He opened the safety pin he attached to the cut flower, gently tugged her dress away from her skin, and pinned the flower to her just above the left breast. He could see she was holding her breath as he did, unsure if she was afraid of getting stabbed or if the deed aroused her.

"Uh!" she sighed.

"What's wrong?"

"My stomach . . ." Vomit erupted and splashed on the concrete at his feet. He managed to jump back in time. "My body . . . feels like it's on fire. What did you—"

The flower. Is it working? "Is there anything I can do?"

"I don't know. Something's really wrong. I . . . ." She jabbered the rest and Steve couldn't make out what she said.

Her dress stretched and tore as her torso enlarged. Steve watched with baited breath, making a mental note of every change, though he doubted he'd be able to turn in the report. Cathy's breasts flattened as hair sprouted from every follicle.

Bones snapped, fingernails and teeth lengthened, and arms and legs elongated until she towered over him. Her mouth enlarged to make room for her new teeth as her nose blackened.

A low guttural growl escaped the beast's lips, signaling the change was complete. A scream echoed from somewhere in the parking lot.

"What the heck is that?"

"Run!"

"We've got to warn the others."

"Cathy? Are you still in there?"

The beast grabbed him by the shoulders and lifted him off his feet.

"Holy crap! It's true."

Steve recognized the voice. It was Louie.

"Help me!" Steve said.

"I don't think so!"

Out of the corner of his eye he saw Louie high tailing it out of there.

As Steve was brought closer to the beast's maw, the wolf sniffed the air around him. It looked deep into his eyes and he wasted no time grabbing the flower still pinned to the dress barely clinging onto the creature's frame. It howled as the transformation reversed.

I don't believe it. This is so . . . so fantastic!

Cathy's half-naked body lay before him unconscious.

"I'm sorry," he whispered as he bent over and scooped her into his arms.

He looked around. No one was in sight. He put her into the backseat of the car. With the flower in his hand he contemplated eating it. When the beast picked him up he could feel its power and he desired it for his own.

Welcome to the pack. "Yes," he said before shoving the flower into his mouth. It tasted like curdled milk, the sap sticking to the roof of his mouth and tongue causing a *tat* sound as he chewed.

He swallowed hard and immediately felt the heat radiating in his body. He looked to his hands and watched the transformation. The sound of his tuxedo ripping filled his ears. All of his senses were triggered with stimulants, the smell of Cathy's perspiration arousing him. He looked through the car's window and with one exhale fogged up the glass.

Steve sensed a foreign presence inside his mind. An instinct he never had that seemed to guide the beast. He needed to tap into it to persuade the creature. The beast wanted to feed and Cathy was the closest meal.

A clawed hand reached toward the glass.

Not her.

It turned around and gazed at the hotel.

Our enemies are in there.

On all fours Steve scrambled toward the entrance. Screams filled the air as he leaped through the glass. Tiny lacerations on his hide from the broken shards healed as fast as they formed. The receptionist ducked down behind the check-in counter as if the wood could protect her from the beast's savagery. A security guard drew his weapon, but he was too slow to get off a shot. The beast ran its razor sharp claws through his skull and continued to run toward the ballroom as the lifeless body fell to the floor.

He approached the double arch top doors and Steve distinctly heard Louie's voice on the other side. He listened.

"I'm telling you. It was a werewolf!"

"Knock it off. If it was true, there'd be some kind of alarm, don't you think?"

Hearing Tony's voice enticed the beast's appetite and Steve felt this was not the time to show restraint. With all its might, the beast slammed its massive paws into the mahogany wood. The doors collapsed from their hinges and crashed inside.

The music was quickly overridden by screams. All eyes were on the beast, but what it desired stood before him trembling.

"I told you," Louie cried.

"I don't . . . I can't . . ." his voice trailed off as he watched the beast raise its claws over its head and then descend them downward, one claw for each of them.

The blow forced their legs to buckle and they fell to the floor. Skin and clothing parted on Tony and Louie's chest. The rest of Steve's classmates scurried to the back of the room in search of another exit. They toppled over each other; friendship was pushed aside as their own survival trumped all else.

Steve took a moment to observe the prom's decorations. The school's colors, blue and silver, were predominately on display in the streamers hung from the ceiling. Balloons were tacked to the walls and table clothes. Steve could feel a toothy grin stretch across its face as the thought of changing those colors to blood red crossed his mind.

"Please," Tony begged, blood spilling over his lips.

How I'd love to be able to tell you it's me, Steve thought as he lowered the beast's muzzle toward Tony's face. Their eyes locked for a brief moment, and then the beast opened wide and bit into Tony's skull. His legs and arms thrashed as teeth broke through the skin, then bone. When the brain was pierced, all functions ceased.

The beast lifted its head, ripping Tony's clean off. In its powerful jaws bone crunched and blood pooled. In a single gulp the beast swallowed the first of many human bits. Blood dripped from its maw, and its long tongue extended outward to lap at the blood-soaked fur.

"Go away! Shoo!" Louie pleaded.

Shoo? Steve laughed inside. *You idiot.*

The claw marks on Louie weren't as life threatening as Tony's as the runt had managed to take a step back. Steve thought how wonderful it would be to bury his muzzle into the cowering buffoon's abdomen and watch blood and sinew fly into the air as he burrowed deeper into his chest cavity, crack open his ribcage and chew the toughest muscle in his body—his heart.

The beast began its decent to carry out the thought.

Wait! He's the only one who saw me and the werewolf. If I kill him, I have no alibi. If I have no alibi, then neither does Cathy.

The wolf growled its displeasure.

I know what you want, and I can't blame you. I'm acquiring a liking to the coppery taste, too. Very well, though most of them don't deserve the same fate as Tony, I don't really have a choice. If this is going to be a partnership, then compromise is necessary. Take as many as you want, but leave him. Now, let's see if we can keep the graduation ceremony under an hour.

The wolf leapt into the air and Steve heard Louie thank God as he was passed over for more bigger and plumper meals. Screams of his classmates as they were ripped limb from limb became the only sound.

Steve had no remorse for their deaths and only one concern: *Guess I'm going to have to turn in the paper on some other monster or else blow my alibi. Maybe Mom will let me see* Death Puppet *if she knows it's for research?*

VOODOO MOON

Homicide detective Murphy Crane pushed his way through the growing crowd in the lobby of the Grand Victorian Hotel. Stepping out of the horde of reporters and angered guests not allowed to return to their rooms, he pulled back his lapel and revealed his badge to the uniformed officer. With the nod of his head, the man allowed him to cross the yellow caution tape and get in the elevator.

He breathed in deeply through his nose; the aroma of rum and tobacco lingered in the air. *I thought this hotel went tobacco free last year?* The elevator doors opened. He shrugged his shoulders and stepped off. A uniformed cop stood vigilante at the end of the hallway. Murphy watched the man's gaze travel over to him; he saved the man the trouble by showing his badge as he approached. "What do we have here?" he asked the beat cop standing in the doorway, though he already knew from the smell emanating from within the hotel room.

"Two bodies, sir. We suspect murder-suicide."

Murphy looked beyond the officer, but saw no other uniformed cop in the spacious living room. "We?"

"You passed my partner by the elevators downstairs."

"Oh, the one keeping the press at bay?"

"Yes. The hotel manager asked us to keep it as quiet as possible until we've got a handle on exactly what went down. Guess he's afraid it'll hurt his business in these hard economic times."

Murphy stepped into the room. "Of course he does. Tourism's down and people have their pick. Some of the finest hotels in Florida have practically given away rooms. However, the manager has no say on what we tell the press. Got it?"

"Yes. You want me to address them?"

"Not just yet. I'll entertain the manager so long as it suits me," Murphy answered and his train of thought derailed. *It smells like a drug deal gone bad.* His sensitive nose picked up a faint formaldehyde aroma. *Crack cocaine, maybe.* "You and your partner were the first on the scene?"

"Yes, sir."

"May I have your names?"

"Of course. Name's Johnson and my partner is Talbot."

"Any signs of drugs or money?"

"No, sir."

"What about forced entry?"

"No, sir."

Victim must have known his attacker then, or was expecting him. "What about witnesses?"

"None, sir. When back-up came we covered the floor and neighboring rooms to the stairwell below."

"Who called it in?"

"The maid, Robin Dearman. We have her in the adjoining room waiting to speak with you."

"Excellent work. How far into the room did she make it?"

"As you can see" —the officer pointed to the two bodies sprawled out on the floor just several feet away from them— "she didn't have to go in too far to realize what had transpired."

"Anyone else been in the room?"

"No, sir. The scene's ready for you to do your thing."

"Coroner?"

"On his way."

"Good work, officer. I'll take it from here."

"Thank you, sir."

Murphy withdrew a pair of surgical gloves and slapped them on. Then, taking his notepad out of his blazer pocket, he jotted down the time he arrived, the officers' names, and ID number. "Officer Johnson!"

"Sir?" the man said, still standing in the doorway.

"I need Talbot's ID number for my notes."

"Eleven-forty, sir."

"Thank you. I need you to document who's here, when they arrived, what they did, and when they left."

"You can count on me, sir."

Murphy returned his attention to the notepad, quickly scribbling every word the officer had said, then pulled his camera up to position. He focused on the two bodies and took shots of both together in the same frame and individually; knife wounds killed both men and there seemed to be no signs of a struggle, which only reinforced Murphy's suspicion.

From what he had gathered from the hotel manager before entering the building, the victim was Calvin Davis, a young black entrepreneur in town for the marketing conference, but Murphy's instincts told him that was just a front for his drug ring. Though there were no physical traces of product, Murphy's nose never lied.

And if the product was here, then there was a second perp.

It wasn't unheard of for a drug deal to go south. Usually it was someone new to the game, someone with dreams of grandeur, believing they could score the dope without paying for it.

He took several more photos; Calvin's tan shirt was covered in blood from the knife wound to the heart. His attacker still clung to the murder weapon, his throat slashed from ear to ear.

Takes an awful lot of will power to cut your own throat, Murphy thought, then kneeled down to shoot another photo before putting the camera away. His nostrils flared as he caught the strange scent of a mixture of fish and gunpowder. *Couldn't be? Could it?*

In all his years and travels he had seen the darker practice of voodoo decline and become near extinct. Yet, here he was, finding the subtle traces of black magic.

It's been nearly a hundred years since I've known anyone to practice it. Don't get ahead of yourself. We need more to go on.

"Almost finished with the scene?" asked a familiar voice.

Murphy stood and greeted Tony Baxter, one of Florida's leading forensics examiners. He offered his hand and Tony gladly shook it.

"So what have we got?" asked Tony.

"Too early to tell, but I think there's more here than what can be seen."

"You got a hunch, huh?"

Murphy smiled. "I need you to check for Tetrodotoxin in the alleged assailant's blood stream when you do your autopsy."

"You think he ate some bad sushi or something?"

"Or something," Murphy said.

From the hallway he heard the static discharge of Officer Johnson's radio. His ears tingled in anticipation.

"All units, report of one-eight-seven and possible two-O-seven on Citrus Trail. Closest unit please respond. Witness on scene claims to have seen a black man adorned in white face paint and wearing a white top hat. Officers approaching scene be on the lookout."

Homicide and possible abduction, Murphy thought and then wondered about the face paint and the cigar smoke in the elevator. Though he had thought it unlikely, it was too much of a coincidence. Someone was masquerading as a Bokor, the evil counter-part of the houngan voodoo priest. *I need confirmation.*

"What's wrong, Murphy?" Tony asked. "You look deep in thought. Is there something you're not sharing with me?"

"No. But I've got to go."

"What about the scene?"

"I know . . . I'm sorry, but could you wrap it up without me?"

"Yeah, man. Of course."

"Thank you," Murphy said, and started for the door.

"I'm not doing the paperwork," Tony called after him.

Murphy simply waved his hand to acknowledge hearing him.

As he passed Officer Johnson, the man held out his arm to stop him. "What about the maid who called it in?"

"Take her statement, will you?" He pulled out a business card from his wallet and offered it. "Call me if you need me. I'm heading to that one-eight-seven now."

"But . . . how'd you . . ." He took the card and asked no further questions.

Murphy made it outside without further delay and peered up at the moon illuminating the night sky. *Two more days*, he thought, then headed toward his car. For the life of him he could not understand what Haitian voodoo was doing in the Sunshine State, and why someone would have the gall to flaunt it.

Perhaps he's here for the same reason I am? Because outside of New York, it's one of the largest melding pots of culture.

Thirty years ago he had moved to Homestead, Florida, to be close to the Everglades, a region dedicated to preserving wildlife. A region where he could shed the façade of man, embrace the wolf within, and roam wild without the constant fear of killing an innocent.

Though he loved being a cop, he knew it wouldn't last much longer. Born a werewolf, he aged much slower than a man since his first transformation, and he was already dying streaks of gray in his hair to alleviate suspicion. Soon he would have to retire and possibly move on. He could collect a pension and remain in Florida for several years after retirement, but he had been the stay-at-home type before, and it didn't take long for cabin fever to set in. He was a social creature and craved interaction.

Being a cop redefined him, the only profession that appeased both of his personalities. The rewarding satisfaction of saving and protecting an innocent, the thrill of the hunt on the heels of a perpetrator, the only thing man and wolf could agree upon. There was nothing else like it. In the late eighteen hundreds, after fighting in the Civil War, he had been a farmhand on a Louisiana plantation; during the first half of the twentieth century he was a cotton mill employee in

Fall River, Massachusetts, and when the factory burnt down he moved to Oregon and lived near Williamette River, where he was a construction worker. He got out of town before the Big Pipe Project, an undertaking to reduce sewer overflows.

I suppose I could start over in another state. Enroll in the academy and work my way back up through the ranks. I would think it easier the second time around. He smiled.

He turned off SW 344th Street and onto Citrus Trail. Guided by the swirling red and blue lights of a parked cruiser, he pulled over, turned off the car, and stepped out to greet the uniformed cop standing outside talking with the neighbors. The houses seemed even closer than usual for a Floridian sub-division; he thought for sure he could stand between them and touch both. He flashed his badge and proceeded to enter the residence.

"You don't want to go in there yet," the officer said.

"Why?" Murphy asked, making a mental note of the man's ID number for his report.

"There's a dog in there guarding the body. Won't let anyone near it. I put a call in to animal control."

"I'll handle it."

"Are you crazy? That thing's a ninety-five pound Doberman!"

"Relax, would you. I got it."

Murphy walked into the house and was greeted by the same mixture of rum and tobacco he smelled back at the hotel and to the low, guttural growl of an angry canine. The Doberman sat beside its master; his head leaned forward, teeth barred and ears straight up. The body on the floor lay still, eyes shut. The only sound of breathing came from the dog.

"Easy, boy," he cooed as he approached. "Who did this?"

The dog let out a soft whimper as its ears folded back. Murphy continued his approach and knelt down to look the animal in the eye and placed his hand upon its head. He made the connection and images flashed before him. A man adorned in black with skull paint on his face. An exchange of cash and white powder. The young couple sitting down to partake in the drug, while the strange man sipped his rum from a glass in his bony fingers, then puffed on his cigar. Betrayal. The couple collapsed to the floor after a single hit.

"How'd you do that?" asked the uniformed cop, breaking Murphy's connection with the dog.

He glanced at the coffee table, but whatever drugs they took were gone without a trace. He patted the dog gently on the head, and said, "He knows an alpha male when he sees one." He stood and turned his back to the body.

"Well . . . that's some trick."

Murphy whipped out his notebook and began writing. "What's your name, officer?" he asked, ignoring the snide remark.

"Brown, sir. Eric Brown."

"Good to meet you. So we have a male, Caucasian, no visible signs of trauma and a missing girlfriend. Is that right?"

"Yeah. The neighbor reported a man carrying out Mr. Stommel's girlfriend over his shoulder. Looked as though she was unconscious."

"And how did the neighbor witness this? There's no sign of a struggle here. For all we know they let the perp in. So what got her snooping?"

"She was just taking her trash out. She claims the man saw her, smiled and winked, then went on his way as if she didn't matter."

"And what's her name?"

"Kimberly Eckard."

Murphy scribbled it in his pad. *This is more than just a two-bit criminal dabbling in voodoo. The level of arrogance is just astounding. It's almost as if . . . . What's his problem?* The officer's eyes grew wide as he took a step back. Murphy turned around to see the eyelids of Mr. Stommel's body had opened to expose white irises.

The body sat up. The Doberman whimpered, then bolted to another room, its nails clicking against the wood floor.

"Mr. Stommel, are you all right?" the officer asked as his hand reached for his sidearm.

"Don't do that. He's not a threat."

The officer relaxed his hand. "How do you know?"

Murphy doubted the man would understand the truth. "He's drugged." *Probably look at me like I'm some kind of stupid if I mentioned zombie.*

This was it, the proof he needed. Should he let the zombie get close enough, he was certain he'd smell gunpowder mixed with puffer fish entrails on his breath. He thought back to the Mambo who lived in the woods that surrounded the Louisiana plantation. How introverted she was. She saw right through him when they had met, and the two became friends, each keeping the others' secret. He probed his memories of the voodoo priestess' teachings and the name "Baron Samedi" appeared as the veil to the past was pulled back. *The loa of sex and resurrection. The Haitian equivalent to the Ferryman with a fondness for tobacco and rum. It's got to be him. But how? Has to be someone masquerading. It's gotta be.*

The zombie stood on wobbly legs. Once it was upright and steady, it stepped forward.

"Mr. Stommel, would you like me to call you an ambulance?"

The zombie slave ignored the cop's question and stepped passed him and out the front door.

The cop turned to Murphy. "Where's he going?"

Murphy shrugged and followed.

"What's wrong with his eyes?" asked a little girl standing beside a woman Murphy could only assume was Ms. Eckard.

What are they still doing outside? Taking out the trash . . . pht . . . more like neighborhood gossip.

"Ma'am, you really shouldn't be out here," Eric said as he stepped outside.

"Is he all right?"

"Ma'am, please go inside," Eric said.

Murphy just watched and jotted down notes as the zombie walked straight toward the woman. Its head tilted to the left in curiosity as it raised its arms to shoulder length; in a few more steps it'd be upon her.

Ms. Eckard, obviously unnerved by Mr. Stommel's behavior, put a hand on her daughter's shoulder and tucked her behind her. "Charlie . . . Charlie, what are you—"

The little girl screamed as the zombie's hands clasped around her mother's neck. Tears pooled at the base of her eyes as she kicked Mr. Stommel in the shins.

"We've got to do something," Eric said as he rushed to the woman's side.

Murphy stood there. Memories flashed before him when he saw the little girl cry. Memories he had buried deep down and locked away. A thirteen-year-old boy, naked, scared and cold, knelt beside his dead mother. The flesh was peeled off the left side of her face with claw marks in the muscle tissue, and the eye missing from its socket. Her chest was an empty crater, the rib cage cracked open and pointed toward the heavens with intestines strewn around the body from the creature responsible for digging out its favorite parts.

"Let. Her. Go!" Eric demanded as he tried to pry the zombie's hands from the woman's neck, but the creature simply ignored him.

The skin on the woman's face was darkening as a bluish hue stretched across her features.

"Mommy!"

Murphy snapped out of his self-pity and leaped over the railing on the front porch. With the agility and strength of the wolf, he pushed Eric aside, removed the zombie's hands from around the woman's neck, twisted the creature around and sent him crashing into the stucco wall. The zombie grunted on impact and fell backward.

Ms. Eckard leaned forward as she rubbed her neck and took deep breaths. The air wheezed through the strained airway.

"Are you okay, Mommy?"

The zombie sat up.

"What is going on?" Eric asked as he withdrew his gun and aimed it at Mr. Stommel.

"I told you to put that away." Murphy knelt down and took the sobbing girl's chin in his hand. He tilted her head upward and looked her in the eyes. "Get your mother inside and lock the door."

She nodded, grabbed her mother's hand, and obeyed.

Murphy withdrew his handcuffs from his belt. "He's drugged. It's not his fault. We just need to wait for the drugs to pass through his system."

"Or we can take him in to get his stomach pumped."

"Now we're on the same page," Murphy said, impressed by the cop's quick thinking.

Mr. Stommel was on his feet again and as he turned around, Murphy slammed him into the house once more, pulled his arms behind him, and slapped the handcuffs on.

"I've never seen anyone move so fast," Eric said.

"Thanks. I workout."

"So I see."

"Would you mind taking him to the hospital?" he asked as he guided Mr. Stommel toward him.

"I don't know. He's kind of creeping me out."

"When's back-up coming?"

"There was an accident on I-95 and with the other calls . . . I honestly don't know."

"The quicker the drugs are out of his system, the quicker we have our answers. I'd rather not pull rank here."

"Okay . . . okay," Eric said, gyrating his hands in front of his chest as he spoke. He escorted the zombie to his squad car.

So the Bokor left orders for Charlie to kill the witnesses. Either he underestimated the time his drug would take affect or how quickly we'd arrive on the scene. Regardless, he won't make that mistake twice. I need to act, but where to start?

Even with his heightened senses, the smell of rum and tobacco was too faint outside with the mixture of countless other odors.

I need a stronger mark. What I need is the wolf's full power.

"Stop struggling . . . will you . . . lower your head . . . I could use a hand here."

Murphy smiled as he watched the zombie's head continuously bump into the roof of the car as the beat-cop tried to shove him into the back seat. He walked over to them and put his hand on the back of Charlie's neck. "I'll hold his head down. You push him in, okay?"

The cop took a deep breath. "Okay."

Murphy applied pressure and the zombie's head lowered, then he nodded and the cop shoved him in.

"You should have let me shoot him."

"Just get him to the hospital." Murphy pulled out another business card. "Call me when he's clean and ready to talk."

"What are you going to do?"

"I'm going back inside. See if I can find a lead and make sure the dog's okay."

"Good luck." The officer walked to the driver's side of the squad car, got in, then pulled away.

Once inside, Murphy sought out something belonging to the woman, a piece of clothing, toothbrush—anything that held her scent. The Doberman followed him room to room and watched every move he made.

"You could help, you know."

The dog barked and darted off. Murphy followed. It scooted low and crawled under the bed. When he came out the other side, a pair of pink panties dangled from its mouth.

"Well all right, then," he said, kneeling down. The dog brought the lingerie to him. He took the panties and raised his eyebrows. "Kinky, but it'll do." He placed the panties to his face and breathed in deeply.

With the scent committed to memory, Murphy walked over to the dresser on the opposite wall. He looked long and hard at his reflection as he contemplated his next move. Should he play defense and wait for another crime scene and hope for a break, or should he tap into the wolf lying dormant within and go on the offense? He didn't like doing it, but this was one of those rare occasions he'd consider letting the beast out. Without the full moon the change would not be complete. His body would be in a flux between man and beast, with both personalities fighting for dominance. The beast was a wild animal, unpredictable and dangerous.

He turned to the dog. "Will you follow me? Keep me in line?"

The Doberman hunched forward, playfully wagging its tail, and barked.

"All right, then." He turned back to the mirror and stared deep into the eyes of his reflection. *Wake up! Time for you to earn some redemption.*

Murphy's palms slammed down hard on the dresser as each breath grew heavy. The irises of his eyes changed. The roundness stretched to an elliptical shape and the brown softened to a yellowish hue. His crew-cut blond hair grew wildly to shoulder length and covered his now-pointed ears. Pain surged in his gums as his canine teeth elongated and protruded out of his mouth. Fingernails lifted and fell away as claws capable of stripping flesh from bone emerged from under the skin. While he still had a rational mind, he swept the DNA samples off the dresser and deposited them into his breast pocket.

A maniacal chuckle reverberated in his throat as he gazed upon himself. Half-man, half-beast, he sniffed the air and found the trail, then turned to the Doberman. "Think you can keep up?" His voice lost its charm, now gravelly and low.

He darted to the window and leapt threw it. Glass shattered and rained on the ground. Tiny lacerations formed and healed before his feet touched down. With his footing secured, he ran east, hot on the scent. The Doberman followed through the now-open window.

He darted in between a group of women walking on the sidewalk. They shrieked as he passed by; the swift breeze hiked up a skirt and one of the women stumbled in her high heels.

"Hey!"

"What, you think it's Halloween or something!"

"Pervert!"

He snarled and gnashed his teeth in return and made a move toward them, but the Doberman barked and ran interference. The beast growled his displeasure, but returned to the hunt. Though the beast seemed angry with the dog's defiance, Murphy could tell it appreciated running with the animal, the pack mentality of the wolf finally being appeased after a century of solitude.

Tongues flopped to and fro as they ran; spittle flew in every direction. The scent was now stronger. They were close. They turned off the main road, down a dirt path and came upon a chain link fence. Without missing a step, Murphy crouched and put all his strength into a single bound. He cleared the fence with ease. The Doberman barked and he stopped, then turned back. The dog looked left then right and spotted a blue-metal dumpster overflowing with trash. It leapt onto a pile of trash bags and sprang forward so quickly he didn't lose his footing, then bounded off the upper rim of the dumpster. It landed safely on the other side of the fence, its legs folding at the perfect time to absorb the impact, but it took a second before running toward Murphy.

Together again, the two ran toward a decrepit building. Murphy remembered it used to be a storage warehouse for a furniture store long since bankrupt. Graffiti covered nearly all of the first floor of the building, a montage of whimsical portraits and fancy letters spelling a variety of curse words and gang names. Out of arms' reach from the vandals, the once-red brick had been stripped of its vibrant color from the Florida sun and blackened with mold. Shards of glass decorated the ground surrounding the building from the broken panes. No one cared enough to board them up. The light from a bonfire danced on the walls of the second floor and Murphy smelled the body odor of at least a dozen squatters inside.

He crept to the side of the building and shimmied along the wall until coming upon a side door; the metal dented and bent inward, allowing him to crawl inside. The Doberman followed as stealthily as he could into the stairwell.

A roar of excitement from up above caused the dog to jump back. It looked up with its ears tipped back and eyes wide.

"It's okay, boy," Murphy said in the softest voice he could, though his vocal cords still sounded as if they were made of sandpaper. The dog didn't seem to mind.

Murphy led the way up the concrete steps. He hugged the wall, concealed in the shadows. The metal balusters and railing were too rusted to trust. When he reached the top, he caught sight of two sentries. His right hand shot behind him to signal the dog to stop. He obeyed.

"What you dink's up with, Moliere?"

"Not sure. There's definitely sum'ding different about 'em."

"'Tis an improvement, though."

"Oh yes. Not so serious all de time."

"Certainly a lot more fun."

"Ay!"

As the two men came within striking distance, Murphy leaped out of the shadows. He landed behind the two men, grabbed them by the sides of their heads, and slammed them together. Bone on bone, a loud thwack echoed in his sensitive ears and the two Haitian men fell to the floor in a slump. Before exploring the second floor, he dragged them into the stairwell. The Doberman gave the men a sniff down; once it determined they were of no threat, it followed Murphy.

A formalized percussion filled the air. He followed the beat, but remained in the shadows until he came to the source. Men pounded on drums and gongs, while women danced and shook rattles.

What are they celebrating? he thought. He watched closely.

The Doberman tugged on the bottom of Murphy's pant leg. He looked down at the dog, which made eye contact with him, then turned its head toward the right. Murphy followed his gaze and saw a young woman, naked and bound to a bed frame in the adjacent room.

He patted the dog on the head and walked toward her. Even from this distance he could tell her chest wasn't rising and falling and, as he approached, the familiar scent of blood came to his nose. The tantalizing aroma excited the beast within and it took every ounce of willpower to not run over there and tear into the carcass.

Poor thing, he thought, seeing her bosom covered in crimson. *I imagine he slit your throat after he raped you, or possibly during.* Without a description of Charlie's girlfriend there was no way to be certain this was her, but his instincts and her aroma told him otherwise.

What a shame. Such a beauty, too. The Hispanic girl's long black hair lay around her angelic face, sopping with blood. *The kill is fresh.*

The dog growled and Murphy turned around. He was stared down by the barrel of a gun.

"Dude! What's up with your face?" asked the man.

Murphy sensed the Doberman's animosity and foresaw its next move.

The dog leaped, teeth gnashing.

Murphy reached out.

The man stumbled back out. The gun went off.

Murphy caught the dog in midair and spun around, putting his back to the assailant. The pain from the solitary bullet was a minor inconvenience, but it was well aimed and would have proven fatal to the loyal companion. After spending all those years taking lives, it filled Murphy with hope sensing that the beast put a life before its own. It released the dog, and in a whirl tackled the man to the ground and bore into the right side of his neck and shoulder. The man managed to fire off another shot, but it was wild and struck the neighboring wall.

The Doberman growled and crouched low, ready to pounce, as more men came investigating.

"Shoot it!" one of them ordered and gunshots filled the air.

Murphy stood his ground, using his body as a shield to protect the Doberman. Hot lead pierced his skin and burned his flesh; he could feel the metal move as his supernatural body pushed them back out. As one bullet hole started to heal, another took its place.

"Enough!"

The gang parted to either side of the room and a man in a white tuxedo and top hat stood at the doorway. His face was painted white in a skull pattern and framed by ropy dreadlocks. Even with the crowd, Murphy's keen nose told him this stranger was no man. Masked underneath the rum and tobacco was the faint scent of brimstone. The dog whimpered and stepped back.

"Baron Samedi, I presume," Murphy said and several of the men were startled at the sound of his menacing voice.

"Very good," said the man. "You are a marvelous creature. I am surprised, though, that you so easily work with the thing that killed your mother."

Hot air whooshed through Murphy's nostrils as he tried to keep his anger in check. He knew he could lay to waste everyone in the room, tear them limb from limb and leave nothing but quivering piles of flesh in his wake, but he could not guarantee the Doberman's survival, the first living creature to show him any sort of compassion in nearly half a century.

"And how touching that you brought that mangy mongrel with you. I should have killed that whimpering pest when I had the chance."

The beast within Murphy growled its displeasure with the statement. "If you're truly the loa of resurrection and sex, why the parlor tricks?"

The Baron let loose a deep belly-laugh that seemed to reverberate in his throat. "A supernatural creature is asking me if I'm real. What a trip. First, I do not have dominion over the souls I do not escort to Hell, and secondly, you have any idea how much trouble the undead are?"

Murphy just stood there, barely listening and plotting his next move. He thought about clawing his way through the crowd, but thought he'd stand a better chance protecting the dog if he just plowed through the wall.

"No?" the Baron continued. "Then let me show you." He extended his right hand toward the dead woman. The Baron's eyes reddened like hot coals on a fire.

The woman sat up and her face contorted in a vicious snarl. She grabbed the Haitian man closest to her and sank her teeth into the back of his neck, and pulled him on top of her.

"Help me, Moliere," the man pleaded as he struggled to pull himself up, but the woman's cold legs wrapped tightly around his waist. He managed to put two rounds into the side of her waist, but as more of his blood coated her face and bosom, the less strength he had. "Please," he said before blood filled his airway and the struggle came to an end.

The other men stepped away from the bed and back peddled toward the door as the woman shoved the dead weight off her and onto the floor. She perched herself on all fours and mashed her teeth together, letting loose an animalistic growl.

Just great! Murphy looked at his clawed hand and hoped all he needed to do was destroy the creature's brain.

Baron Samedi's eyes glowed with Hellfire once more and the dead woman's flesh ignited in flame. The zombie rolled off the bed and writhed on the floor as the flames consumed her flesh. The heat from the fire caused Murphy to shelter his face with his arm. Just as it appeared, the fire vanished and left nothing but ash.

"As you can see, true zombies are unruly. Death is cold. Icy. The undead are not ravenous for food, but the warmth that living flesh provides as it slides down their gullet. Though momentarily at best, living blood warms them and when a victim's flesh no longer generates that warmth, they search for their next victim. Any more questions?" he asked Murphy, who couldn't think of anything but getting out of there unsinged. He hadn't expected that kind of power. "I'll take your silence as a no. Now, a creature such as yourself should be working with me, not against."

"What exactly are you doing here, and in that body?"

"This weak-minded soul invoked me in hopes of accomplishing the American dream. I swallowed his soul and in turn his friends and cohorts will reap the benefit of his sacrifice so long as they are loyal and serve their purpose."

The henchmen, one-by-one, exited the room as if sensing the imminent confrontation.

"You should join me, Murphy Crane. Together we can find your wayward father and bring him to justice."

My father!

"Yes. He's still out there. Don't you want to punish him for raping your mother? For leaving you two without so much as a warning?"

Murphy had heard enough. He wasn't about to stand there and let this arrogant pig dredge up over a hundred years of repressed memories. He lunged forward, claws outstretched and ready to rip flesh from bone.

With cat-like reflexes, the Baron grabbed him by the wrists, spun him around, and playfully kicked his backside. The force sent him stumbling forward and Murphy could tell the man had held back, but how much he didn't know.

The Doberman leapt into action and was swatted away with a backhand. It crashed into the wall and lay still on the floor.

"NO!" Murphy roared and attacked again. Once more his hands were caught before they could rip the Baron asunder, but this time he was kicked in the gut. The strength of the blow sent him hurling backward. He hit the wall behind him with such force the brick collapsed under his weight and he fell two stories to the ground. His leg twisted at the knee, broken. Crumbled brick rained down on him as he sat up to right the leg. He grabbed the leg with both hands and jerked it back in place and let loose a howl. Within seconds, the pain was no more.

The Baron's men came running out of the building, guns blazing. Hot lead pierced his hide, but they were nothing more than a nuisance. He charged headlong into the mob; his arms flew wildly as he passed through the crowd. His razor sharp nails tore through muscle; limbs dropped and throats sprayed arterial fluid. Within the span of a minute, the Haitian gang had their numbers cut in half. The surviving members either fled back into the building or ran off, leaving their weapons behind.

"Enough of this," the Baron said, standing in the center of the hole in the wall. He jumped down. His body descended slowly—ghost like.

Murphy watched him closely.

When his feet touched the ground, he extended his hand toward the sky. "I want to see your full power."

With the wave of his hand, the dark shadow covering the final crescent arch of the moon receded. Murphy's heart thundered in his chest upon seeing the soft glow of the now full moon. The animal within stirred, demanding release. He grabbed the buttoned folds of his shirt and ripped the fabric off his expanding chest. His face elongated into a muzzle. Muscles bulged. Bones cracked and popped out of their joints to reposition themselves in unnatural angles. Hair sprouted from every pore.

"Yes . . . now show me your power so that I may make it my own."

The wolf leaned back on its haunches and howled at the moon before dropping and running headlong at the Baron. The Baron twirled his body out of the beast's way, grabbed it by the scruff and used the spiral momentum to toss the beast into the air. It crashed through another brick wall. The gang members inside screamed and ran deeper into the building.

"Disappointing." The Baron approached him methodically. He punched the wall as he stepped through the opening, sending a stray brick straight at the beast's head.

The beast showed its agility by catching the brick with its teeth, then crushed it between its powerful jaws. Tiny stone particles spilled from its lips. Not sure of what its next move should be, the beast waited for the Baron.

"What's wrong? You tired of playing with me already? All right, I'll make the next move."

The Baron ran at the wolf; the wolf ran toward him. They collided. The wolf's right paw was caught, but the left clawed down the Baron's chest. Deafening screams filled the air. The wolf dropped to its knees and covered its ears. It stared up at Baron Samedi and saw the screams did not come from him, but from *within* him as if a window to Hell had been opened and the tortured souls called out for help. The Baron clasped his hands together and raised them high above his head, then brought them down upon the beast's skull.

The wolf fell to the ground, darkness creeping over him. It struggled to stand, but received another crashing blow.

We cannot win, Murphy thought. *He is the lord of the dead. He can't be killed. What am I to do?* Then he remembered the practice of the Jivaro people of the Amazon rainforest and how they used to shrink the heads of their enemies to trap their soul inside. It was a long shot, but he had no other alternative. *But how am I going to get close enough to remove his head?*

No sooner than he thought about it, the Doberman came running out from the shadows and clamped its teeth onto the Baron's calf. As the Baron knelt down to pry the dog off, Murphy lunged upward and clamped his powerful jaws around the base of the Baron's neck and bit down. Blood pooled along his gum-line and filled his mouth as his teeth pierced and severed the flesh. The head fell to the ground and rolled away. The body slumped to its knees. More screams and white smoke billowed from the open wound and Murphy caught the shapes of faces within it. A green flame ignited along the neckline, searing the flesh closed and the screams were silenced.

Murphy scooped the severed head with his open maw and ran off. In full wolf form, Murphy traversed the city in the shadows and via rooftops. With the best of his ability, the Doberman kept up the pace using the streets below.

As the morning sun rose over the horizon, Murphy hopped the fence to his backyard. He lived in a bungalow near the beach, a modest residence for the perpetual bachelor. There, the transformation reversed. The claws, teeth and hair receded and a calming peace came over him as the beast went dormant once more. The Doberman barked from the other side of the fence. Murphy walked toward the gate with the severed head tucked behind him covering his bare backside and his left hand concealing his manhood. He peered over the fence, and with the coast clear, he lifted the latch, opened the gate, and whistled for the dog. The Doberman came bolting around the corner and once inside his yard, Murphy secured the gate and made his way toward the back door. He kept a spare key under the doormat for such occasions.

Once inside, he placed the head on his kitchen counter and went to get dressed, but not before lighting a fire in his stone fireplace. He could feel the Baron's gaze on him as he walked away, but he didn't care. It would be something he'd need to get used to, though. He stepped out of his closet, fully clothed, to the Doberman sitting at his bedside, tail wagging.

"You hungry, boy?"

The dog barked.

"Suppose I'm going to have to come up with a name for you, huh?"

He stood, tail still wagging.

"No dog food, I'm afraid, but I got a ham bone in the fridge you're welcome to."

The dog ran off to the kitchen.

"Guess that settles it."

He followed the dog into the kitchen, and retrieved the ham bone he had been saving to make pea soup. "I'll get you something with more substance after I take care of our little friend." He handed it over and the dog trotted off to the center of the living room.

With the dog happy, Murphy pulled out a pot from a cabinet under the counter, filled it with water, and put it on the stove. He set the temperature to high and grabbed a knife from its cradle. Then, with his free hand, he grabbed a hand full of dreadlocks.

"Penny for your thoughts," he said as he stared into the unblinking eyes of the Baron. "No cocky retort? I'm surprised. Let's not put this off any longer."

He turned the head around and jammed the blade into the base of the neck, then made a slit up to the back of the head so that he could peel the skin and hair from the skull. Then, carefully, the eyes and lips were sewn shut. By the time that was done, the water was boiling and ready. He dropped the head in, covered the pot, and set the timer for ninety minutes.

This'll give me time to get some sand and stones, he thought.

* * * *

Murphy made it back from the beach with three minutes to spare. He had collected enough stones and sand to finish his shrunken head. None of his belongings were chewed up by his new roommate and he was very pleased. On removal from the pot the head was a third of its size, the skin rubbery to the touch. The stones went into the water in its place.

Grasping the dangling flesh of the neck and sliding his fingers into the folds, he turned the skin inside out, scraped off all the adhering flesh, and then turned the skin right-side-out. He sewed a slit up the neck line, then removed the hot stones and shoved them into the neck, not caring about scalding himself; time was of the essence if he was to trap Baron Semedi's soul inside the head. He rolled the stones inside the bag of skin until the head shrank to a point where the stones could no longer move. He returned the stones to the boiling water to reuse them, and filled the head with the sand collected on the nearby beach. Once the stones were hot enough, he took one and applied it to the outside surface to seal and shape the head's features. When a stone was cool to the touch, he took another and continued to work until he was satisfied. Then he singed off the fine facial hairs.

"There, that looks like you, or rather the man you stole from this world. Don't worry. I'll reapply your ceremonial war paint."

The Doberman suddenly stood up and ran to the back door, barking.

"What is it, boy?" He looked out the window to see five walking corpses, men and women in various stages of decay, and one legless zombie crawling, his flesh bloated and covered in seaweed. The group surrounded the bungalow. He held the shrunken head at eye level. "Guess they don't call you the lord of the dead for nothing, but how far does your influence reach?"

He darted to the front of the house and found another four shambling zombies closing in on his white picket fence.

Murphy recognized one of the females by her clothing: a jogger reported missing two weeks ago. Her shorts were ripped in the middle and he'd bet anything she had been raped. Given her condition, cause of death was undeterminable, but it was clear she'd been abducted and ditched as suspected. Her legs and arms had deep chunks of flesh missing, a sure sign of animal mauling. Her skin was dry, wrinkled, and pressed tightly against her bones, the decay heightened by the Florida heat. Murphy felt a tinge of guilt for not checking the neighboring woods to his house, but the area was nowhere near where she was last seen.

Couldn't have known, but I'll be paying each neighbor a visit when this is over, he told himself. He looked to the sky. The sun had just cleared the horizon. He heard a scream come from his neighbors, and though he wanted to help them, he had bigger problems and couldn't afford his secret getting out.

"Looks like we're trapped," he said to the Doberman still standing at his side. He walked over to the fireplace and hung the shrunken head over the open flame to cure, then pulled down his shotgun from over the mantle. He looked to the dog and said, "Think we can hold out 'til nightfall?"

The Doberman barked in agreeance.

Murphy smiled as the perfect name dawned on him. *I think I'll call you Moondoggie.*

LADY OF THE FOREST

"ARE YOU SURE your brother was last seen in these woods?" the young woman asked as she pushed a tree branch out of her way.

The man sighed. "Yes, I'm sure. The police found his camping equipment by the lake, but no sign of him. I can't believe they're just giving up."

"I'm sorry, Jack, but it has been two weeks. Maybe it's time you—"

"Don't say it!" he shouted, cutting her off. He stopped in the middle of the path of Virginia State National Forest and turned back to face his wife. "You and Marty are the only family I have left. I'm not about to give up on him. Alive or dead, I need to know."

It was her turn to sigh. "Why was he out here alone, anyway? Who the hell goes camping alone?"

Jack knew she was insincere by the use of vulgarity. She only cursed when she was extremely ticked off.

Shrugging it off, he replied, "Our father always took us into these woods for camping trips; this was like our second home. Every year since Dad's death, Marty has come out here alone for a weekend to honor that memory. Look, Karen, I told you to stay home. You have no one to blame but yourself."

"And what if you disappear? What will I do? Did you think about that?"

"No, I haven't."

"Well, I have, and you're stuck with me. And as long as we're out here, you're stuck with my complaining!"

Frustrated, he turned around and continued his hike.

"I'm getting tired, though. Would it be possible to stop?" she said.

"All right. There should be a clearing up ahead where we can rest. Probably best to just set up camp. Think you can make it?"

"Yeah."

As the young couple continued to walk the narrow, winding trail, an eerie silence blanketed the forest. There were no birds chirping. No insects orchestrating their music. No tiny woodland creatures scurrying past them. They were alone, and Jack took notice, and he could not shake the feeling of an icy stare. Somewhere, hiding in the shadows, something was watching them.

He stopped and looked to the sky. The ancient trees stretching toward each other with their plethora of leaves made it difficult, but there were tiny pockets scattered throughout the forest canopy allowing in enough daylight to guide them. However, the sun would soon be setting and was already adding a pinkish hue to the atmosphere.

Karen walked passed him, playfully slapping him in the gut with the back of her hand as she did.

"Hey, where are you going?" he asked.

She stopped and turned. "To the clearing. I know you'll catch up."

"Listen," he said.

"To what?"

"Exactly. None of the animals are making any noise."

"Who cares," she said, continuing on her way. "Come on, you're just being paranoid . . . AH!"

Jack's eyes went wide as his wife's arms shot upward, her body disappearing into the earth.

"Karen!" he shouted, watching her vanish. He ran and dropped to the edge of the crater. Peering into the darkness, he called to her. "Are you all right?"

Nothing.

"Karen . . . Karen!"

Again, nothing.

"Oh, dear God, please let her be all right," he said, rummaging through his backpack, looking for his flashlight.

"I'm okay!" she shouted, breaking the silence.

"Where are you?"

"I don't know. It's too dark!"

"Find your flashlight. I put it in the outside pouch."

"Okay!"

Stealing a quick glance at the sky, he mumbled, "Thank you."

"I found it. It looks like some kind of cave. Jack? Are you still there?"

Jack's eyes opened wide as several large wolves surrounded him. He wanted to shout to his beloved, but fear paralyzed his vocal cords. All he could do was watch as they drew closer, baring their fangs and growling with intent to murder. He rummaged through his pack again, this time looking for his hunting knife; it was the only weapon he thought to bring along.

As the pack of wolves came upon him, Jack found his knife. Clutching it with his right hand, he waved it in the air in an effort to ward them off, but the beasts didn't stop advancing. Suddenly, another wolf jumped directly in front of him. The creature's fur was an odd dirty blond color, instantly reminding him of his brother's hair. It growled at the oncoming wolves. Several backed off, but two of the largest continued: one with midnight black fur, the other a mixture of gray and white, both larger than any wolf Jack had ever seen.

The wolves lunged toward the blond wolf in unison. It met their advance and knocked the black wolf to the ground with a mighty blow from its right paw, but the other got through its defenses with a quick sidestep and clinched its teeth into the back of its neck. The blond wolf howled in pain.

"Jack, are you all right? What's all that commotion?" Karen's voice was panic-stricken.

He didn't answer.

Instead, Jack got to his feet and plunged his blade into the hind leg of the gray wolf. It released its bite and turned toward him. It stared at him, growling and baring its blood-soaked fangs. It barked before leaping into the air.

Jack acted quickly. Rather than trying to block or dodge the animal's attack, he received it. He pushed himself backward on impact, driving the knife into the beast's stomach all the way to the hilt. He pulled upward, slicing the beast open. Intestine and blood washed over him. It let out a soft whimper, and then its dead weight fell onto his chest, making it difficult to breathe. As he pushed the animal off him, he noticed the other wolves turning tail. The blond wolf had the black one by the throat, its mouth encompassing almost half the neck. With one good twist, the wolf's life slipped away as its throat was torn out.

The blond wolf turned to Jack, blood dripping from its muzzle as well as from the wound on its neck. Jack's fear washed away as he stared into the wolf's eyes, emotion residing within them. He could see compassion and fear. That gaze. It looked . . . familiar. As the wolf slowly walked toward him, he lowered his knife. The wolf lay before him; he knelt down, embracing it.

"Marty?" he asked, staring into his brother's eyes.

The blond hair began to fall off. The skin underneath began to bubble and blister as it changed shape. The wolf's muzzle receded. The sound of bones cracking drowned out Karen's pleas for him to answer her. In mere minutes, Jack was staring at his brother's naked flesh.

"Hello, Jack," Marty said before coughing up a mouthful of blood. A large chunk of flesh was missing from the side of his throat, blood flowing profusely.

"You're hurt," he said as he took off his already blood-soaked shirt and placed it against his brother's wound. Though he had the burning desire to ask his brother what he had gotten himself into this time, it could wait until after his wounds were attended to; they were reunited with Karen; and after they were out of this forsaken wood.

The blood flowed relentlessly, saturating the shirt within seconds.

"Listen . . . you have to leave this place," Marty said.

"What happened to you?"

"I met a woman. The most beautiful woman I've ever seen. She was at the lake getting a drink. When I saw her, I just had to have her."

"You're not making any sense."

"Listen," he said, coughing up more blood. "She is cursed. Any man who gives into his desires, who obeys his animal instincts and tastes her nectar, becomes an animal himself."

"That's impossible."

"No! It's true. Every creature in this forest was once a man. Look at the others."

Jack took his eyes off his brother and saw the two wolves Marty had protected him from were now men as well. "This is not possible."

"You see . . . you must leave."

"Karen is trapped in that hole. I'm not leaving without her."

"She's stopped screaming. It's too late for her. Save yourself. I love you, bro . . ." His head slouched backward in Jack's arms and his eyes glossed over.

"Marty . . . Marty!"

A single tear dripped down his left cheek, splashing on his brother's face. Realizing there was nothing he could do for his brother, Jack returned his attention to the hole. "Karen . . . Karen, are you still there? Answer me!"

There was nothing.

"Hang on, Karen, I'm coming." Without thought, he grabbed his backpack and jumped into the hole.

Jack landed on his feet, but the impact knocked him on his backside. Using his flashlight, he sliced through the darkness, trying to get his bearings. "Karen!" Getting no response, he stood and traveled deeper into the cave, his knife held out in front of him.

An awful sound echoed in the cavern: the sound of chewing. Panic settled in and Jack sprinted, fearful he was too late. As he ran further, he saw light emanating from an opening. However, his short hopeful thought was ripped from him upon seeing three wolves tearing at his wife's carcass, growling and snarling as they devoured her flesh. He stopped dead in his tracks, his wife's vacant eyes staring at him.

He turned his head to the right and vomited, drawing the wolves' attention. They growled their displeasure at having their meal interrupted.

Fighting back his fear, shock taking over, he shouted. "Get . . . get away from her!"

The wolves braced themselves as Jack charged headlong.

"Stop! All of you!"

Surprised to see a woman at the entrance of the cave, Jack obeyed, halting in his tracks.

"Leave it!" she ordered.

The wolves darted off, returning to the forest beyond.

Jack walked to his beloved and dropped to his knees. The tears flowed freely.

"I'm sorry about your wife. They were hungry," the woman said.

Jack didn't reply.

Seeing his wife's abdomen torn open, her intestines strewn about, was more than he could handle. Several rib bones were completely devoid of meat and her left thigh was partially eaten.

"They're not evil. It's just been so long since anyone came to the forest—"

"Who are you?" he asked, lifting his head to gaze at her. He could barely manage the words through the sobs.

The woman's beauty was beyond compare. Her pale white, angelic face appeared deeply concerned for his loss. Her full lips trembled and her emerald eyes glistened, fighting back tears. Her blonde hair fell passed her shoulders, covering her chest. She wore a blood-red gown with a matching cloak. He noticed her large breasts rising and falling as she sighed.

"My name is Catherine," she said, stepping closer to him. Jack noticed her shoeless feet and caught sight of her long slender legs. The gown was seductively slit, exposing her left leg all the way to the hip. He studied her full figure as his head lolled up to look her in the eyes so as not to be rude.

"You're her, aren't you? The one my brother told me of."

"Yes," she answered simply.

"Why do you do it?" he asked, standing abruptly as she came closer. His rubbery legs could barely support his weight and for a moment he thought he'd collapse back to the ground.

"I don't do anything."

"Liar. My brother told me you turned him into a monster."

"I did no such thing. Your brother sought me out. He knew the—"

"Liar!"

"I'm sorry for your loss, but your brother was one of the few who knew my terrible secret. If anyone is a liar, it was him."

"I don't believe you."

"That's irrelevant. The fact is your brother witnessed a rape many years ago. My rape. I saw him watching in the bushes and I knew it excited him. I didn't struggle against my captor. There was no reason to. They all receive their punishment. He witnessed the man transform into a bear after his climax, yet came searching for me. You foolishly believe he came out here, year after year, to honor your father's memory." She laughed. "He came in hopes of seeing me again. When I finally presented myself to him, all he wanted was to lay me, despite knowing my curse."

"So you gave in?"

"Who am I to deny a man what he desires? I've lived long enough to know men take what they want if it's not given freely."

"Not all men," he replied, but understood. Even with the smell of death and urine from the wolves marking their territory, he could still smell her wonderful aroma. He felt the bulge pressing against his jeans, demanding to be satiated, her beauty stirring something primal within him. *My emotions are all over the place*, he thought. "How did this happen to you?" he asked, shaking away the thought of throwing her to the ground and forcing his will upon her.

"I fell in love with a man. Problem was, he was married, and didn't tell me. His wife eventually caught on. To both of our surprise, she practiced witchcraft and laid a curse upon me. That curse turned any man who slept with me into the beast best suiting his disposition. Since her husband gave into his animalistic desires and betrayed his wife, I have been forced to live an existence of solitude, nearly two hundred years now. But even out here, far from the civilized world, men still fancy me, and even those who are well aware of the sacrifice still desire me. Some of their desires are even heightened. They become much more curious of the wonders lying within here," she said, opening her hands and bringing Jack's eyes toward her pubic region. "Your brother was one of those. However, they are fortunate, for when they die, their curse is lifted and they become a man again. Death is not a luxury I have."

"I'm sorry." Jack didn't know what else to say. His mind riddled with various emotions, tugging him in different directions. He grieved for the loss of his wife and brother, swamped with guilt for spending those last moments with his brother instead of saving his wife. He was angry with the woman before him for causing all this, but simultaneously was lustful and aroused by her beauty. *Is this roller-coaster ride of emotions part of her curse? My grief over Karen should outweigh her beauty . . . and yet—*

"I can show you the way to the main road, if you'd like," she said, breaking the silence and snapping Jack out of his inner torment.

"There is nothing left for me out there. Marty and Karen were all I had."

"That can't be entirely true."

"But it is. I don't have any *true* friends, just a bunch of bottom feeders. I'm stuck in a dead end job with nothing to show for ten years of employment. All because I dropped out of college when my father died."

"Those are all things you can change," she said.

"Maybe," he replied, grabbing her by her right wrist. "Or maybe—" He pulled her close and pressed his lips against hers. Her lips tasted so sweet he could only wonder how the rest of her tasted.

He threw her to the ground.

She looked at him discontentedly.

He didn't care.

She would be his for those few fleeting minutes. As he fiddled with his belt, he wondered what animal he would become.

WAR DOG

A HORN ECHOED in the air followed by a voice over the loud speaker. "Game's over, ladies!"

Marcus Wright stared down at the two blue ink spots in the center of his chest. *Screwed up again*, he thought.

"What the hell were you doing? Sleeping?" asked Squad Leader Harris as he came out of the surrounding bush. "Give you a simple task . . ."

You didn't fare any better, he thought.

"How he made it this far I'll never know," said another squad member

"The idiot's been recycled twice. What do you expect?"

"Be careful, he might put a gypsy curse on you."

Marcus just stood there and let his teammates vent; he was used to it by now. Since they learned of his heritage, diluted though it might be, they teased him with their prejudices.

"A true leader assumes responsibility for his men," the opposing squad leader said.

"What'd you say? You gotta problem?" Harris said, charging at the man until he was nose to nose.

"Get a room, ladies," barked drill sergeant Barrow.

"Why do you keep giving us Marcus? We can't be expected to win if—"

"Maybe you should consider it an honor. Maybe I see what you cannot and I feel you need to be sabotaged in order to even the sides. Or maybe I think you're just a whining baby who needs his momma. Is that what it is?"

"Sir, no sir!"

"All of you get back to the barracks. Except you, recruit," Barrow said, eyeing Marcus.

All members of the blue team laughed as they triumphantly walked to base camp, waving the red flag in victory as they did.

"Aren't you getting tired of this?"

"Sir, no sir," Marcus answered, stiffening his back.

"You've failed the Phase Three test twice already. This is your third squad, and I'm afraid your options are dwindling."

"I know, sir, I can do better. Perhaps if I was on the blue squad—"

"Afraid not. Face it, you lack that killer instinct, and that's just something you cannot learn. It's inherent. Changing squads isn't going to make a difference."

"But, sir—"

"Listen, Marcus, I know it sounds harsh, but I've been watching you closely. It's not unusual for a recruit to fail their Phase Three test, but you're on your way to failing a third time and I believe it is because you're holding onto your identity too tightly. It's my job to strip recruits of everything that makes them unique, and rebuild them into soldiers."

"I don't understand, sir."

"And therein lies the problem. Think it over. Dismissed."

"Thank you, sir."

Marcus walked to the barracks at Fort Benning alone and contemplative. The sergeant was right, he knew, but the Army was his only chance at a decent life. The base felt like his one true home since losing his parents to a carbon monoxide leak while away at summer camp. As a twelve-year-old boy, he bounced from foster home to foster home with prospective parents only interested in toddlers and babies. As soon as he was old enough, he enlisted in the Army and finally felt peace.

I have to make this work. I just have to, he thought.

"If it isn't the gypsy queen," Harris said, standing in the doorway with his arms folded in front of his chest. "So tell us, gypsy queen, what did the sarge want?"

"Leave me alone."

"Where was that backbone on the battlefield?"

"It wasn't a battlefield." Marcus shoved his shoulder into Harris, pushing his way through the doorway.

"That's where you're wrong."

Marcus felt two hands slam into his back, knocking him face first to the floor.

"Now tell me, what did Sarge want? You squeal on us?"

"No," Marcus said, getting to his feet. "He wouldn't do squat anyway. Hazing's part of the training, right?"

"Right," Harris said. His cronies, Eric and Tony, nodded in agreement.

"If it makes you feel better, Sarge wanted me to think about why I'm here. Says I lack the necessary 'killer instinct.'"

"He's a smart man, that sarge. Best drill instructor the Army has."

"Yeah, you should just quit," Tony said.

"Or dig down deep for that animal instinct."

Harris nudged Eric in the shoulder. "You're such a dumb twit. We said *killer* instinct."

"What's the difference?"

Animal Instinct! That's a great idea. "Are we finished here? It's getting late," Marcus said.

"Yeah, whatever," Harris said and Marcus walked away from his teammates and headed for his bunk.

As a boy, whenever Marcus would misbehave his father teased and threatened him with a gypsy curse, but always with a smile on his face. When his parents died, he learned all he could about the gypsy blood running through his veins. It was the only way he knew to honor his father and to keep his memory alive. Learning about himself and his family tree also comforted him and warded off the isolation he felt in the foster homes. He had an old library book he had checked out and never returned because of being relocated. The book detailed the history of the gypsies as well as their beliefs, and there was one such belief that could help him now. One of the first things Harris had done when Marcus was assigned to their squad was confiscate the book after seeing him read it. Not that it mattered, for he knew every passage by heart and could recite it easily.

It's worth a try. What do I have to lose?

Marcus withdrew a sharpening stone from his bedside table, sat down with his knife and began sharpening the blade.

"Plannin' on killin' somebody?" Harris asked.

"No . . . not someone." *Yet, anyway.*

"Well, you're not going to need it tomorrow. It's just the training course."

"Always good to be prepared. Besides, maybe it will help me with my problem."

"Couldn't hurt." Harris walked away.

"Goodnight," Marcus said.

When night fell, Marcus snuck out of the barracks and entered the woods, armed with only his knife. In Georgia it was legal to hunt wolves and he knew this undertaking would be daunting, but he had no other choice. Merging his spirit with that of a wolf was the only way he could foresee getting that killer instinct. He searched the ground for tracks, but came up with nothing. He pressed on well into the night but eventually gave up. The forest was as dark as pitch and seeing anything more than ten feet off was impossible. And that was with a flashlight.

Shortly after climbing into bed, exhausted, the alarm went off and a new day began. His morning shower and coffee only stimulated him so much. After so many hours of training, his body craved sleep.

"Come on, recruit, let's see some hustle," the sergeant said through his megaphone.

"Just give up," he heard Harris say from the other side of the twelve-foot wall.

Just a couple of more obstacles, he told himself as he grabbed hold of the rope and hoisted his body. His arms screamed in protest, but he pushed on. Overcoming the pain, he shifted his body to the top of the platform and lay there.

"Move it . . . move it . . . move it. It's not nap time, recruit!"

Marcus grabbed the pulley, then slid down the rope. He dropped to all fours. *I can see the finish line. Everyone's waiting.*

"Are you sleeping?" the sergeant asked as Marcus crawled under the barbed wire.

How could anyone sleep with you barking orders?

"Simply pathetic. I can see you gave my question little to no thought, isn't that right?"

"Sir, no sir!"

"Prove it! Cross that line so we can call it a day."

Marcus grabbed the dangling rope and swung over the mud pit. His legs buckled as he landed and he fell to the ground, his face displacing mud as it pelted the earth. Laughter erupted.

"You just going to lay there and take it?" the sarge growled.

"Sir, no sir," he answered, lifting himself out of the mud. It felt as if his body weighed twice as much as he took several steps toward the finish line.

"C'mon, boy!" Harris teased.

"Push it," said Tony.

As Marcus crossed the finish line, he collapsed once more. Chest tight. Breathing erratic. The sky above him swirled as he teetered on the edge of consciousness.

"Pick him up!" the sarge ordered.

Marcus's teammates helped him to his feet and stood by his side, escorting him to the barracks under the watchful eye of the sergeant. When the men realized the sergeant hadn't followed them in, Harris and Tony mercilessly tossed Marcus on his bed.

Marcus said nothing, too tired to complain, and he knew if he said anything smart that would not be the end of it and only invite more trouble. He dragged himself toward the pillow and drifted to sleep.

He awoke to the sound of rain pelting the roof. Moonlight filtered in through the window above his bed allowing his eyes to quickly adjust to the darkness. Everyone appeared to be sound asleep.

I don't know if it's worth it, he thought. *Last night was a bust, and tonight . . .*

A howl echoed in the night.

Marcus grabbed his knife and headed outside with little regard to waking the others, the rain instantly drenching his uniform. He ran in the direction he thought it originated from and found tracks several yards in.

He knelt down to determine their freshness. *The rainwater hasn't pooled too high. These are fresh.*

A low, guttural growl caught his attention. Looking up, he stared into the wild eyes of a gray and white wolf. He could clearly see the outline of the wolf's ribs. *It's starving*, he thought.

The wolf lunged and ran headlong at him. Marcus stayed down on his knees, knife at the ready. This was it. Either he became a warrior or a meal; there was nothing else for him.

As the wolf leapt, Marcus leaned back and drove his knife deep into the beast's midsection. He received the beast's weight and sliced upward, spilling blood and intestines onto his chest. He fell backward and pushed the wolf's body off him.

I did it!

Marcus ran the blade up the wolf's midsection, the neck, and through the jaw. Then went back, slicing the carcass toward the tail. With that accomplished, he delicately separated skin from muscle, being meticulous to keep the hide intact.

With the animal skinned, he undressed and wrapped himself in the hide, wearing it like a hood and cape. *One more step.* He got down on all fours and lapped the water residing in the wolf's footprint.

A howl forced him to turn around.

It's working, he thought as he stared at the ghostly image of a wolf standing over the carcass. Their eyes locked and for the first time, in a long time, Marcus was not afraid.

"Be one with me."

The phantom image blurred as it ran toward him.

"I'm not afraid," he said as the wolf leapt and disappeared into his chest.

He dropped to all fours, the animal hide burning his skin as it fused with his own. Pain surged through his body as his muscles contorted; his bones snapped, twisted, and reformed;

his fingernails and teeth elongated as his mouth and nose stretched outward. The hairs on his body tingled with life as they intertwined with the wolf's.

With the transformation complete, Marcus stood on his haunches and howled. The forest was alive. He heard the insects marching, the flutter of a bird's wings, and the sound of running water from a brook nearly a mile away.

This was life. This was freedom. This was power.

He ran into the night in search of his first victim.

* * * *

Marcus awoke to the sound of snickering. As his eyes adjusted, he saw the shapes of people hovering around him.

"Gives a new meaning to 'going commando,' doesn't it?"

"Good one, Harris."

"Why am I naked?" Marcus asked, touching his forehead. He had a splitting headache. "What did you guys do to me?"

Harris held his hands out in front of him. "Settle down! We didn't do anything. We found you like this."

An image of him running through the woods hot on the scent of meat flashed before him. "I must have just gotten really hot during the night. I honestly don't remember."

"Regardless, if you're not dressed in five, you're gonna be late. And that reflects on the team." Harris turned away and walked toward the door. The others followed, laughing and giggling like schoolgirls.

A low growl emanated from within, surprising him. "Don't worry," he said, staring out the door, "we'll have our day."

Without regard for hygiene, Marcus got dressed and joined his team at the obstacle course.

"Since you ladies fail to understand that this is a team effort, and a team is only as good as its weakest member, we're running the course again," the sergeant said.

The other guys sighed, obviously preferring a war game to the course, but Marcus didn't mind. This was his time to shine. He could feel the beast eager for the competition.

"Assume the position, ladies," the sarge said and everyone in the squad lined up.

The sergeant fired a shot in the air and Marcus was off, instantly getting ahead of his squad on the straight away run.

"Who lit a fire under his ass?" Harris's voice was unmistakable.

"Beats the hell out of me," Tony said.

"I'm not letting him show me up!" Eric said.

Marcus hustled through the rows of tires, shimmied across the single rope line across the first mud pit with balance and precision, fearlessly crawled under barbed wire and leapt half-way up the wooden wall and climbed the rest without the aid of the dangling rope.

This is easy. I'm not even panting, he thought.

Once at the top of the platform, and with the finish line in sight, he turned back to see the rest of his team still struggling. *They exerted themselves trying to match me. Fools!*

The sergeant got on his bullhorn. "Are you ladies going to let Marcus beat you?"

It felt good hearing the sarge tease them for a change.

"Don't be so smug, Marcus. Team effort, remember?"

Right, Sarge, he thought. *Better wait here and see if anyone needs help climbing the wall.* "Come on, guys." Marcus watched intently as the men reached the bottom of the platform.

"Son-of-a-bitch is cheering us on."

"Knock it off, Harris. He's finally taking this seriously and so should we," Eric said, grabbing the rope.

Harris wrinkled his brow and narrowed his eyes. "Whose side are you on?"

"The team's side."

"Wrong answer!" Harris yanked the rope out of Eric's hands and shoved him to the ground, then ascended the wall.

Marcus looked to the sarge, but he obviously couldn't see the transgression. He locked eyes with Harris. "You rotten, miserable—"

"What are you going to do about it?" Harris asked, pulling himself onto the platform.

"How about I rip your black heart out of your chest and crap it out tomorrow?"

"You're lucky the sarge can see us from here, 'cause I'd knock you off this platform, you little punk."

"Don't stop! Keep moving, else he'll think it suspicious," Tony said as he nudged between the two of them, grabbed the rope and swung to the other side.

Harris threw his shoulder into Marcus as he grabbed the rope on the return. "We'll finish this later."

"Somebody help me," Eric said, struggling at the edge of the platform.

"Sorry, I don't help losers." Harris swung away.

"Nice friend you got there," Marcus said, reaching out.

Eric grabbed his hand. "Damn! What's with the nails? Trim those things."

"Sorry," Marcus replied and hoisted Eric onto the platform.

"Easy! Have you been working out?"

"Not exactly."

"You near pulled my shoulder out."

"I'm just trying to help."

"It's all right, but look at my hand."

There was a nasty gash in the center of Eric's palm, blood running down his wrist. Marcus looked at his own hand and noticed his nails were longer and tapering to a point.

I'll just need to be more careful, he thought. "You ready to finish this?"

"Absolutely."

"You go first. I'm used to bringing up the rear."

Marcus trailed Eric all the way to the finish line and even though he didn't complete the course first, he still managed a far better time.

"More like it. Marcus, I'm proud of you," the sarge said.

"Sir, thank you, sir!"

"And, Harris, don't think I didn't notice that little stunt you pulled. Tonight, while everyone else is sleeping soundly, you will be cleaning the mess hall and I'll be right there watching you."

"Sir, with all due respect . . ."

"Would you rather I write up a formal Article 15, recruit?"

"Sir, no sir."

'Bout time you get yours, Harris.

"Tomorrow you'll be facing off against York's recruits. I expect a coherent team. Understood?"

"Sir, yes sir," they all said.

"Dismissed!"

As they started walking back toward the barracks, the sarge said, "And, Harris, I'll be by at lights out for your punishment."

"Yes, sir," he mumbled.

After showers and dinner the men strategized, going over the mistakes made during the last war game. As usual, Harris took the lead, but surprisingly saved his finger pointing and criticisms. The decision was made to make one alteration to the original plan: to leave Eric as backup for Marcus.

"All right, so you know the plan and what's expected from you?" Harris asked.

Everyone at the table nodded.

Harris stared into Marcus's eyes. "Maybe this time you won't let yourself be overwhelmed."

There it is. Couldn't resist, could you? "I think we'll manage."

Sergeant Barrow stood at the door just as 'lights out' was signaled and he escorted Harris to the mess hall. Marcus did his best to fight back the snicker, afraid of being forced to join him.

As he lay down, ready to sleep, the night came alive. Each heartbeat of his roommates thundered in his ear. No matter how hard he tried, he could not block out the sound. He still needed to master his enhanced senses. He focused on the pleasing sound of an orchestra of insects outside his window. As the beating hearts faded away, the snoring began.

You rotten . . . he thought, sitting up. *I'd rather sleep out there under the stars as nature meant.*

He caught movement to his right and was amazed at how well he could see in the dark. Eric was fidgeting, scratching the palm of his hand. He noticed Marcus staring and stood up from his bed. Eric's eyes were wild with madness and a shock pervaded his body. Eric smiled a toothy grin.

It can't be.

Eric darted off, out the door and into the night.

He looked out the window, up at the full moon in the sky. *The werewolf's curse. I have to stop him. He'll ruin everything. But why haven't I changed?*

There was time to worry about that later. He had to follow him. With his new senses, tracking was easy. He followed the musky scent deep into the woods, away from the barracks.

"Grrrr!"

Marcus stared into the eyes of the largest wolf he had ever seen and couldn't help but wonder if this is what he looked like. *Now that's interesting. No tail.* He remembered reading that men disguised as wolves lacked tails. Sometimes it was the only way of knowing if one was dealing with a werewolf or not.

The wolf took a step forward.

"Easy, boy," he said.

Another step, followed by a low, guttural growl.

"If that's how you want to play it." He felt the wolf inside him itching for a fight. To prove its worth, prove it was alpha.

The change was less painful this time, almost enjoyable. In beast form, he stood on his haunches, extending his arms out to the side, claws at the ready. He howled at the moon. The werewolf before him scrunched down, lowered its head and ears, and whimpered. Its eyes pleaded for forgiveness.

That's right, beast, cower before me.

The wolf slowly approached him, circled around his feet then lay before him.

If it wasn't for his scent, there'd be no telling this was Eric. There doesn't seem to be any trace of his personality, just a wild beast obedient to me. Oh the possibilities.

He barked an order and Eric stood on all fours, then darted off toward the mess hall.

How is it I have all my wits and complete control of the change, yet Eric doesn't?

Marcus headed back toward the barracks, still contemplating. *The werewolf's curse. It must be real and must only pertain to second generation. A single scratch is all it takes.*

He had an idea, one that would turn the tides on Harris. As he passed the mess hall, Eric was in place, ready to distract Harris and Sergeant Barrow should they finish before him. If he was to pull off his plan he needed time and stealth. Entering the barracks, Marcus proceeded to delicately scratch his sleeping roommates. None awoke to his touch. He could picture the slaughter, every wall decorated in crimson if one of them woke up prematurely and sounded the alarm. He'd have to fight his way through, and where would he go then?

With the deed done, he transformed back into a man and signaled for Eric. Still in wolf form, he entered the barracks and lay beside Marcus's bed, keeping to the shadows. *We'll be the perfect platoon.*

Morning came fast, and after breakfast it was time to face the blue squad.

"This is the last war game before finals. Show me what you've learned, ladies," Sergeant Barrow said.

"All right, everyone take your places," Harris said and the squad looked to Marcus.

He nodded for them to obey. Harris stood there dumbfounded as the men carried out their orders.

"What the hell just happened?" he asked.

Marcus stepped toward him, getting in his face. "You're not the big dog around here anymore."

"We'll see about that." Harris headed off to join the others.

Marcus smiled, pleased with himself and his plan. He was surprised to find the men already falling into place. It was instinct. Never in his life did he have this much confidence, this much respect.

Blue squad's trying to end this early, he thought, catching their scent. *They're relying too much on past experience.* A slight rustle in the bushes off to his left confirmed his suspicion. He took a knee, aimed and fired.

"How the—" someone shouted.

"You know the rules, come out of there."

"Two more to the right," Eric said.

The man Marcus hit walked out of the brush, a bright red stain in the center of his goggles.

"No wiping!"

"No duh," the man said, then walked away.

He's out. Now for the other two. Marcus sidestepped to Eric.

"Can you pinpoint their location?" Eric asked.

"Not quite. If they'd just move . . ."

The distinct sound of the nitrogen-powered paintball gun gave their location away, but Eric was in the line of fire. Marcus acted quickly, pushing Eric behind an aluminum wall, then took a knee again. Another paintball was fired. He leaned to his left and the paintball missed its mark. He fired two shots of his own.

"What the . . . . How was that . . . . Must be cheating!" The two men walked out from behind the brush, each sporting a red stain on their chest.

As if that's the only way you guys could lose, right? You're not even worth it. Go cry to Momma.

"Excellent work," Eric said.

"Thank you. Let's see if the others can claim victory for us."

The men didn't disappoint. Within the hour the blue flag was captured and brought to the red team's side, Harris the only casualty.

"Marcus, I'm proud of you. You've shown tremendous improvement," the sarge told him afterward.

"Thank you, sir."

"Harris, I expect you to be less overzealous tomorrow."

"Yes, sir." Harris sounded defeated.

"All of you, fine work. Let's call it a day. Tomorrow we see who becomes a man."

"Sir, yes sir!"

Nothing could bring Marcus down from his high, not even Harris's persistent whining as to why the others were hovering around Marcus rather than him. Seeing Harris shunned as he was amused him. He thought about converting

Harris, but his men had done a fine job, and tonight was the last night for the full moon.

Tonight they feast.

The men went to bed at lights out. None of them stirred until Harris's snoring broke the silence. Marcus drew the curtain and moonlight filled the center of the room. The pack huddled in close and transformed.

"What's going on?" Harris asked, sleepy-eyed.

Marcus smelled the fear as Harris's gaze circled his bed. The beasts surrounded him, a wall of teeth and claws. Harris swallowed hard and when the scent of urine wafted to his nostrils, Marcus barked and the pack descended.

* * * *

"Congratulations, men, you have survived Basic Training."

"Sir, thank you, sir."

"It's a shame Harris decided to go AWOL. I expected better." The sergeant looked to Marcus. "He could have learned something from you. Third time's the charm, right, soldier?"

"Sir, yes sir!"

"Tell me, what career choice have you made? Where will you be going for advanced individual training?"

"I don't know about my squad, but I'll be staying right here for infantry, sir. I think I'd be best suited on the front lines."

"We're staying too, sir." The rest followed in.

"Excellent. With more soldiers like you, we could win this war."

Marcus smiled. *That's the plan.*

SHADOWS OF THE WOLF

"No. I can't."

Damn it, Francesca. "I thought you were ready," Paul said, leaning in, putting his weight behind him in an effort to try and stop her from pushing him off. "I never would have taken you up here if you hadn't said—"

"I know . . . I am . . . but I don't want my first time to be in a car. And especially not with others around."

"A *car?*" He pulled away. "This isn't just a car, babe, it's a classic '67 Mustang Fastback fully restored."

"That doesn't mean anything to me. You know that." She put her hand on his chest and rubbed it in a circular motion. "My first time's supposed to be special. It should be in a bed."

"I suppose you want candlelight, too?" He took her hand by the wrist, pulled it away from him, and placed it on her thigh. The gesture wasn't helping matters; it only increased his arousal.

"I'm serious," she said, dragging the word.

"As for the other cars, what did you expect? It's the weekend." *What a waste. She looks so good.* He looked down at her chest and had to consciously stop himself from licking his lips. *Just two buttons standing between me and those perfectly shaped—*

He propped himself upright in his seat and turned the ignition on.

"Where we going? I can still . . . you know."

"If you're serious, I think I know a place."

"Where?"

"My brother told me about a cabin up on Blue Ridge." He pointed across the cliff to a neighboring mountain. "He used to take his dates there. Says he's only seen the owners there two or three times a year and they keep the key in a potted plant behind the house."

"You think it's empty now?"

"Worth a look, right? Unless you want to try and sneak past my parents."

"No. That's out of the question. I'm not doing anything like that with your parents around."

"The night's still young, your dad said to have you home by midnight. You wanna chance it?"

Francesca smiled with her dimpled cheeks and said, "Why not?"

That's my girl, he thought, then revved the engine. Paul put the gear in reverse and backed away from the lookout.

"I hope no one's home," she said, putting her hand on his thigh. She glided it back and forth, coming oh so close to his happy place, then falling away.

You and me both, babe, he thought as he drove down the mountain.

Though Francesca didn't know it, Paul was still a virgin as well. She had assumed he was experienced with the ladies given the reputation of several of his exes, but he was too embarrassed to correct her. He didn't lie, nor led her to believe he wasn't. He just let it slide and never mentioned it. Tonight was the first time he actually pushed for it, but only after she had whispered her desires in his ear while they watched *Blood of the Dead*, the new zombie flick playing. He had read the book and enjoyed it immensely, the first part of a trilogy, and had waited months to see it on the silver screen, but despite his love for the shambling ghouls and their never-ending lust for living flesh, the need to become a man triumphed, and they left the theater before the half-way mark.

Her boldness in the theater proved that even after seven months of dating, Francesca could still surprise him. She had shocked him when she sent her best friend, Abigail, over to him during a lunch break to ask him out. He had admired her from afar the entire school year, her beauty making him, and several other guys who were man enough to admit it, apprehensive. He accepted without thought. She had surprised him three months into their relationship the first time she performed oral sex on him, and he hadn't even asked or hinted that he wanted it. He remembered the feeling of wanting to marry her at that moment, then remembered the joke about that little cliché.

She amazed him in all she did: her kind-heartedness, her intellect, her dexterity. Though he had no clue as to what he had done to deserve her, he was thankful. He was not the best looking, best dressed, or best anything. He was of average build, a borderline 'A' student, not involved in any sports, his only highlight being the Mustang he and his father refurbished over the summer between junior and senior year and she had made it painfully clear she could care less about it.

Nobody's perfect, he thought.

Feeling a greater appreciation for her, he took his attention off the road for a brief glimpse and was disappointed to see her long black hair had fallen over her shoulder, concealing her ample cleavage at this angle.

Soon, he told himself, then returned his attention to the road in time for the bend.

"I think I see it," Francesca said with enough enthusiasm for the both of them.

"It's pretty big for a cabin, huh?"

"I'll say. And I think it's the perfect place for you know what."

A heat permeated from his cheeks and he couldn't resist the smile forcing its way on his face. He hoped she didn't think him a dork for it.

The road circled around the log cabin and down a slope. He followed it, hoping to keep the car out of sight of passersby. As he drove, he marveled at the structure. The light of the full moon was hindered by clouds, but that only added to its charm. The cabin was a rustic beauty built into the side of a hill. Paul pulled up close to the building, just a few feet from the door.

"The lights are on," Francesca said.

"They're probably on a timer. If you're scared, you can wait here and I'll go take a closer look."

"Okay, keep the engine running just in case we need to bolt."

"Good thinking," Paul said before he stepped out of the car. He thought about not closing the door, then realized how foolish that was because if someone was home, they had already heard the car.

Mindful of his footsteps, he approached the back door and peered through the single-pane glass. He had a clear view into the cabin's kitchen and great room.

No one's here, man. Get on with it. There's the pot Jimmy mentioned.

It was a rather large, but cheap, plastic pot meant to look like terracotta with a variety of marigolds and pansies. He strained his neck as he scanned the foliage until a metal tin, propped against the inside rim, caught his eye.

Perfect, he thought as he popped the lid and revealed a brass key. He opened the door and stepped inside. "Anybody home?" he asked. "We mean no harm."

Paul walked through the kitchen and into the great room. *This is beautiful.* He took notice of the vaulted ceilings and a stone gas log fireplace centered on the opposite wall.

"Hello!" he asked again, fully expecting someone to jump out and grab hold of him, but no one responded. He shrugged his shoulders and walked outside to fetch Francesca, on the way returning the key to its rightful place.

"Well?" she asked, leaning her head out the open car window.

"It's clear, babe."

"Really?"

"Yeah, c'mon."

Together they entered the cabin. Paul gave Francesca a minute to gawk and fantasize about owning such a place. He could see her desire written plainly on her face, her wide eyes and drooping lower lip. It was as if her head was on a turnstile, swiveling to and fro trying to see everything.

There aren't many properties like this in Virginia. "Let's go upstairs," he said, taking her hand in his.

"Lead the way."

The master bedroom was located right at the top of the stairs with an adjoining bathroom. The bed frame was a carved mahogany with wrought iron accents.

"Is that a Jacuzzi tub in there?" Francesca asked, stretching her neck to its max.

"I don't know," he said, releasing her hand. "Go find out."

She darted off, giggling.

"It is," she squealed.

"What was that?" he asked after hearing a metallic clang.

"I didn't hear anything," she said, returning to the bedroom.

"Listen." He leaned over the handrail outside the room.

Ching-ching.

"There it is."

Ching-ching.

"It's coming from downstairs," she said as she approached.

Ching-ching.

"We better check it out," he said.

"No, we should probably get out of here while we can."

"It's probably just an animal, Francesca. Do you really want to give up this easily?" He puffed his lips and opened his eyes wide.

"Don't look at me like that," she said, turning away.

"C'mon," he said, dragging the word.

"Okay, we'll check it out."

Ching-ching.

"It's getting louder," Paul said as they took their first few steps down to the main level.

She gripped his arm. "What do you think it could be?"

"Probably a raccoon or something. Sounds like it's coming from behind that door."

"You go first," she said, stepping behind him.

He smiled and reached for the door handle.

"May be we should just go back upstairs and ignore it?"

"Seriously? You know you won't be able to."

She nodded. He opened the door.

Odd, he thought. The basement light was already on and though he tried to step lightly, the stair creaked under his weight. The metallic sound's intensity increased and became a constant clatter. Paul picked up the pace and took the steps two at a time.

When he was at the bottom, he said, his voice barely audible, "Francesca . . . I need you."

She came down the stairs. "What is it? Is it bad?"

She gasped.

The sound had been coming from a woman trapped inside a steel cage. She was bent low at the knees, with her palms pressed against the concrete floor. Paul would have found her beautiful if not for the toothy grin and white foam clinging to the corners of her mouth. Tongue flopped out, she panted as if she was a dog.

"Are you okay?" Francesca asked as she approached the cage.

Why is she here? And where's the bastard who put her in there?

Francesca checked the lock on the door. "It's okay. We'll help." She reached in for reasons unknown to Paul.

"No. Don't!"

The woman lunged at the cage and swiped at Francesca.

"Oww!" Francesca clutched her arm and stepped back.

He stepped toward her. "Are you all right?"

"Yeah," she answered, inspecting her arm.

Three thin lines ran down the inside of her forearm with a faint trace of blood on the surface. "It's just a scratch."

"I know. I'll be all right." She turned toward the woman in the cage and asked, "Who did this to you?"

The woman said nothing and continued to pant.

"Probably some ugly, redneck hillbilly in overalls and a few missing teeth. Someone who couldn't get a date if his life depended on it."

"That's a little harsh," Francesca mumbled as she looked away from him. He let it slide.

Paul scanned the room. The basement was one open room with two support beams staggered along the center. The cage was centered on the backside wall of the cabin. On the left hand side was a workbench with a vinyl surface and the biggest vice he had ever seen, the wall above covered in pegboard and housing a variety of tools. He made note of the hacksaw should they not find the key to the padlock on the cage door. On the other side of the room was a gurney and medical cabinet. Scattered, broken pieces of brown glass were on the floor just a few inches from the cabinet.

It was a bottle . . . but of what, he thought as he approached the largest piece; the sticky paper label had kept it intact. He picked up the piece and turned it over to read it. *Tranquilizer.*

"Well . . . this'll explain her behavior," he said, holding the piece out to Francesca. "He's been keeping her drugged. Who knows how long she's been down here."

"He's treating her like an animal, but it looks like the effects of the drug are wearing off. I imagine she'd be more docile if he had just given it to her. Either way, we have to help her."

"I don't know . . . maybe we should go and get the sheriff."

"We can't leave her," she snapped.

Paul looked toward the cage. The woman was motionless, crouched down and panting. "What if he comes back?"

"Exactly! The sheriff might not make it here in time."

"If he was going to kill her, he'd have already done it."

"How do you know? This could be his tenth victim for all we know."

"Fine!" he said, throwing his hands in the air. The look on her face, the glaring eyes and pursed lips, told him arguing was futile. "Help me look for the keys. Check the cabinet, I'll look over here."

While Francesca searched the medical cabinet, Paul searched the workbench, opening all its drawers and tiny compartments. He came up empty. Nothing but nails, screws and screwdrivers, pliers, and ratchets and an assortment of socket adaptors.

Looks like it's gonna be the hacksaw, he thought, eyeing it once more.

"Any luck?" Francesca asked.

"There's this," he said, holding up the saw for her to see.

"You up for it?"

"Depends." He fought back a smile.

"On what?"

"If you're going to make it worth my while."

She crossed her arms in front of her chest. "You think this is the time to be joking around?"

Guess not. "I'll get to work." *Stupid idiot, you make a joke of everything. Why do you always do that?*

Paul inspected the chain and the lock, and decided he had a better chance at sawing through a chain link rather than the lock's arm as it seemed to have a smaller diameter. He rested the blade against a link and gently scored the metal.

Ching-ching.

Paul jumped backward, startled by the woman's aggression. "What the hell, lady?"

"Don't be upset. It's not her fault. She doesn't understand we're trying to help."

"I'm a little past upset." He eyed the woman, then returned to the chain. He worked slow and steady at first; making himself a nice groove so the blade wouldn't slip when he gave it more vigor.

The woman remained in the center of the cage as he increased his momentum. After fifteen minutes of steady sawing, his shoulder started to protest. Tightness spread in the muscle and all he had to show for his effort was a fine layer of silver dust on the web of his thumb and index finger, with a little excess on the floor.

"This is going to take forever," he said.

"If you're tired, I can take over for a bit."

"I don't think this is such a good idea. We're taking an awful big risk."

"Let me try," Francesca said in a soft but firm voice.

"All right," he replied, handing her the saw. "But we won't be doing her any good if we get caught ourselves."

Francesca immediately went to work, the blade flying back and forth within the groove Paul made.

"You're going to burn yourself out faster that way."

"This was all you found to use on this?" she asked. The arm holding the saw dropped to her side.

Paul stepped toward her and reached for the saw. "Let me take over again."

She allowed him to take it. "I'll admit, it's tougher than I thought."

Paul continued to work the chain over and was approaching the half-way mark when the sound of a diesel engine pulling up to the cabin caused him to stop. He swallowed hard, but he tried not to show his fear for Francesca's sake.

"What are we going to do?" she said.

"I want you to hide."

"Where? There's no place down here."

The front door slammed shut.

Crap! No time for her to hide upstairs. "Get a hammer out of the drawer. We'll fight if we have to."

She nodded and obeyed. Paul looked up to the ceiling, following the thumps of the footsteps. Francesca returned to his side, hammer clutched in front of her chest with both hands. He stepped in front of her as a shield when the door at the top of the stairs opened. The silhouette of a man filled the doorway.

He's not searching the place. He knows we're trying to save her.

"Whatever you're doing, I suggest you stop it. This isn't what it looks like." The man took a step. "Just so you know, I have a gun. Don't make me use it."

Francesca leaned in close and whispered, "What are we going to do?"

"Nothing yet."

The man reached the bottom of the stairs and trained his shotgun on Paul. He was nothing like Paul expected: clean-shaven, black hair trimmed short, blue jeans with a brown belt and a non-flannel, button down shirt. In his hand holding the barrel of the gun was a brown paper bag. It was pinched tight at the top and Paul could make out the shape of a bottle.

More tranquilizer, I bet. Not big enough to be booze.

The caged woman snarled at the sight of the man. Though he looked like any other neighbor, she seemed to know otherwise.

"You kids step away from the cage. It's dangerous," the man said.

"The only thing dangerous here is that gun," Francesca said from behind Paul.

Paul put his hands up. "Let us go. We won't say anything."

"I can't do that," the man said.

"Yes, you can," Francesca said. "You can let us all go."

"My wife stays."

"Your wife!"

Paul winced at the sound of Francesca's high pitched accent on the last word. "How could you treat her like this?" he asked, taking his eyes off the man to look at the woman, who was pacing the perimeter of the cage. Her gaze locked on her husband with malicious intent. *She's been in there so long she believes herself to be an animal.* He turned back toward the man with a gun.

"You think I like locking her up? You have no idea what you're talking about."

"Then enlighten me," Paul said.

The man shook his head as if he contemplated the thought. "I'm afraid you're stuck here 'til morning. Now" —he waved the barrel of the gun to the right— "step aside."

"What are you going to do?"

"I need to give her some of this," he said, raising the bag.

The gun's not loaded with bullets. It's got to be tranq darts. But I don't think I can risk it.

The barrel was shifted from Paul to the caged woman. She snarled and leapt at the cage door. It buckled under the weight, but held.

"Easy, Maria," the man said softly as he took aim.

If you're going to do it, do it now. Paul lunged forward and gripped the barrel.

"Paul!" Francesca shrieked.

"What are you doing?" the man asked as he struggled to maintain his grip. "You're making a mistake."

"Give me the gun," Paul demanded.

"No!"

The gun fired. A pinch in Paul's abdomen. Heat. Francesca screamed.

Paul winced as he pulled the dart out of his gut. The caged woman slammed her body into the steel door. The chain snapped, the compromised link unable to withstand another blow.

"What have you done?" the man said as his wife darted up the stairs on all fours.

The room swayed and Paul fell to the floor. Everything seemed distant; he didn't know how long he'd remain lucid and feared for Francesca.

"You shot him!" Francesca said.

"He'll live, but not if we don't get inside there. As soon as she sees the moon, we're doomed."

The man grabbed Paul by the left shoulder and dragged him toward the cage. He tried to grab the man, tried to fight against him, but his body refused to obey.

"We are not going in there," she said adamantly.

You tell him, babe.

A howl echoed in the night.

"What was that?" Francesca asked.

"What I was trying to keep locked up. Get inside or I'm closing it without you."

Paul tried to tell her to listen to the man, but only a moan escaped his lips.

"What is it, baby?" she asked him, leaning toward his mouth as if doing so would allow her to understand him.

It took every ounce of strength and will to lift his hand and point to the cage. She nodded.

"Okay," she said, then grabbed Paul's other shoulder and together she and the man dragged him inside the cage.

Fingernails scraped along the outside wall and the man immediately went to work on the lock. He pulled a key out of his pants pocket, disengaged the lock, and tightened the chain. All Paul could do was watch helplessly. His life and the life of the one he loved most was in the hands of this man who, moments earlier, he thought a psycho.

"Thank God there's enough slack in this chain. If your boyfriend had cut a few links lower we'd be utterly . . . well . . . you know."

Darkness closed in from the corners of his eyes as the lock was engaged and the man stepped toward the center of the cage. A loud thud caused Francesca to scream and the man to raise his gun. The upstairs door crashed at the bottom of the steps; splinters of wood and dust flew into the air. A shadow stretched along the wall. Paul's vision blurred. All was dreamlike as a silhouette of a wolf the size of two men grew larger with every creak of the stairs. Unable to fight the drug any longer, the last thing he felt was Francesca taking his hand in hers.

* * * *

Paul awoke with a start. "Look out!"

"Easy," Francesca said in a hushed voice. "It's okay. We're safe."

He took a moment to gather his bearings. He sat in the passenger's side of his car. The morning sun coming over the horizon stung his eyes. He looked out the side window and saw Francesca's house. His head swung round to look at her.

"I'm too scared to go in. My father's going to kill me."

"How'd we get here?"

"You were so brave. After you got shot with that tranquilizer, I clubbed that sicko with the hammer. I dragged you out of there and called the police, but I got us out of there before they arrived."

"What about the monster?"

"Monster? There was no monster," she said, one eyebrow raised higher than the other.

"I could of . . ."

"You were probably trippin'. Who knows what kind of drugs he was using and how much."

"I guess," he said, though he doubted it. *Why would she lie, right?* "What about the woman he had captive?"

"She got outta there. Probably ran off in the woods. I better go. Are you gonna be okay driving home?"

"I'll take another minute, but if your father charges out here with that crazed look, I'm gone. Lucid or not."

She chuckled. "I wouldn't blame you. Call me when you get home, okay?"

"I will."

She kissed him lightly on the lips and exited the car. He watched her head up the walkway then saw the front door open and her father fill the doorway. The man looked at him with daggers in his eyes and he quickly scooted over the shift and into the driver's seat, turned the engine, and smoked his tires as he pulled away.

I hope he takes it easy on her. It'll be easy enough to prove if he doesn't believe her.

When Paul got home he, too, had some explaining to do. After hearing his story, his mother made a big deal of it and was about to call the sheriff for confirmation, but his father talked her out of it. He looked mighty pleased with him. There was a wide smile on his face and Paul could almost read his mind. *He'll be even happier when I finally do become a man*, he thought as his father dismissed him to talk privately with his mother. He walked out of the living room, rounded the corner and walked up the stairs to his room all the while wondering what kind of punishment they'd lay down.

Can't worry about it now. Could be worse. The vision of the shadow on the wall inside that basement returned. *I could be passing through the lower intestine of that creature I saw. It was so real.*

He threw himself down onto his bed, still groggy from the tranquilizers. *That was some powerful stuff.*

He folded his arms behind his head and leaned into them. He closed his eyes for a moment and an image of a gray wolf with jaws large enough to swallow his head came and went.

"I've got to go back." He sat up and a knock wrapped against the door. "Come in."

"Hey, champ," his father said as he opened the door and entered.

"How bad is it?" Paul asked.

"Well . . . your mother's not happy. Not happy at all. But I convinced her that you're seventeen—"

"Almost eighteen."

"Yes, almost eighteen and there are certain freedoms you should have. However, we both agree that staying out all night is not one of them."

"But—"

"Last night will be an exception. Your mother called the sheriff, but couldn't get a hold of him as he's not in right now. Your mother couldn't get specifics, but it's safe to assume you're telling the truth."

"I really should go out there and try to help. Francesca was scared and panicked."

"Understandable. If you feel it's something you should do, then go ahead. I'd go with you, but I have to go into the office."

"On a Saturday?"

"Yeah, I know, but we have a huge Navy contract to bid on. It could mean work for a lot of people."

"Good luck, then."

"Thanks . . . and should you be out all night who knows where with Francesca again, I don't need to tell you—"

"No, Dad, you don't."

His father smiled and nodded, then left the room. Paul was about to follow him, but when he stood, he got a whiff of himself and decided to shower and change his clothes.

Once he was ready, his father had already gone and his mother was on the phone. He waved to her as he walked by.

Out of the corner of his eye he saw her put her hand on the receiver and raise her hand to halt him, but he pretended not to see and carried on his way. She said nothing, so he was guilt free.

He drove to the cabin, obeying the speed limit for the first time since passing the driving test, knowing cops would be on, and around, the scene. When he arrived, he was shocked to see no officers there, no yellow caution tape, no anything. He drove around back, hoping to find someone, but he was alone.

He parked in the same spot he had last night and went straight for the flower pot. The key was still nestled in its hiding place. He grabbed it, then opened the front door. Though he wasn't sure why, he put the key back before heading downstairs.

Well at least I know part of it happened, he thought as he approached the cage door. The chain was broken, as he remembered, but the lock was open. *Strange. Why did Francesca lie? There's no way she called the police. And now that guy is long gone. I should call her.*

He retrieved his phone from his front pocket and as he dialed, he thought about what he would say should her father answer it. He flipped it closed. *Better to just show up. That way I can at least get a word in.*

He left the cabin and headed for Francesca's place. She lived in one of the more rural areas, nearly a forty-minute drive from the base of the mountain. When he arrived, he knocked on the door expecting Mr. Madaffari, but no one answered.

"Hello," he said after checking the knob and the door opened. "The door was open."

Paul closed the door behind him and stepped into the foyer. He craned his neck to look up the stairs and saw no one; looked to the right and found nothing in the den; then turned to the left and saw a pair of feet on the floor behind the sofa in the living room.

"Are you all right?" he asked as he dashed into the room.

Francesca's father lay face down on the floor in a pool of blood. He knelt down beside him and gently rolled him over. The cold blood soaked through his jeans.

"It wasn't a dream," he whispered, seeing Mr. Madaffari's throat ripped out by a single bite. "Francesca!"

Fearing the beast had somehow followed them, he dropped her father's lifeless body, stood and turned around in time to see an aluminum baseball bat careening toward him. It hit in the center of his forehead and darkness claimed him as his body fell backwards.

When he awoke, Francesca hovered over him. Her beautifully sculpted naked body calmed him for the briefest of moments.

What's going on? he thought. His arms and legs felt stiff. He tried to move them, but soon realized he was tied to her bed frame. He was cold and naked. As she placed the palms of her hands on his chest, he noticed the scratch the caged woman had given her and the brown hair growing from the wound.

"Figured it out, have you?" she asked as she pressed her weight against him. There were tears in her eyes. This demeanor of hers seemed forced.

"Why did you lie to me? I thought you were better than that."

"You really gave me no choice."

"What?"

"By the middle of the night I was experiencing . . . unnatural urges. I figured out what was happening. I was becoming like her. You called that woman a monster. What choice did you give me?"

"No . . . I . . ."

She shook her head. "Even now, your contempt is evident in your eyes."

"And what about your father? Did you kill him?"

"And Mother, too. She's in their bedroom. They wouldn't shut up. Kept scolding me like I was a child. I just wanted them to shut up. I—" She sniffled. "I exploded. Then I . . . I liked it. No, wait. I didn't! I did."

"Then you are a monster."

"Well, I still love you, and if you survive this, we can still be together. It'll mean we were indeed meant for each other."

Hope filled her eyes. Her sudden swap between mad dog and princess made a shiver run through him.

"Survive what? What are you going to do to me?"

"I'm going to do what I promised. We're going to make love." She shifted her waist toward his pelvic region. He felt her warmth encompass him. "You'll be my first. And we'll do it by moonlight." She opened the curtain as she continued to gyrate on him.

Paul looked out the window over her bed and wondered how long he had been out, then he felt movement across his thigh and waist. He straightened his head to see Francesca bathed in moonlight. Her skin bubbled as thick hair sprouted and covered her body. Her ears elongated and tapered to a point. Joints popped and twisted. A wail turned into a howl as her mouth stretched toward him, her button nose blackened over and her blunt teeth unrooted and rained down upon his chest as sharp, canine teeth forced their way through the gums.

"Francesca . . . please . . . if you're in there, let me go. I love you," he said.

He looked into the beast's eyes.

She leaned in.

He prayed it was for a kiss.

ANIMAL BEHAVIOR

"Do you think we'll get one?" Nicky Schmidt asked as he watched, from afar, Leah Tipper hand out invitations to her annual Halloween party.

"How am I supposed to know? Am I a mind reader?"

Nicky looked at his friend, Jonah Morgan, and wished for once he could drop the sarcastic attitude.

"What?" Jonah asked. "C'mon, it was a stupid question. You know she really hasn't spoken to us lately."

"You think she's still pissed about last year? I mean . . . she should have been flattered."

"Right. I thought girls loved when guys fight over them."

Nicky's gaze returned to Leah and her tight rainbow-striped sweater, the fabric leaving none of her curves to the imagination. "Yeah . . . well . . . she's different, I guess."

Jonah wailed his balled fist into Nicky's right arm. "Don't look at her like that. What have I told you about that?"

Nicky clenched his teeth as the pain spiked. "When she finally says yes to your indecent proposal, then I'll stop looking at her with sex in my eyes, deal?"

Jonah released a nasal laugh. "You're a real douche. I don't know why I let you hang with me."

"'Cause I'm the only one who'll put up with your crap."

"True." He shrugged. "Be cool, she's coming over."

Leah stepped up to them. Without saying a word, she produced two envelopes from her backpack and held them out. "I don't want a repeat of last year. Understood?"

"Of course. I'm over you anyway," Jonah said.

"He means thank you," Nicky said, taking both envelopes. Jonah narrowed his eyes at him for a second only, then returned his attention to Leah.

Oh crap. Nicky saw Jeremy Talbout approach. His brow wrinkled in disgust and his lips pursed.

"Why you giving them an invitation? You already know what they're going to be," Jeremy said.

"Well, in all honesty," said Jeremy's best friend, "that pathetic white make-up has got to be almost gone by now. After all, this would be, what, the fourth year you've dressed up as skeletons?" Michael made quotation marks with his fingers, emphasizing "skeletons."

Jonah stepped directly in front of Michael, getting in his face. "Maybe you should tell your friend here about that missing tooth of yours."

Nicky saw Leah's eyes open wide and immediately stepped in between the two. "Now, now, no worries here." He gave Jonah the *look*—the single raised eyebrow and flared nostrils—as he pushed him away. "No worries, Leah, they'll be no fighting here or at your party."

Jonah's anger left his face as he obviously realized Nicky's intent. "Yeah, I'm sorry, just a temporary lapse. These guys aren't worth it."

"So you're okay that Jeremy is my date for the party, then?" Leah asked, a devilish grin on her face.

She's testing him, Nicky thought.

Jonah added through clinched teeth, "I'm over you."

"Good. And just so you know, there will be a costume contest, but no pressure, okay?"

Jonah nodded.

"See you losers around." Jeremy grabbed Leah's hand. "C'mon, babe."

"What does she see in him?" Jonah asked as the others walked away.

"I really don't know, but you better behave or we're not going to be able to go. There'll be other girls."

"Okay, *Mom*."

Nicky ignored the sarcasm. "We should get to class."

"Yeah. Thanks for stopping me from doing something stupid. Had I cold-cocked him, Leah probably would start dating them both."

"Stranger things have happened." Nicky smiled. He knew what his friend was getting at. Leah had done the complete opposite of what both of them had thought. In the movies, the girl always fell for the tough guy, but Leah had comforted the loser of Jonah and Jeremy's fight, and the two became close friends.

Nicky knew any chance Jonah had with her was gone, but he would never admit that out loud. What Leah and Jeremy had was more than a high school crush, anyone could see. They took their time, got to know each other, and love blossomed the way it was meant to.

The school day finished without another incident. Their paths never crossed with Jeremy and Michael's, though Nicky had observed Jeremy staring at them in the cafeteria during lunch. He said nothing, afraid it might instigate another confrontation.

They walked home the usual way, cutting through the Pennsylvania woods that surrounded Central High School. It was a serene alternative to the noisy, crowded bus. Products of single-parent families—Nicky and his sister without a mother and Jonah without a father—neither had anyone to go home to, so there was no rush. They had attempted to hook their parents up on several occasions, the fantasy of being brothers too good to pass up, but neither parent was ready for a commitment.

Looking around, Nicky didn't understand how most of the other kids were too afraid to enter the woods. Yes, they were home to all manner of critters, but the scariest animal they ever saw was a fully-antlered buck. As they walked, Nicky did his best to derail any conversation of Leah and or Jeremy.

"Shh! Did you hear that?" Jeremy stopped and listened.

"No," Nicky whispered. "What did you hear?"

"Not sure. It sounded like a dog."

Nicky stood still and strained to hear, then he picked up on the sound. "It's coming from over there." He pointed to his left. "It sounds hurt."

"Let's check it out," Jonah said, slapping the backside of his hand into Nicky's gut as he started to jog.

"Wait up," he called after him. Fallen autumn leaves crunched and crumbled under their feet as they trampled through the woods. A wolf's howl caused both of them to stop dead in their tracks.

"We should go," Nicky said, seeing the gray wolf off in the distance.

"Something's wrong." Jonah took a step. "I think it's hurt."

Nicky grabbed him by the arm. "Dude, if there's one, there's more."

Jonah looked around, obviously realizing he spoke the truth. "Um, I don't see any. C'mon."

Nicky let his arm go and followed closely behind, his head rotating back and forth. He saw nothing. No squirrels, no birds, and no deer. *That's just too strange.*

Though the trees were already barren, and the forest floor offered little in the way of hiding spots—just a few boulders and shrubs—it did little to calm his nerves. They were fit, but Nicky doubted they could out run a pack of wolves.

The wolf growled in protest at their approach, and as they got closer, Nicky saw the bear trap clamped around its front paw. The wolf barked and nipped at the air even though they stood several feet away.

"What do we do?" Jonah asked. "Do we help it?"

"We can't risk it. It could bite us before we even got close enough. Or maul us after we've released it."

"You want to just leave it? We should at least put it out of its misery."

"And how do you propose we do that?"

Jonah scanned the ground. "Ah ha!" He darted off a few feet away, bent over and came up with a tree branch. It looked to be around five inches in diameter.

"No," Nicky said, shaking his head.

"Why not? You got a better idea?"

"Yeah, let's just leave."

The wolf growled and tugged on the bear trap. The chain rattled from the slack, but it held strong and secure. The trap's jaws dug deeper into the bone; the wolf whimpered and licked at the wound.

Jonah looked at him. "If we don't do this, it'll gnaw off its own foot, then bleed to death as it tries to walk off. That's a terrible way to go for any creature."

Nicky knew he was right, but it didn't make it any easier.

"Turn away if you have to," Jonah said as he stepped up to the wolf.

Nicky just stood there, eyes wide. He thought he wanted to turn away, but for whatever reason he was transfixed, his morbid curiosity getting the best of him. With unblinking eyes he watched as Jonah raised his club overhead and smashed it down on the wolf's skull. It whimpered and collapsed, but it was still alive.

"Hit it again!" Nicky said, fearing the beast's suffering was worse now.

Jonah brought the club down on it three more times. Each time he raised the club more blood and grue clung to the end. He raised his makeshift weapon once more and waited.

"It's done," Nicky said, walking over to his friend and placing his hand on Jonah's wrist. He guided his friend's arms down and Jonah released the club.

"I wasn't strong enough to do it in a single blow."

Nicky patted him on the back. "It couldn't be helped."

Jonah stared at the carcass. "What a mess."

"I'll say," Nicky said, looking at the wolf's cracked skull. Part of its scalp still clung to the club lying at their feet. Inside the cranial opening, there were slimy curves and folds of the brain tissue. To his surprise, he wasn't disgusted. In fact, the sight recalled a piece of information he had once read: "Did you know some Europeans believe you can become a werewolf by eating a wolf's brain?"

"What? C'mon . . . get out. You serious?"

"I don't know how serious it is. I read it online."

"That would be friggin' sweet, wouldn't it? Imagine!"

"I suppose."

"Think you could do it?"

Nicky felt his lip curl in disgust. His stomach twisted at the thought. "I don't know, man. You?"

"I could probably do it. Do you know if you can cook it, or do you have to eat it raw? I don't think I can eat it raw."

Nicky felt his jaw go slack. "You seriously considering it? Dude, I read it on the *internet*. The internet, okay? It's the same place that claims Bigfoot stalks the earth and some guy named Bubba John gets kidnapped by aliens six nights out of seven."

"Six nights out of seven, huh? Hey, I'm a Bigfoot fan. Love werewolves, too. Sheesh, man, why not? Think about it: we'd have the best Halloween costumes ever."

"Okay, first off, I ain't eating that," Nicky said, pointing at the carcass. "Secondly, there was already a full moon this month. Third, it stinks. I hate that dog smell."

"Who's to say you need a full moon at all? Why can't *any* moon work?"

"We have only one moon."

Jonah looked at him crossly.

"You know what I mean. Besides, I didn't make the rules," Nicky said, crossing his arms.

"No, Hollywood did. You're being a douche. What's it going to hurt?"

"It's disgusting!"

"It was your idea!"

"Na-ah! I was just shooting the breeze. Seeing it reminded me what I read, that's all. I never—"

"Fine. Then go home. I'm going to make a little campfire and have me some brains." He clapped his hands in front of his chest and rubbed them together greedily, a sickening joke for sure, but Nicky wasn't going to give Jonah the satisfaction of knowing he was getting to him.

Nicky steeled his nerves and watched in disbelief as Jonah gathered some rocks and twigs. He thought about leaving him, but the idea of Jonah getting sick and being deep in the woods alone kept him planted.

"So you're staying?" Jonah asked as he dropped his loot.

"Yeah."

Jonah said nothing more. He placed his rocks in a circular pattern and placed the twigs in the center, forming a tepee, and shoved some dry leaves into it. He pulled out his mother's silver flip-top lighter from his back pocket—stolen from her dresser after she finally quit a twenty-year smoking binge—then lit the decaying foliage. Smoke drifted in the air from the lit leaves and finally the structure was consumed by flames.

"So how're you going to do this?" Nicky asked.

"Like roasting marshmallows," he said, grabbing another stick.

"Do you think the hole is wide enough?"

Jonah grabbed the wolf by the scruff and lifted the head slightly off the ground. "Probably could be bigger, but that club started to splinter. I don't think it could handle another blow."

Nicky walked over to the trap and tried to pry it open, but it wouldn't budge. "Help me with this." *Can't believe I'm doing this. I'm a sick, sick puppy.* He smirked at the bad pun.

Jonah grabbed one end, careful not to cut himself on an exposed metal tooth, and Nicky put both hands on his end. The two pulled in opposite directions. The jaws moved slowly, but with a little sweat and endurance, the mechanism opened enough to slip it off the wolf's leg.

"On three," Nicky said.

"Wait . . . what?"

"Let it go on three so we can use it to smash in its skull."

"Oh, okay, got ya."

"One . . . two . . . three." Both of them released the trap. The jaws snapped shut, making a metallic *thwang* as the device fell to the ground.

"Could have easily lost a finger or two in that thing," Nicky said.

"No kidding." Jonah picked the trap up and aimed it at the wolf's skull. He brought it down and the wolf's cranium caved in on impact. As he straightened his back, the trap came away dripping blood, a piece of brain matter clinging to its edge.

Nicky turned away, his stomach turning slow and sure like an old-fashioned ice cream maker.

"It feels so slimy," Jonah said.

Nicky turned to see what he was talking about and quickly regretted it. The sight of his fingers probing inside the wolf's skull was the final straw. He turned away and yakked partially digested sloppy joes and tater tots.

"What's wrong with you?"

"Me?" Nicky said, wiping his mouth on his sleeve. "What's wrong with you? You're the one sticking your hands in there."

Jonah pulled out a slick, spongy-looking pinky-gray glob and held it out for him to see. "I take it you won't be joining me, then?"

"I don't know." He walked away.

"If you don't, I'll show everyone at school your sister's picture. You know the one."

"Dude, you wouldn't."

"Of course I would. And your sister is sure to find out you gave it to me."

Nicky thought about that. If Maria knew he'd taken that Polaroid in the middle of the night, she'd kick his butt, then his father would take a crack at him too. He hadn't been the one who snapped the picture—Maria's girlfriend Kelly had during a sleepover—why, he didn't know—but he was spying nonetheless and got an eye full of both of them. "Fine. Let's get this over with."

Jonah smiled triumphantly as he walked to the fire. He crammed the stick into the chunk of brain matter and hovered it over the fire. When the surface was completely blackened, he asked, "You think it's ready?"

"I don't know. Looks like burnt burger. Try it." Nicky fought back a smile when he saw the look of apprehension on Jonah's face. "Well?"

"All right, all right." Jonah plucked a sizable piece off and shoved it into his mouth.

"How is it?"

He chewed for a few moments before answering. "It's . . . quite good, actually."

"Let me try." Nicky pulled off a piece and stared at it long and hard.

"Well? What're you waiting for?"

Nicky closed his eyes and plopped it into his mouth. It was slightly bitter, but had the familiar taste of pork.

They each took another piece and continued until the hunk of meat was gone.

"Should we cook some more?" Jonah asked.

"Nah. We should get out of here. The smoke has gotten high. Someone might think it's a forest fire."

"Good point." Jonah stood and raked his foot along the ground, kicking dirt onto the fire. He kept it up until it was smothered. "We should stick together. Why don't you sleep over at my house tonight?"

"Okay."

As they walked not a word was passed between the two. There was tightness in Nicky's stomach, an uneasy roiling. He didn't feel like he was going to throw up again, but it was an odd feeling he was unfamiliar with, sort of a cross between being full and satisfied, but nauseous all the same. Jonah's right hand was pressed against his stomach, and though Nicky wanted to ask if he was okay, he was afraid if heard otherwise it might put him over the top, and another bout of vomiting would come about.

If he wants to tell me, he will, he figured.

When they arrived at Jonah's house, Nicky felt some relief and he noticed Jonah's hand was by his side so he assumed he was feeling good, too. As expected, Jonah's mother was nowhere insight and the two headed upstairs to Jonah's bedroom.

Nicky looked around the room and wondered where he was going to sleep. The floor was covered with discarded clothes, magazines, video game cases, and an empty potato chip bag. He watched his step and walked over to the terrarium on Jonah's desk.

"You gonna hold her this time?" Jonah asked.

The Chilean Rose Hair tarantula in the five-gallon tank sent shivers dancing down Nicky's spine. The spider was nestled inside a tree hollow Jonah had carved. He loved and spoiled the thing, feeding it cockroaches and the entrails of other vermin. The spider stared at him, daring him to stick his hand inside the tank so she might sink those fangs of hers into his tender flesh and pump venom deep inside his veins.

"I don't think so," he finally said.

"What a girl! You know it loves ya when it doesn't bite."

"Same can be said for a normal pet . . . like a *dog*!"

Jonah waved his hand, dismissing the idea. "Agh!"

He knew he was being silly. The venom stored in the arachnid wasn't potent enough to kill a person unless they were allergic. Statistically speaking a person had a greater risk of being mauled to death by a dog then dying from a venomous bite. That knowledge did nothing to lessen his anxiety of touching the creature.

"So . . . any requests for dinner?" Jonah asked.

Nicky tilted his head in apprehension. "You cooking?"

"Yep."

"More brain?"

"Ha ha."

"Nah. It's okay. I've changed my mind. I'm going to head home. I'll call you—"

"Don't be silly," Jonah said with a smile. "If it'll make you feel better I'll toss in a frozen pizza."

"That'll do."

"All right, then . . . it's not delivery!"

The two laughed heartedly.

"What's wrong?" Nicky asked when Jonah stopped.

"You smell that? Sunflowers." Jonah pushed passed Nicky, making a bee-line to the window. "What's she doing next door?"

"Who?" Nicky asked as he walked over to his side. "Leah?"

"Yeah. That's her, right?"

"I think so."

The two stared out the window; Nicky saw Jonah was as perplexed as he was as to why she was in the neighborhood.

Jonah turned from the window. "I'm going out there."

"No, wait!" Nicky grabbed him by the arm. Jeremy had just appeared from the bushes that ran along the side of the house. "She's not alone. Better to stay here."

"Aw, man. What a douche." Jonah leaned against the sill, his body filling the window frame. "Do you remember seeing Lily at school today?"

Nicky gave it some thought. "No, I don't."

"Yep. She just slid an envelope into the mail slot. Must be an invitation to the party."

"You should get out of the window before they see you," Nicky said unable to see.

"Too late."

"Dude!"

"She's staring at me. I knew it. She's still interested in more than friendship." He paused, then Jonah mumbled. "Same to you!"

"What is it?" Nicky pushed his way to see.

"He pegged me off when he noticed I was the one she was looking at. Jealous prick."

"Ah!" Jonah stepped away from the window as Leah and Jeremy got in Jeremy's Cavalier.

Nicky watched them drive off all the while wondering how Jonah knew she was out there. How could he have smelled her when he was inside and the window was closed?

"Pizza time!" Jonah said as he started to leave the room.

"Are you sure you smelled her?"

"Positive. She wears that sunflower perfume. "

"But how?"

Jonah paused. The look of concentration allowed Nicky to see the mental wheels turning. "It must be working," he finally said.

"Working? The wolf thing? I don't feel any different and I don't smell sunflowers."

"I don't know, man, maybe it's different for—"

All sound vanished. Jonah's lips were still moving but Nicky couldn't hear a word. "What's happening?" he tried to say, but he couldn't be certain words formed.

I'm deaf. He gets super smell, I go deaf. No fair. He tried to tell Jonah, and he wasn't sure if words came out of his mouth until Jonah just looked at him dumbfounded, raising his hands palms upward as if saying, "What?" *Mute, too, great!*

Jonah put his hand on Nicky's shoulder and said something; he assumed Jonah was asking if he was okay.

No, I'm far from okay.

He looked around the room for a pen and paper. He stepped toward the desk and grabbed a pen resting in between the number and function keys of Jonah's keyboard, and one of the many loose papers cluttering the desk.

He scribbled: HEARING'S GONE. YOUR FAULT. He turned and held the paper up for Jonah to see.

"You serious?"

Nicky managed to read his lips and nodded.

"Dude, it's not my fault." Nicky read his lips again. "We need to get you to a doctor." Just as suddenly as it was gone, his hearing returned, though the sound was muffled as if Jonah was in the next room.

"Wait," Nicky said, digging his index finger into his ear canal. "Say something."

"I love you and want your baby."

That's better, he thought. "Always a jokester."

"You heard me? You're okay?"

"I think so. What the heck was that?"

Jonah just smiled that full-faced, devilish grin. "It's working. It's really working!"

"This is scary, man. How's it working? Shouldn't my hearing be amplified not diminishing? I don't think—"

"Don't think, man, just go with it. Good thing you're sleeping over. We'll keep an eye on each other."

"I suppose," Nicky said, but he had his reservations.

"You worry too much. C'mon, I'm starving all of a sudden. Let me get that pizza in the oven."

After dinner, the two watched the usual hack-n-slash movies on cable television, a true sign of the season. Jonah's mother let them be, locking herself in her room once she got home from work. They fell asleep on the couch with the TV still on.

Nicky awoke abruptly, disturbed by the vision of him sneaking into Mrs. Morgan's bedroom and ripping her throat out with his teeth while she slept peacefully. The dream felt so real, he could still taste the blood in his mouth. He wiped his hand across his chin to check for blood, but found none, fresh or dried. *Must've bitten the inside of my cheek*, he reasoned.

Still . . . He peered over his shoulder to the closed bedroom door. *I better check on her.*

He got up slowly so as not to disturb Jonah and stood from the couch. With each step he placed his feet as gently as he could against the hardwood floor. The cold floor sent shivers up his spine from the large hole in the heel of his sock.

Please don't squeak, please don't squeak. He chanted his mantra as he turned the doorknob. The brass knob complied and his mantra changed. *Please let it've been a dream.*

He opened the door just enough to shimmy through. His eyes already adjusted to the darkness, and with the aid of the soft light from the television filtering in, he quickly saw Mrs. Morgan. His eyes went wide and it took him a moment to realize he was holding his breath. She lay there upon her bed, the sheet draped just below her left breast, even through her bra her nipple erect from the cool autumn air.

Don't be a pervert, he told himself, *you came in to see if your dream was just that: a dream.* Though he fought to take his eyes off the mesmerizing sight, he did so long enough to see her chest rise and fall. *Good. Just a dream.*

A soft whimper from the other room caused him to look away. He stood in the doorway and waited, but Jonah remained on the couch.

Better not push my luck. He stole one last glance. *Man, she's beautiful. Wonder how far Dad got with her?*

With one hand pressed against the door, he gently pulled it closed. Not a sound was made, but another dog-like whimper piqued his curiosity. *What's going on over there?* he thought as he returned to the living room.

As he came around the edge of the couch he saw Jonah lying on his side, almost in the fetal position, his legs and arms twitching as if he was running on all fours. When Jonah whimpered again, Nicky reached out, grabbed his ankle, and gently shook it.

"Wake up, man. You all right?"

"Huh!" Jonah sat up. "What's wrong?"

"That's what I want to ask you. You were whimpering."

"Really?"

"Yeah. What were you dreaming of?"

"Running through the woods, chasing a deer." He looked toward the floor with his lips pursed and brow furrowed. "Did you have a similar dream? Maybe it's another sign."

"No . . . my dream was . . . different."

"What was it?"

"Short version, I killed your mother." Nicky could tell he didn't like hearing that.

"Weird."

"Yeah."

"We should probably shut that off and go to my room. If my mom wakes up and finds us out here, she'll be pissed."

"All right."

Jonah turned off the television and the two quietly passed through the living room and hallway, and as they walked up the stairs, Nicky whispered, "You think your dad regrets leaving your mom?"

"What kind of question is that?"

"I don't know, it's just —"

"My mom ain't the easiest to get along with. And that's all I'm going to say on that. I don't like thinking about it. You got it easy. Your mom died. She didn't leave you by choice."

"Your dad didn't leave *you*."

"Yeah, yeah, zip it. Okay?"

Nicky said no more. Jonah climbed into bed and he slid into the sleeping bag on the floor.

Though Jonah managed to drift off to sleep with relative ease, Nicky struggled with the level of violence in his dream. Fighting was Jonah's thing, not his. He knew there was something more than a simple excuse of not falling asleep while watching a horror movie. He had seen demon hunters rage war; vampires treat humans like cattle; zombie hordes devour the flesh of the living; werewolves stalk their prey countless times prior to going to bed in the past. He couldn't recall any of them infiltrating his dreams.

What if he's right? What if it is working? How far will it go? Will I even be me anymore? Sleeping really didn't seem like an option anymore.

When dawn broke he was already downstairs making a pot of coffee. The aroma alone instilled vigor within him. Mrs. Morgan's door swung open and she stepped out of her bedroom. She was in the middle of tying her robe, and Nicky couldn't help but stare, hopeful to get another peek.

"You making coffee?"

"Yes. Yes, I am." Though he tried to fight it, the smile on his face just wouldn't go away.

"Smells good. Enjoy your movies?"

"Yeah. You should have watched them with us."

She waved her hand. "Oh no, I can't handle those things."

"That's too bad."

"You excited?"

He slouched in his chair, hoping to see into the fold of her robe. "'Bout what?"

"The party tomorrow night."

"Oh yes . . . very much so."

"I think there's still some of that make-up left."

"I don't think we'll need that," he said.

She smiled and walked passed him toward the cupboard. She opened a cabinet door and stretched for a coffee mug.

Nicky's gaze locked on her taut bottom and a sudden punch in the arm startled him. He turned to see Jonah giving him the eye.

He smiled and Jonah simply nodded his head.

With her coffee in hand, Mrs. Morgan returned to her bedroom.

"Have a good day," Nicky said and got a backhand wave in return.

"Douche," Jonah whispered in his ear. "You keep flirting with my mother we're going to be late for school."

"Sorry. I don't know what it is. I'm, like, extra horny."

"Well, keep it in your pants. Take a cold shower or something."

"Might be a good idea. I'll pour my cup, let it cool, then come back for it."

"And, please, don't be masturbating in my shower." Jonah smiled and Nicky couldn't help doing the same.

"I make no promises," he joked as he left the room.

Upstairs, he turned the water on in the shower and undressed. "That's new," he said, staring at a fresh patch of hair in the middle of his chest.

He shrugged it off and stepped into the shower, the steamed air awakening him further. As he proceeded to wash himself, clumps of black hair formed at the shower's base. He checked his front, but found nothing peculiar other than the first patch. He twisted his waist as far as he could and saw a clump of hair traveling down the back of his leg with the flowing water and suds.

My back, he thought and shot his hand around. *Uh*. His hand came away from the dense, wet hair. The hot, steamy air in the shower began to smell like wet dog.

He pulled the shower curtain slightly to the side to yell for Jonah, but was startled to find him already standing in the bathroom checking himself in the mirror. In Jonah's reflection there was two pearly white incisors protruding over his bottom lip and his ears were tapering to a point.

"Dude," Jonah said.

"Guess I can't complain."

"What's wong wif you?" A bit of drool fell over his bottom lip from the effort to form the words.

Nicky said nothing; he simply turned and showed him.

With his hand over his mouth, Jonah said, "At leath you can 'over it up."

"You can wear a hat to cover your ears, and . . . I guess . . . just don't say anything."

"Ya wight!"

"I know . . . I didn't really believe you could be quiet for ten minutes let alone a whole day. Sorry."

Jonah turned back to the mirror.

Nicky felt bad, Jonah looked so ridiculous he wanted to laugh. "Just stay home today. I'll take notes for you."

Jonah walked out of the bathroom, defeated. Nicky wanted to stay with him, but knew if his father found out he cut school after being out on a school night, there'd be hell to pay. He could handle the punishment, but it would cost him his father's trust, and that was one price he wasn't willing to pay.

Once finished in the shower, Nicky toweled off and got dressed. Thick, blotches of hair clung to the towel. He picked them off and tossed them in the trash, not wanting to raise any awkward questions from Mrs. Morgan.

The bathroom door suddenly swung open. "They're back to normal!"

Nicky looked at the wide smile on Jonah's face as he pointed to his teeth. "Not your ears, though."

"No problem. Like you said, I'll wear a hat."

The only hat Jonah had was a rainbow-colored, pompom-top beanie his aunt gave him last Christmas. It did its job, but looked ridiculous. Afraid of incurring Jonah's wraith, Nicky fought back the need to laugh as best he could, but a nasal snort escaped.

"What?" he asked.

"You gotta take the pompom off, man."

"And what do I say to Aunt Linda when she asks about it?"

Nicky shrugged his shoulders.

"Just . . . shut up, okay? It's working, right?"

Nicky nodded.

"Don't be like that. You know I didn't mean don't speak."

"All right. Are we ready, then?"

"As ready as I'll ever be."

They walked to school, taking the hike in the woods so as to be away from prying eyes. Though he didn't want to see it, Nicky couldn't help but think about the carcass they had left behind. *Would anyone else do what we did?* He said nothing about it to Jonah, and, surprisingly, Jonah didn't bring it up either.

When they got to school they did their best to avoid everyone, but it appeared as though Jeremy and Michael were looking for them. The two stormed up to Nicky and Jonah, their lips pursed and brows wrinkled.

Great, just what we need. He whispered to Jonah, "Be cool. The party's tonight. We don't need any attention brought to us."

"What the hell's your problem, man?" Jeremy asked, then shoved his hands into Jonah's chest.

Jonah stumbled back a step, but remained upright. "I don't want no trouble," he said, shocking Nicky. He had fully expected him to immediately lay into Jeremy.

"Nice pompom, baby. Does the baby want his—"

Jonah's balled-up fist silenced the teasing and Jeremy went down.

"You stupid—" Michael came in with a right hook and Nicky reached out and caught it. He squeezed tightly on the hand and Michael's knees crumpled under him, tears welling in his eyes. "Letgoletgoletgo."

Nicky released his hold, feeling guilty for hurting him. He hadn't meant to, but his newfound strength surprised even him. Jeremy was still crying, curled in the fetal position and clutching his mouth.

"Anyone watching?" Jonah asked.

Nicky looked around. They were in an alleyway off the main courtyard. No one was around, and no one was coming to see what all the commotion was about. "It's clear."

Jonah unzipped his fly, stepped into position, and peed on Jeremy.

"What are you doing?" Nicky asked.

"Marking my territory," he said, then turned it on Michael.

"Cut it out," Michael said, holding out his hand to protect his face from the yellow stream.

"That's enough!" Nicky said.

"All right. I'm done anyway." Jonah shook it off, then zipped up. "Feel free to tell on us. But something tells me you'll want to save yourselves the embarrassment."

As Jonah walked away, Nicky whispered: "I'm sorry," then followed his friend to class.

"Sorry I lost my cool back there. You think they'll tell?"

"I doubt it."

"I'd hate to be the one who ruined the party for you."

Nicky smiled. "You're a true friend."

They took their seats in English class and waited. Several minutes passed and Leah walked in glaring at the two of them.

Wonder what they told her? Nicky thought and fully expected her to storm toward them and renege on her invitation, but she took her seat at the head of the class and said nothing. Michael and Jeremy came in right behind Mr. Swanson.

"Mr. Morgan, you know how I feel about hats in my classroom."

"I know, sir, but can you make an exception just this once? I'm cold."

"If I make an exception for you, I'll soon be doing it for everyone else. Besides, it is not cold in here. Now take it off."

"Can't do that, sir."

Oh boy! Nicky's gaze bounced back and forth between them. He cursed himself for not checking to see if Jonah's ears had returned to normal or not. He had meant to, but the scuffle with Jeremy and Michael distracted him.

With his hands on his hips, Mr. Swanson said, "Come again?"

"I have my reasons and I'm not taking it off for anyone."

"Is that a fact?" Mr. Swanson said and made a fast approach.

He's going to pull it off! What are we going to do? What's everyone going to say? Thinkthinkthink. Vulcan! Yeah. A Vulcan party or . . .

"You take that hat off now, mister." Mr. Swanson grabbed the pompom and pulled. Jonah reached to grab it and keep it on his head but Nicky had already seen the tips of his ears and signaled to him.

Everything was all right.

"You can get this back after class." Mr. Swanson returned to his desk, tossed the hat into his top drawer, and began the day's lesson.

The rest of the school day came and went. The hallways were filled with talk of the Halloween party, the food, the music, the costumes. Leah's parents were well off and the party was to be catered and there was even talk about a cash prize for the best costume. Most of the students complained they still had one more day to get through, and even though that day would be a Saturday, they wanted to fast forward to the party tomorrow night.

Jonah thought it would be a good idea for him to sleep over again, and Nicky agreed. He wasn't sure his father would go for him staying out two nights in a row, but it turned out he was okay with it. Given the close call of the morning, they locked themselves in Jonah's room, afraid of any sudden changes to their bodies. Mrs. Morgan came and went as she pleased and they didn't need her walking in on them in the living room with a clawed hand, muzzle, or a wagging tail.

The night was uneventful until Jonah's sudden painful moan awoke Nicky.

"What's wrong?"

"My skin," Jonah replied, feverishly scratching his arm. "It itches!"

Jonah's bed was lit with moonlight from the half-moon perched high in the sky outside the window. Nicky's gaze gravitated toward the moon and upon seeing it, his heart slammed in his chest.

"You still with me?" Jonah asked.

He couldn't respond. His attention was locked on the half-moon. He felt the urge to rip his skin off and run wild in the neighboring woods. To hunt. To be free. To live.

"Nicky?" Jonah scooted his body to the far side of his bed and stared wide-eyed at him.

The world faded away, replaced by searing pain as if his flesh was on fire. His muscles rippled under his skin. Hair sprouted and consumed him. Bones cracked, popped, and reformed. His pajamas ripped as his body enlarged, tattered rags still clinging to him in parts. He looked to his hands; the hair growth had stopped at the wrist, and his exposed skin was now dark brown. His finger nails blackened, thick and long. As the transformation from man to wolf completed, a hunger like no other permeated his belly. He growled, low and menacing, as he stepped toward Jonah's bed. Jonah tucked his legs into his chest, afraid. Nicky sniffed the air and recognized Jonah as a member of his pack, then leaped out the open window and ran into the night.

* * * *

"Nicky! Nicky!"

His eyes opened to see Jonah running toward him. He was face down on the ground, surrounded by mud and crumpled leaves, his hands looking normal again. Jonah dropped to his knees and slid the rest of the way to him.

"You all right, man?"

"What happened?"

"Dude! You're a werewolf!"

"Yeah," he said as he sat up. His clothes were ripped, but still covering his unmentionables.

"It was beautiful, man. What a sight to see."

"Did you change?"

"No. But I was able to track you by scent, so it's only a matter of time, my friend. And I could run a lot faster, but not as fast as you on all fours."

"Were you scared?"

"Me?" Jonah hesitated. "Yeah … I was scared. But only for a minute, 'cause you came right up to me, and you recognized me. You believe it? You actually recognized me and left me alone. We can do this."

"Do what?"

"Be werewolves, man. Obviously we're not savage beasts like they are in the movies. They have it all wrong. It didn't take a full moon either. We can go to the party and win that money."

Nicky shook his head. Though he didn't remember much of last night, he believed he didn't hurt Jonah, but he couldn't be sure he didn't hurt anyone or anything else. "I don't think that's a good idea."

"No, it's not a good idea, it's a brilliant one. I can't wait to rub it in those guys' faces when we win."

"You go. I'm not putting anyone in danger like that."

"C'mon, where's your sense of adventure?"

"The same place as your morals."

Jonah narrowed his eyes. "You can't be serious. Even if we lost control and tore everyone limb from limb, who cares? They're nothing but a bunch of posers and wannabes. They're all worthless and will never amount to anything. But you and me … we can be gods among men."

Nicky couldn't believe what he was hearing. He knew Jonah to be a hothead, but this bloodlust was beyond him. He was indeed changing, but more on the inside than on the outside—like himself.

I can't let him hurt anyone. I should rip his head from his shoulders, hold it up high, and let the blood spill all over my face and run down my throat. Wait … what the … Nicky shook the image away.

"What's the matter? You look pale all of a sudden," Jonah said, leaning in close.

Maybe he's not the only one changing on the inside, Nicky thought as he looked Jonah in the eye. There was concern on his friend's face, so he decided there was still hope. Jonah would need his support and understanding, and together perhaps they could overcome the bloodlust within each of them. "I'm all right," he finally answered.

"You scared me for a second there."

"Gods aren't supposed to be scared of anything," he said.

"I suppose you're right. Little over-the-top, huh?"

Nicky cracked a smile. "I'd say."

"If you don't want to go to the party, maybe you're right—"

"We can go."

Jonah balled his left hand into a fist and tucked his elbow into his chest. "Yes! You won't regret it."

"We'll see."

As they ran through the woods, heading back to Jonah's house, they tested their newfound agility and dexterity. It was a game to them. They leaped and somersaulted over tree branches, pounced off tree trunks and twirled in midair. Nicky felt like Spider-Man.

All of his senses were alive. The wind carried so many smells: the sweat of a deer, car exhausts, and fresh baked bread from the bakery on Market Street. He could hear squirrels chattering as they ran to higher perches in the trees as they ran past, and Jonah's heart thundering in his chest as it pumped adrenaline through him.

This is amazing, he thought, right on Jonah's tail.

They spent so much time testing their bodies they lost track of the hour. When they finally got to Jonah's house they had less than an hour to get showered, dressed, and out the door or otherwise be fashionably late.

With Jonah's mom out and about, they had to walk. When Leah's house came into sight, the sun was just setting and it was darker than usual; the moon was hidden away, tucked behind the heavy cloud cover. The house was decorated with fake, white and black spider webs; orange and black streamers; skeletons propped against the porch railings; and tiny ghosts dangling from tree branches. Fog drifted from the doorway and crept down the front steps. They heard the music pumping inside. Their strut adjusted to the beat.

Jeremy stepped outside the front door dressed as a surgeon with blood smeared on his chest. "Too embarrassed to use the same costume four years in a row, so you decided why bother, right?"

"Don't you worry your pretty little head," Jonah said. "We brought our costumes and if you play your cards right, you'll get to see 'em."

Nicky's fingernails dug into the palms of his hands, drawing blood. He breathed in deeply through his nose, held it, then released. *Bastard was probably looking out the window waiting for us.*

"Never mind him," Leah said, stepping past him.

Nicky's jaw went lax as he found his gaze locked on the provocatively unbuttoned candy striper outfit. *Must be betting on her cleavage to win the best costume prize.*

"C'mon in," she said, stepping to the side and pushing Jeremy away. "Food's on the left, drinks are in the cooler on the floor. Or, if you're brave, there's some blood-bath punch on the table."

"Thank you, Leah," Jonah said with a smile, "you're a great hostess."

Nicky looked to Jonah to see if he caught the smile fighting its way onto her face and by the smug look he got, he knew he had. Jonah bumped his shoulder into Jeremy as he passed him but Nicky stood there, face-to-face with him, staring him in the eye. The thought of him plunging his hand into Jeremy's abdomen and pulling out his small intestine and choking him with it put a twisted smile on his face.

Easy, he told himself. *The thoughts are growing more and more violent.*

"What are you smiling about?" Jeremy asked.

"Oh . . . this and that," he answered and walked past him.

The lights in the room were dimmed with a strobe light flickering against the walls. Jonah was at the food table. Nicky joined him.

He inspected the food. There was a variety of the usual party foods with a pumpkin-shaped cake, but there was also some specialty dishes. Each dish had a place card marking the Halloween appropriate name and its contents. In reading them he was reminded of an article in the paper that had given the recipes. There were blood sausages; monster eyeballs (deviled eggs with green food dye, topped with a black olive); blood-splattered brains (goat cheese covered with tomato pesto); bone marrow with coagulated blood (cream cheese dripping with cranberry sauce); bloody fingers (shrimp in cocktail sauce); and a chocolate fondue with strawberries to make bloody itty-bitty hearts. "Wow! What a spread."

"Right? The punch tastes like ginger ale and cranberry juice," Jonah said.

"Too cool."

"Aren't you glad you came now?"

"It's still early," Nicky said. "And in case you hadn't noticed, Jeremy's burning a hole in the back of our heads."

"Let 'im stare."

"You think the moon will come out enough for us to . . . you know?"

"We'll have to play it by ear. We'll keep checking, then show that pompous goof true terror."

"Don't push your luck."

"What are you girls talking about?" Michael and Jeremy stepped right up to them.

A low, guttural and echoey growl came deep from Nicky's diaphragm; the beast within begged for release. Michael trembled. Jeremy looked around to see if anyone else heard it. Even Jonah was surprised by the sound.

Jonah patted him on the back and said, "Let it out."

Nicky turned to him. "You feeling it, too?"

Jonah nodded, a toothy grin stretched across his face.

"What are you talkin' about?" Michael poked Nicky in the chest with his index finger, angering the beast further.

I don't want to be a monster, he thought.

"What's the matter? Cat got your tongue?" Michael slapped him across the face with an open palm that embarrassed Nicky more than it hurt.

"You gonna let him do that?" Jonah asked.

"No," he said through gritted teeth.

As Nicky gave in to the beast's urges, he thought, *Time to decorate these walls proper.*

MIMIC

"Please…stop it!"

"You stop," Frank replied as he continued to torment him.

"C'mon," Bill said, stretching the word as he twirled the edge of his mustache. "I can't."

"I'll stop when you stop. Promise." Slouched in his chair, across the aisle in the neighboring cubicle, Frank continued to twirl his mustache with a wide smile stretched across his face. "What do you call this again?"

"It doesn't matter. It's a sickness. And you're just playing me. Now stop!"

"I can do this all day. It's starting to feel good actually."

"Ahem!"

Frank stopped twirling his mustache and sat up straight at the sight of the stout man standing over him with his arms crossed against his chest.

Thank God, Bill thought as he was finally able to break free from his debilitating disease. This was one of those rare moments when he appreciated Gary Muir, his over-demanding supervisor. The man was all business twenty-four seven, he stood there, lips pursed, left eyebrow raised with that condescending tilt to his neck. Never in his seven years of employment at the call center had Bill seen the portly man smile.

Gary dropped his arms to the side and placed his hands on his hips, all the while sucking in his bulbous gut to expand his chest, a pitiful attempt to assert his authority. "I see you learned nothing from our last conversation, huh, Mr. Stone."

"No sir…I ah…"

"Save it. Clock out and go home."

"Sir?" Frank tried to argue.

"Now!"

Frank lowered his head, then opened his desk drawer to retrieve his car keys. Though he was the victim, Bill couldn't help but feel guilty.

"As for you," Gary said, turning toward Bill, "I suggest you keep your eyes locked on your screen during working hours to avoid future embarrassing moments."

"Yes," he said with the nod of his head and turned around.

"Let's go, Frank. I'll see you out myself."

Though he could see the tops of several of his co-workers heads peeking over their cubicle walls, not wanting to add insult to injury, Bill fought the urge to turn around and watch Frank leave.

Serves him right, Bill thought. *Maybe this is exactly what he needs to stop it.*

Bill suffered from two diseases, but the one Frank exploited was the one he just could not tolerate. Echopraxia the doctors called it, an involuntary imitation of observed movement. How many hours had he wasted tapping his foot; drumming his fingers against the desk; picking his nose and making googly faces all in the name of fun as Frank had once said? But the two had completely different definitions of the word. It was torture. Plain and simple.

"Don't let him get to you," said the voice of an angel. "He's just a jerk."

Bill's head slowly lolled up, his gaze taking in the office beauty, Sheila Walker. Her red suit jacket pulled taught across the shoulders creating fantastic cleavage under the matching blouse. He took a deep breath, inhaling her scent — dew kissed sunflowers bathing in golden sunshine. A low, guttural growl passed over his lips.

A smile stretched across her face. "Did you just —"

"What?" he said, arching his back straight and playing innocent.

"Never mind." She walked away from him and his gaze locked on her sashaying ass.

What a beauty, he thought as his head drifted side to side in rhythm. When Sheila turned the corner he was free to return to his monitor to register the next phone number.

Despite himself, Bill had to admit the workday dragged without Frank across the way. There was nothing to break up the monotony of soft sales calls, the haggling of consumers, and demands of removing names from their database. The second hand of the clock moved slowly as he stared at it with unblinking eyes. Each click echoed in his ears like thunder booming overhead, until finally it was six o'clock.

With no words passed between him and his replacement, Bill grabbed his cooler and car keys, then headed toward the elevator and made his way to the parking garage. Usually, Frank walked with him. Joking and laughing at his expense, but the humiliation was between the two of them and he'd gladly take that over the deafening silence that blanketed the garage.

The heels of his shoes clopped against the concrete floor as he walked the aisles, but there was another sound. Distant, but distinct. He stopped and listened. "Hello?"

Bill peered over his shoulder, then looked to the left and then right, but saw no one. "Is anyone there?"

His stomach tightened as the hairs on the back of his neck went rigid, his dormant instincts telling him something wasn't right. After years of having the sixth sense, he learned to trust it and quickened his pace.

By the time he reached his Toyota Camry his heart pounded in his chest and sweat beaded his brow. With a fumbling hand, he unlocked his front door, climbed in, and slammed his palm against the pushrod. The car's engine roared to life and he quickly backed out of his space and followed the arrows toward the exit.

"Okay," he said aloud in a calming voice, "settle down. You're safe…for now."

Bill leaned forward and peered out the front window as he drove. The setting sun cast a yellow and pink hue against the heavy cloud cover, and though he could not see the encroaching full moon, he could feel its power.

He traveled I-95 through the heart of South Carolina. A quarter of the moon peaked out from behind the clouds and if he didn't pullover and venture deep into the woods soon, the beast scratching under his skin would tear through flesh and steel and attack the first car it came upon.

"I can't have that."

Whether it was his repetitive disease or the beast's natural instinct, he didn't know, but he returned to these woods every full moon. Thirteen years ago, on a camping trip forced upon him by his mother to fit in, he learned his father had lied to him. Monsters did exist. He had come face-to-face with a beast, cold and calculating like a man, but wild as the wolf.

Sensing the change upon him, Bill pulled over and got out. He made it several yards into the woods when he heard the sound of another car door closing. He sniffed the air.

"What the hell are you doing out here you crazy son-of-a-bitch?" Frank asked from the forest's edge.

What is he doing here?

"Hey, c'mon. Where are you…there you are!"

"Go home, Frank." The gravelly sound of Bill's voice told him it was too late. The beast within had Frank's scent and would chase him until his innards were ripped from his chest and strewn between its razor sharp fangs.

"I've got a bone to pick with you," he said as he continued to walk closer.

"Stay back!"

"Don't be like that. I would never hurt you."

"It's not me I'm worried about."

"Oh! Big man." Frank stepped right up to him and Bill took a retreating step.

Feeling the moon's light upon his backside, he said, "Please Frank. Leave."

"Why didn't you say something to Gary?"

Bill's head twisted to the right as the sound of bone snapping echoed in his ear.

"Hey man, what's wrong." A reassuring hand landed on his shoulder, but it was quickly pulled away when the bone underneath buckled and cracked. "Bill, what's happening?" Frank took a step back as if finally realizing the danger.

Bill looked over his left shoulder and saw the illuminated full disc high in the night sky. His heart hammered in his chest just before his knees jerked inward. He fell face first in pain, but managed to catch himself by bracing his palms against the cold, damp earth. The fabric of his clothes tore as his shoulder blades popped and rotated. His fingernails lifted from the flesh as sharp claws extended from the tips. They burrowed into the soft soil as Bill pressed down, bracing against the pain.

A pain-filled roar turned into a high-pitched howl as his jawbone elongated. Teeth rained down as canine incisors filled their place. His nose collapsed on itself, leaving a blackened lump of flesh and his ears tapered to a point. Every follicle on his body burst to life as dark-brown fur sprouted and covered his entire body.

"Bill…you're a . . . .," Frank said as the beast stood on its haunches before him.

The scene reminded Bill of the night he found himself in Frank's shoes, staring down the beast in wonderment and disbelief after he snuck away from camp to pee. Fear had clutched him in its cold embrace, but when the beast charged toward him, his disease shook the icy tendrils that kept him rooted to the spot and, he too, charged. He ran headlong into the claws and teeth of the beast. It pinned him to the ground and ripped into his shoulder, then left him to bleed. He had figured the beast found no sport in him and abandoned the kill for a more suitable hunt.

"Bill, are you still in there?"

Of course I am, he thought, but was unable to answer. In response, the beast growled.

It took a step toward him and as it did, it discarded the tatters of clothing still clinging to its body.

"Please," Frank begged. "I won't tell anyone . . . I promise . . . just . . . let me go."

Sorry, you had your chance, Frank, Bill thought as the beast took another step. Though he was not in control of his new form, he was still conscious — an unwilling witness to the beast's brutality.

"No, no, no, no, no," Frank said as his hands waved frantically in front of him.

The beast stopped suddenly and copied Frank's movement, its razor sharp claws slicing through the air rather than Frank's flesh.

Frank's eyes went wide with the realization. "You *are* still in there," he said with a smile.

He stopped waving his hands and the beast quickly darted toward him. Frank acted quickly and started hopping backward. Without missing a beat, the beast followed the movement and hopped backward, increasing the distance.

"Oh man . . . ."

Let's see if you still think so when you're too tired to keep this shit up, he thought.

Frank's gaze drifted toward the forest's edge where he left his car. Bill doubted he could make it. The beast would easily regain ground on him the moment the trance was broken. He knew the beast's power well, had seen extraordinary feats of strength and speed over the years.

"If I run," Frank said as he continued to bounce up and down, "you'll overtake me, won't you?"

The beast could not respond, somewhere in the transformation the ability to speak was lost. It could only mimic Frank's movement.

"There's no way I can jump like this all night," he said, obviously strategizing. Suddenly, his jumping ceased and he bolted for the car. Free from the spell, the beast roared and dropped to all fours.

We've got you now, Bill thought, saliva foaming along the brim of his massive maw. *I'm going to slice that shit-eating grin off your face.*

Frank skidded to a halt, turned around, and extended his right hand outward, palm up. "Stop. . ."

. . . The beast halted as well and threw out its paw. . .

". . . in the name of love." Frank's arm waved through the air and the beast was locked in another trance. . .

". . . be-fore you *break* my heart. Think it o. . . o. . . ver. Think it o. . . o. . . ver."

The beast's hips swayed with Frank's as the two performed The Supremes dance routine and when they were done, Frank led them into the funky chicken.

Great, humiliate him, Bill thought as he sensed the beast's anger boiling. The more Frank tormented the monster, the more it craved his flesh. Bill knew Frank would not be able to maintain the act, he'd falter sooner or later, but the beast could go all night if need be and the more frenzied it became, the less of Frank the authorities would find.

Winded, Frank stopped his perverted little dance and leaned forward, placing his hands on his knees. The beast charged forward as Frank breathed deeply.

"C'mon," he said, stretching the word. "Give a guy a break." He jumped backward and the wolf followed, but given its strength, leaped three times as far as Frank had. "Phew," Frank said, then took another breather.

Again the beast charged and again, Frank jumped back, but this time with a sweeping upward angle.

He's trying to get closer to his car, Bill thought and the wolf growled its displeasure. Realizing it didn't need to see its prey to tear him limb-from-limb, the beast lowered its head and stared at the ground as it ran toward Frank.

"Oh shit!"

It was fun while it lasted, Frank. You get an A for effort.

Though Bill could hear the sound of Frank's footsteps against the ground and the crunching of leaves underfoot, the smell of Frank's sweat seemed to be growing stronger. Too strong considering the gap that was between them.

Frank's running ceased and suddenly he was underneath Bill, between the beast's legs.

Giving up I see, Bill thought as the beast raised its right paw high above its head.

Before it could plunge its claws into Frank's abdomen and rip out his intestines, Frank scratched his own face. The beast saw the movement and copied it. Pain surged as its claws sliced through its own flesh. Skin and muscle peeled away with ease. One razor sharp nail passed through the corner of its right eye, and the spongy tissue rolled out of the open wound and dangled in its whiskers. It howled in pain as it stepped backward.

As gently as it could, the beast caught the swaying appendage in the palm of his hand and pushed it back in place. Once inside the vacant space, the beast closed its eyelids and waited for its supernatural healing to make him whole.

The roar of a car engine interrupted the silence blanketing the forest, and the beast could wait no more. It dropped to all fours and ran to the forest's edge and came upon the car. Dust and debris scoured its face as Frank's tires spun wildly on the shoulder of the road. Now blinded in both eyes, the monster relied on its hearing and sense of smell to follow the automobile until it could open its eyes again. The horn of Frank's car wailed as if that would deter the beast from exacting vengeance for the indignity suffered.

With the pain all but gone in his right eye, the beast opened it and dug down deep to close the ever growing gap. Frank's car swayed on the open road as the distance between wolf and metal closed. It ran up to its rear bumper and swatted the faux chrome away with a single swipe. The car swerved, but maintained its speed. The beast ran up alongside the vehicle and threw its shoulder into it. Again the car veered off course, but remained upright.

The beast hit it again. And again.

"Cut it out!" He could hear Frank shout.

Thanks to the long, straight road, the wolf managed to reach the front of the car, slow and steady. It slammed its head into the passenger's window, shattering the glass.

"My deductable," Frank squealed.

The beast barked, its jaws snapping wildly, splashing the driver with thick globs of spittle. Steel moaned in protest as claws ripped into it. The door creaked and flew away, a shower of sparks erupted upon its impact with the pavement.

A clawed hand reached toward Frank, who kept his eyes on the road up ahead rather than the looming danger.

"I'm sorry about this, Bill. Maybe we can laugh about it tomorrow."

The car veered to the left and the beast craned its neck to see the large oak tree Frank had made a beeline toward, but it was too late. The half of its body still dangling out of the open car door slammed into the massive trunk and the car's momentum caused the beast to wrap around the tree. Bones popped as its back broke on impact.

Mind-numbing pain embraced him as the beast's body flipped around the tree and tumbled down the embankment, while Frank continued on his way home. When he finally stopped, his legs and arms spasmed uncontrollably. The damage severe, his healing would need a lot of time to mend his spine.

Good on you, Frank. You survived. . . this time.

As he lay there, staring up into the starry night, twisted and mangled, he couldn't help but wonder what sick, childish games Frank would force him to do now that he knew the whole truth.

That son-of-a-bitch is gonna find a way to get me to lick my balls.

MIND, BODY, AND SOUL

JESSE BARNES AWOKE to darkness and pain.

Where am I? Am I tied up?

His body trembled with vibrations from the music that thundered in his ears. The soft glow of an emergency pull cord told him all he needed.

I'm in a trunk. But who . . .

He remembered a strange man approaching him and asking for a light.

Then nothing.

Someone must've hit me from behind while I was at the grocery store. But why? And where are they taking me? I haven't done anything . . . except . . . the bank robbery. He looked at the pull cord. *They've come for me.*

At the time, he didn't know that the bank he worked at for seven years was owned by the Mafia.

All I wanted was a little payback.

Life had been great for Jesse; he was on the fast track to becoming *the* financial consultant to Chicago's elite at one of the city's most prestigious banks. The majority of the bank's customers loved and requested him, no matter how many were in line before them. At his peak he averaged a twelve percent return on investment on the funds he recommended to his clients. No one was better.

Then the economy took a turn, all stocks plummeted and everyone lost. Corners were cut, jobs were downsized, companies restructured and there was no longer room for a fallen hotshot at Iniquity Bank of Chicago. He pleaded for at least a teller job, but job competition was fierce and he was overqualified, so they sent him packing.

When his daughter was born, his wife quit her job to be a stay-at-home mom. At the time, they were financially secure, but without steady income, their savings dwindled to nothing. Her job search was no better than his; a four-year absence from the workforce was not what companies were looking for.

With one of their cars already repossessed, the foreclosure notice on their suburban home was the final straw. He was the man of the house, the sole breadwinner, it was his responsibility to clothe, feed, and protect his family. So he devised a plan, and his former employer inadvertently made it easy for him by not changing any of the security codes upon his dismissal.

Had I known then what I know now, I would've understood why they felt it was not necessary. Who in their right mind would steal from Victor Bianchi?

During the most successful times people smoked, drank and gambled, and during the most trying times, people smoked, drank, and gambled. Victor Bianchi understood this and found a way to turn a profit in these industries.

The man was untouchable, the only crime boss left in Chicago. He and his crew seemed to be the only ones thriving in this economy. He shared his good fortune with the right people: police officers, whose hours had increased while their pay decreased; judges that ruled against overzealous District Attorneys that thought they could bring down the notorious Bianchi; and Building Commissioners that approved the plans and permits to build his empire—all of whom wanted to give their wives, children, and mistresses the things they wouldn't normally be able to, but were able to with a supplemental income.

How did I not know he owned the bank? How did it slip by me?

It wasn't until during the heist that his former boss revealed the secret, but it was too late by then, the job was already in progress and going smoothly.

Jesse had recruited a couple of the other bank employees that had lost their jobs as well. He knew the risk he was taking by asking them, as they could have easily turned him over to the authorities, but he couldn't do it alone and they were all too eager to help. Mitch Almeida had been one of three janitors employed by the bank, and on his paltry salary he was quickly put on the streets after termination. Rounding out the trio was Jake Holden, a rookie teller who lost out to his female supervisor when she agreed to take a demotion when her position was eliminated.

Without a flaw in the plan, Jesse had questioned the ease of the robbery, but having all that money in his hands distracted him.

I should have been prepared for this. Did they take Michelle and Lisa?

The thought of his wife and daughter suffering for his mistake was too much. Jesse didn't care about himself, but for his family he would fight. He struggled against the ropes binding his wrists behind his back, bit at the duct tape on his lips in the hopes of grabbing the pull cord with his teeth and disengaging the lock and jumping out, but nothing budged. Added to that, his breathing was becoming increasingly difficult as a soft haze of cigar smoke encompassed him.

I've got to get out of here!

When the car finally stopped, Jesse's fidgeting did, too.

Wonder where we are? Did they bring me to Victor so he could be the one to dish out my punishment? What will he do to me? Boil me in oil. Give me a pair of concrete shoes. Carve my hide and feed me to his dogs. Oh God, don't let him hurt my family. He can do anything to me, but let them live.

The trunk opened and two of the largest men Jesse had ever seen stood before him. Behind them, the full moon stood prominently in the dark sky.

"Let's go," one said as he grabbed Jesse under the arms.

The other grabbed his legs. They hoisted him up and he was draped over one of their shoulders and carried away from the car.

Jesse looked around, trying to figure out his bearings, but he didn't recognize the wooded area around them. The men said nothing as they carried him deeper into the woods.

Once they were in a clearing he was tossed to the ground. The two men took turns kicking him. His hands were still behind his back leaving his midsection exposed. Most of the kicks landed there, breaking several of his ribs, but a couple landed against his face and skull. Darkness engrossed his vision, but the removal of the duct tape snapped him back to consciousness.

"What do you want?" he asked, barely able to get the words out through the pain and the fire now lit inside his chest.

"Our boss wants his money. Where is it?" one man said.

"We've got your whole crew. If you don't talk, one of them will," said the other

Jesse swallowed. His mouth was dry. "We divided it up. I don't have—" A low growl followed by a tug on the ropes behind him stopped him in mid-sentence.

"What's that doing here?" one of the big boys said.

"I don't know. Grab it!" the other said.

"I'm not touching it. It could be rabid."

"Do I have to do everything?" The man grabbed the wolf pup by the scruff and lifted it toward his face. "It's cute. Think I could keep it?"

"What for?"

"Could be intimidating?"

"Believe me," Jesse said, "you're intimidating enough. Let it go. It was just playing."

"Thank you, but flattery isn't going to help you. And don't tell me what to—Ow!" The man dropped the pup. As the pup scurried away, he aimed his gun and fired. The pup yelped and toppled over. The man walked over to it and finished the job with his massive boot. Jesse heard bone crunch beneath the heel.

Two more growls, this time coming from the right.

"Look what you did," the other man said as two adult wolves walked out from the underbrush.

Before the wolves could pounce, two shots rang in Jesse's ears. Without a sound, the wolves fell.

The big man towered over Jesse. "Let's get this over with. You were going to tell us where the money is."

Jesse prepared himself to speak. Taking a breath with his ribs broken felt like his lungs were expanding against iron bars. "I want to know if my family's safe first."

"Our boss sent us and our buddies out to get you and your crew. They're being interrogated elsewhere and if none of you tell us what we want to know, then our orders are to ask your loved ones." The man grinned then raised his eyebrows up and down a couple times like some kind of hotshot.

Michelle, Lisa. "I'll tell you where my share is," Jesse said. "It's buried in my backyard under the birdbath, but I don't know where the others stashed theirs."

"That's not your concern. Frankie, I'm callin' it in. Keep an eye on him."

"A'right." Frankie's gun was trained on the center of Jesse's forehead.

The other goon dialed as he walked away.

What is he talking about that he can't say in front of me? I've got to get out of here. My family needs me. He tested his bindings. *That pup, I think he loosened the rope.* Jesse fidgeted a moment more. *Yes!* He wiggled his hands free.

"I think that wolf is still alive," Jesse said.

Frankie turned to look and squinted against the dark. "I don't think so."

As he turned back, Jesse grabbed a handful of dirt and tossed it in Frankie's eyes.

"Son of a—"

Jesse stood, aiming the top of his skull at the goon's head. The blow landed, knocking both of them to the ground. The world around him spun and he was forced to close his eyes. An image of Michelle and Lisa being terrorized by the two goons that kidnapped him flashed before him. Rage burst within.

He stood.

A gun fired.

Jesse fell to the ground, heat radiating at the center of his chest.

The big guy who had been talking on the phone came up to them. "Frankie, what are you doing? You let this runt overpower you?"

"I'm sorry, Moe."

"Get to the car, we've got orders."

"What about him?"

"I'm taking care of it." As Frankie walked away, Moe knelt down beside him. "Nice try. I understand why you fought. I'd fight, too, so I'll tell you what I'm going to do. I'm going to let you bleed to death here while we go meet up with some friends to go dig up Mr. Bianchi's money and then have a little fun with your girls. Orders are to leave no witnesses. You understand, right?"

"No . . . please . . ." Breathing was near impossible, making talking difficult. Blood spilled from the corners of his mouth. A chill swept over him as his warm blood pumped out of the hole in his chest. *No. It can't end like this.*

"You think about all the nasty things we're going to do to those precious to you," Moe said.

Jesse reached out to try and grab Moe by the ankle, but his arm fell limp before he could latch on. Moe just laughed and walked away.

This is it. I'm going to die alone and my family is going to be tortured.

There was a rustle in the nearby bush; he strained to turn his head in order to see what it was. He feared it was another wolf, hungry and intent on feasting on an easy meal.

It's still alive. It's going to finish me off, he thought as the wounded, male wolf crawled toward him.

He tried to speak to scare it off, but only a gurgling sound came out. The wolf crawled on top of his chest; excruciating pain shot through his body from the weight.

Warmth spread through his body like wild fire as their blood mixed together.

What's happening?

The wolf's flesh melted into his.

Where's he going? Why's he falling into me? What—We're becoming one.

Hair sprouted from every pore. Jesse's fingers lengthened and tapered off into vicious claws. The sound of bones cracking and reforming echoed in his ear. The pain in his chest faded. He stood on his haunches.

Finally whole, the beast slowly approached its fallen pup. Jesse lifted it up and cradled it against his chest, feeling the loss of a child, then carried it over to his mother and laid him beside her. He looked to the moon high in the sky and let loose a bloodcurdling howl before chasing after the two men. The wolf inside him had a new family that needed protecting. Jesse could sense its rage, both man and beast united with the same goal—revenge.

With the heightened senses of the wolf, Jesse tracked the Italian thugs through the woods with ease, guided by the aroma of the cigar smoke. Frankie stood by the car and Moe traversed the hill toward the road. Jesse jumped onto a nearby tree and catapulted off it.

"Look out!"

Moe turned around. A clawed hand arced downward. The razor sharp nails of the beast sliced through skin and muscle, decapitating his head. It plopped into a pile of fallen leaves and the body rolled down the hill.

Frankie ran to the body; Jesse assumed he needed the keys. He dropped to all fours and charged, running at him headlong.

"Stay away!" Frankie drew his gun and fired a barrage of bullets.

The beast zigzagged, dodging most of the bullets. Jesse pushed through the pain caused by the hot lead, staying the course. He leaped into the air and drove his body into the goon's. As they fell to the ground, he clawed at his midsection, disemboweling him.

Frankie rummaged with his small intestine, trying to shove them back inside. When he spoke, blood spurted from his mouth in thick glops. "What have you . . . done? . . . . What are . . . you?"

Jesse lowered his muzzle toward Frankie. The goon's scream turned into a gurgle as his throat was ripped apart with a single bite. Blood geysered as the body convulsed, then all functions ceased.

Blood dripping from his mouth, Jesse sniffed the air. He approached the car, took in the scent of the tires, and followed the road. He kept to the shadows as he made his way back.

At such a late hour, few cars appeared on the road and Jesse struggled to keep the beast in line. Each passerby teased the creature. The wolf wanted to hunt, to feed, to answer the call of the wild and show its dominance, but Jesse's will overpowered the animalistic urges and kept the beast on course.

Please let me be in time, he thought as he turned down his street and his house came into sight.

From this distance he couldn't hear any screaming but he could see three men: two in the living room and one in the kitchen. The beast approached the ranch-style house with stealth, hopped over the picket fence and stared into an adjacent window.

Michelle and Lisa were bound and gagged by the fireplace. The men appeared to be waiting for something, their guns at the ready.

Must be waiting for Frankie and Moe. Thank you, God. Now if only I could get in there without Michelle and Lisa seeing me like this. Guess it's unavoidable, but I need to at least draw those two away from them.

The beast leaped through the kitchen window, tackling the lone goon standing beside it and immediately tore the flesh from his bones. Blood splashed on every wall; tendons and muscle clung to the beast's claws. The man screamed, then fell silent.

"What the hell?" asked one of the other two men as Jesse came into the room. The man opened fire, the other joining his side. The bullets pierced Jesse's hide and hurt only for a second, and then the bullets were pushed out as the wounds healed.

The men trembled. "It can't be. It just can't."

"We've got to get out of here."

"What about the money?"

"Screw the money!"

In a single leap the beast knocked both retreating men to the ground. One of the men was directly under him and the other just ahead of him. Jesse heard his wife and daughter's muffled screams of terror. His heart broke. He wanted to tell them it was all right, to hold and coddle them, but first he needed to eliminate the threat.

He bit into the back of the neck of the man underneath him. The head separated from the body and toppled over. A rush of blood painted the floor, then the flow tapered off to a slow trickle. He feared this vision would haunt his daughter for the rest of her life, but knew because of it, she would live a fulfilled one.

"Get away!" The last thug thrashed his legs at the beast, kicking it repeatedly in the head, only infuriating it further.

As another blow attempted to connect, Jesse clamped his massive jaw on to the man's calf. The man screamed and fired a shot point blank, right between the beast's eyes. Jesse yipped as the force of the bullet sent his head backward.

Freed, the man staggered out of the living room and into the hallway toward the front door. The beast growled as it got to all fours. It charged, leapt on to the right wall of the hallway, then leapt to the ceiling, bounced off and landed on the man.

The man squealed as he was tackled to the floor. The beast plunged its paw into his back, grabbed his spinal cord and yanked. Tendons and nerves popped as they snapped. Discs separated under the pressure and the spinal cord was tossed aside as the man's last breath exited his body.

Sighs and whimpers from the other room caught the beast's attention and it turned back down the hallway, still hungry for the kill. Something shifted inside and Jesse wasn't sure if he remained in control.

No. You mustn't. Not my Wife. Not my daughter.

The beast continued its approach.

They're your family too now.

Michelle scooted her body in front of Lisa's. Jesse's heart ached. He didn't understand why the beast was disobeying him.

Stop, damn you!

Michelle trembled as she pushed against her daughter. The beast sniffed the air around them and reached out its clawed hand.

I'm sorry. I tried. I love you both.

The bindings around Michelle's wrist fell to the floor with the flick of a finger.

Thank you.

She quickly pulled the gag out of her mouth, turned around and went to work on Lisa's bindings. "Run!"

The beast's head swiveled as the little girl ran passed him.

"Leave her alone!"

The beast lay at her feet, whimpering.

"Honey, wait." She looked upon the creature, confusion written on her face.

Jesse felt the beast's rage subside and the transformation reversed. The brown, wiry hair covering his body fell away, exposing his naked flesh. His canine teeth returned to normal. The claws retreated into his flesh and his fingers shortened.

"Jesse?" Michelle said.

"Yeah," he said softly.

"I don't understand. What happened to you? You're a . . . a . . ."

"I can't explain it and we don't have much time."

"Daddy!" Lisa ran to him and he scooped her into his arms.

"I'll get you some clothes," Michelle said.

"What's wrong?" he asked Lisa as she started to sob.

"You lied, Daddy. You said there were no such things as monsters."

He released his hold and looked into her blue eyes. "I'm sorry, honey, I didn't know."

"It's okay," she said, wiping a tear away. "The monster saved us from the bad men."

"Yes, he did."

"Where did he go?"

"He's gone for now. Go check on your mother for me."

"Okay."

As she bolted away, Jesse went outside, not caring if a neighbor saw him in the buff. He knew someone had to have alerted the authorities to the gunshots and he needed to move quickly.

He scanned the yard. *Doesn't look like they dug up the money yet. Good!* He kicked over the birdbath and tore into the soft earth. As Michelle came outside with a pair of jeans and a T-shirt, he uncovered the duffle bag and pulled it free.

"What is that?" she asked.

"I want you to take this and you and Lisa go visit your mother."

"What did you do?"

"There's no time to explain. The cops are—"

"What did you do?" she asked again, shoving her palms into his chest and almost knocking him over.

I really screwed up, he thought. He felt ashamed. The tears in her eyes caused him heartache. "I only wanted what was best for us."

Michelle shook her head as if knowing what he'd done. "No."

"Take this. There's almost a half a million in here."

The tears came on stronger. "No."

"Go to your mother's. I'll be there after I clear this whole mess. I promise."

"You're going to get yourself killed . . . or worse. What if you don't come back to me, or you don't come back as you, but that—"

"Don't worry. I don't fully understand what's happened to me, but I know it had no desire to hurt you or Lisa. It's still me. I swear. Now go, before the cops come and ask questions you don't have the answers for."

"Promise you'll find us."

"I promise. I love you guys too much."

She kissed him, long and passionate. Though he wanted nothing more than to kiss her longer, he pushed her away.

"When will you be back?"

"I don't know. A few days tops."

"I'll see you then." She stole another kiss, then left him to fetch Lisa and be on her way.

He got dressed in time to wave them off. He could see Lisa's teary eyes as she and Michelle pulled down the driveway and he knew she didn't understand what was happening, but he also knew she was young and once he saw to it they were protected, she'd forget all about this night. Several of his neighbors were outside on their porches trying to get a glimpse of what was going on. He ignored them as he walked down the street.

I've got to get to Jake's. There might still be time.

Jake was forced to move back in with his parents after losing his job and they lived a half a mile away from them. As he approached their house he caught the faint scent of cigar smoke, the same cigar he smelled when he was locked in the trunk.

Can't be the same goon. He's dead. Bianchi must have shared his cigars with his whole crew. That's the only explanation, but either way, it means I'm too late.

With caution he approached the front door and tried to open it.

Locked. I'll go around.

When he reached the back patio, he noticed the door was ajar. He tilted his head and leaned closer to hear movement within, but there was none. He sniffed the air and the scent of blood filled his nostrils.

Looks as though they've already come and gone.

He pushed the door aside as he entered. Nothing was out of the ordinary in the living room so he moved forward through the house, the scent of blood growing stronger. He followed it to the upstairs bedroom where Jake's parents were bound and gagged at the foot of their bed in a puddle of blood, their throats slashed.

I'm too late. "I'm sorry," he said, hoping somewhere, somehow, they could hear him.

Off in the distance Jesse caught the sound of a siren. Fearing they were coming here, he leapt out the window. He landed safely on his feet, broken glass scattering around him.

"Freeze!"

There's no time for this. He rushed the uniformed cop. He managed to fire off a shot, but Jesse twirled his body and maintained his momentum. The bullet grazed his left shoulder and only burned for a second before his superior healing went to work. He rammed the man with the right side of his body. The cop went down and Jesse continued to run.

"You can't run forever. Victor Bianchi will find you," the cop shouted after him.

Jesse stopped. The sirens were getting closer. "You work for Bianchi?"

The man nodded.

Jesse approached the man and helped him to his feet. "You can take me to him?"

"Yes, but we need to go now."

He's not supposed to be on the scene. That's why he didn't use his siren. He's only working for Bianchi right now. Better be careful. "Let's go."

"My car's parked on Mailer."

Good. We can get out of here undetected. "What are we waiting for?"

Jesse walked side-by-side with the crooked cop, his eyes never leaving the pistol trained on him, though he knew by now ordinary bullets were a minor annoyance at best.

Victor Bianchi won't know what hit him, he thought with a smile.

He climbed into the backseat of the patrol car and kept quiet. He wanted the man to believe he was in control and not the other way around. This was his chance to meet Victor face-to-face and put an end to the mob so he and his family could live in peace.

The officer called Victor and set up a delivery location. He explained how he singlehandedly captured Jesse, and all he could do was smile at the over exaggeration.

Someone's trying to get a bonus.

Within fifteen minutes they were at the building where Jesse's life had begun to spiral out of control. The cop ushered him inside the bank and there was Victor Bianchi sitting in the center of the lobby surrounded by his goons, the smug look on the crime boss's face stirring the beast within. Jesse felt it scratching under his skin, begging for release.

"Seems I've underestimated you," Bianchi said. "You've proven very resourceful."

"Maybe you shouldn't have fired me."

"I have no control over who comes and goes here. I pay people to handle that part of the business for a reason. You're friends are dead and the money they took from me is back in the vault where it belongs. Now ... where's the rest of my money?"

"It's safe."

Victor nodded to the cop and the man pointed his gun down and fired. The bullet went straight through Jesse's right knee. Hot, searing pain shot through him as his leg buckled, but he remained on his feet.

"Where's Frankie and Moe? What did you do to them?"

"I'll show you." Jesse released himself to the wolf.

Victor and his men watched wide-eyed as man transformed into beast. The cop beside Jesse took a step backward as he aimed his gun at the beast's head. Victor stood and his men circled around him.

With the transformation complete, the beast stretched out its arms and roared. The crooked cop bolted for the door and Jesse let him go for he would soon be unemployed anyway. Besides, killing a cop, crooked or not, would rain down a new kind of terror onto his family.

"Kill it!" Victor ordered and his men opened fire.

The beast leaped into the air and into the center of the circle the men were forming around their boss. Victor ducked. The beast pulled back its clawed hand and spun. Several heads fell to the floor, followed by the decapitated bodies. The men who survived the attack dropped their weapons and ran for the door.

Victor tried to run as well, but he was grabbed from behind and lifted off his feet. "Please . . . no. I'll give you anything. Anything!"

The beast brought him face-to-face and growled.

"You think this'll be over when you kill me? Well, you're wrong. Another will rise to take my place and he'll want the money you stole. You'll never be safe unless you join me." With a cheap grin, he added "I could use someone like you."

He's right. We'll constantly be looking over our shoulder. On the run. What kind of life is that? My girls deserve better. Besides, it's not like I couldn't use the money, and it would give me the chance to see the extent of Victor's reach. Wipe out the threat completely.

Gently, Victor was put down. "You've made the right decision. Consider the money you stole from me a down payment."

The transformation reversed.

"This is the beginning of a beautiful partnership," Victor said with a twisted smile.

DOG FIGHT

Jesse Barnes watched as his two creations battled to the death in the steel cage. Newly turned wolf pitted against the current champion. His hands gripped his knees and his shoulders tightened in anticipation of the next blow.

"You want to fight, don't you?" asked Victor Bianchi, his voice cold and uncaring.

Jesse kept his gaze locked on the fight. "The wolf wants to prove it's alpha."

"Understandable. You know if you did, though, you'd have to wear one of those, too. Gotta keep it sportsmanly, you know?"

"I've got no problem with that. It's an irritation and only serves to keep the beast in a frenzied state."

Victor placed his arm around him. "Sorry my friend. You're far too valuable to gamble with."

Though Victor's touch no longer repulsed him, Jesse would not consider them "friends". Their relationship was purely parasitically symbiotic. One used the other and vice versa.

"Think the newbie stands a chance?"

"That's where my money is." Jesse's eyes flinched as his newest creation took a blow to the left side of its neck. The lock on the silver muzzle spun around the latch and a chunk of fur fell to the blood-stained mat as the werewolf's body crashed into the reinforced steel. *Damn*, he thought, *was I wrong?*

The reigning champion, Thomas Barrett, charged in for a killing blow. The man had been turned five months ago. He had gone so far into debt, Victor Bianchi had come up with the underground fighting arena as a chance for him to work it off. Of course, fight clubs were a dime a dozen, and Victor needed his to be the cream of the crop—the be all end all of fighting—so he forced Jesse to do the unthinkable. And frankly, Jesse knew after seeing monster on monster violence, who would settle for anything less?

The newbie—Jesse hadn't yet learned his name—ducked an upward swipe and capitalized on his opponent's mistake by raking his large claws across Thomas's abdomen. The crowd roared their approval as blood splashed across the mat. For a second, Jesse saw the tubular tissue rise to the surface as the skin folded outward, but Thomas quickly pressed against the wound with one clawed-hand and jabbed with the other. His blow landed against the silver muzzle, rocking the newbie's head, but causing little harm.

"C'mon!" shouted an overzealous spectator. "My girl's going to kill me if I lose that money!"

"Sit down!" another spectator said, tossing popcorn at the disgruntled man.

As the man sat back down, the fledgling werewolf launched an assault of his own. He stepped forward and stabbed his claws into Thomas's right shoulder. The beast howled in pain as the newbie dragged his nails through the fur and flesh. Four, wide streaks ran down from the shoulder to the hip. Blood ran, matting Thomas's brown fur and joined the crimson stain on the once white mat.

This is it, Jesse thought as the newbie removed its left hand from Thomas's desecrated flesh and plunged its right hand straight into Thomas's chest. Silence blanketed the crowd sitting on the bleachers surrounding the ring. Their eyes wide, mouths gaped open in disbelief, they watched and waited for their champ's next move, but all Thomas could do was whimper in pain. The newbie pulled its arm back, removing the reigning champ's heart.

A pain-roar erupted and subsided as Thomas dropped to his knees, and was replaced by a roar of triumph from the arena's newest champion. It was apparent who bet on whom by those who applauded the victory and those who lowered their heads in shame.

On cue, three guards fired tranquilizer darts at the victorious beast, each hitting its mark on the werewolf's chest. The wolf yelped and swiped the darts off itself, but it was too late. As one of the guards fumbled with his keys to the cage, the beast wobbled on unsteady legs.

"Hit it again!" Victor said.

The closest guard—a three hundred pound man built like a freight train—was more than happy to oblige. He smiled as he reloaded his weapon, then fired. With a whimper, the beast fell to its backside. The cage door swung open and another guard stormed in, berretta aimed at the losing beast's head. He fired a shot into its skull. The body jolted from the impact, then lay lifeless once more.

When the guard nodded to Victor, signaling all was well and under control, Jesse's boss stood. "Ladies and Gentlemen, we appreciate you coming out tonight. I'm sure fortunes were lost and gained on this magnificent fight and I hope to see you again next month. Goodnight!"

Victor gave Jesse that look — arched right eyebrow, pursed lips, and flaring nostrils told Jesse it was time.

God I hate this part, he thought as he stood. Jesse followed Victor out of the arena and up to the second floor.

Housed in a two story warehouse, the arena had a maximum occupancy of twenty-five hundred, but Victor Bianchi turned no patron away. Most nights, the calculated figure set forth by the fire marshal based on the building's size and exit routes was often ignored, and seating arrangements turned into standing room only as the spectators salivated with primal lust.

Directly above the arena's steel cage, the ceiling dropped away. Upstairs, the fighters were kept in separate cages beneath a wide skylight that allowed the light of the full moon to encompass Jesse's creations. There was no hiding from the change, and no escape from fighting. Once you were in debt with Victor Bianchi, the only release was death—a fact Jesse Barnes still struggled with.

In the room above the cage, Jesse found a man tied to a chair. Arms behind his back with his head slumped forward. Two guards stood beside him, both were rubbing their knuckles.

"Meet, Frank Roche." Victor extended his right arm, palm up.

At the sound of his name, Frank lifted his head. His right eye swollen shut; a deep, purplish discoloration surrounded the area. Both cheekbones were raised as fluid collected in the underlining fatty tissue. His lower lip was puffed out with a trail of crimson running down his chin and staining his white undershirt, and his nose had an unsightly crook.

Jesse narrowed his eyes. "Was that necessary?"

While one thug shrugged his shoulders, the other said, "Just passin' the time."

"You realize you're playing with fire," Jesse said. "The beast will remember you."

"Just turn 'im," Victor ordered.

With a heavy sigh, Jesse released the mental restraints on the beast within as he stripped off his clothes. The thugs looked away, his natural gifts shaming them. Victor, as always, watched with unblinking eyes.

Jesse's heart thundered in his chest as the beast relished the moment. Muscles rippled under his skin as they reshaped themselves. Bones cracked and popped out of place—the sound echoing in his ears—they shifted and reformed into something new. The hairs on his arms lengthened and covered every inch of flesh, his fingers elongated and tapered off into vicious claws. And in a matter of seconds, the pain faded and he stood on his haunches.

The beast turned its head and stared into Victor Bianchi's eyes. Their gazes locked, the two thugs drew their guns.

"Lower your weapons."

"But boss," one argued.

"Do it."

The thugs obeyed and stepped away from the beast's intended target.

Victor stood his ground. "I know you want to eviscerate me. I can see it in your eyes."

A low, guttural growl reverberated in the beast's throat.

"Today is not the day," he said, voice dull and flat. With the nod of his head in Frank's direction, the beast broke eye contact with Victor and stared down at the bound man.

"No," Frank whispered as he shook his head. "I'll pay! I swear. . . I'll get you the money!"

"It's too late for that. You were given too many chances, and you failed each time. Like I told you when you first came to me, one way or another, I get my money."

With three powerful strides, the wolf stepped up to Frank.

"You can't do this!" Frank begged, but the beast was not known for mercy. "Please!"

Feeling its bloodlust, Jesse willed the creature to not rip him to shreds. Instead, the wolf grabbed the man by the shoulders and hoisted him up, chair and all. Frank's brow wrinkled as he closed his eyes tightly. Jesse smelled the urine as it traveled down the man's leg before he heard its trickling splash against the concrete floor. The beast growled, the fear enticing its killer instinct.

Just a nip, Jesse commanded.

"Oh God!" Frank uttered, his head scrunched into his shoulders. Tears streamed down the man's cheeks, his body quaked with fear.

Jesse could only imagine the images flashing in Frank's mind. The realization that monsters were real and the dark was something to fear was a tough pill to swallow. The man's sobs only infuriated the beast more. Compassion was not a trait it was known for, and it had no sensibilities to reason with.

Opening its wide maw, the beast obeyed Jesse's command of only a bite. Frank screamed as the large canine teeth pierced his shoulder and bicep. Blood filled the bottom of the creature's jaw; the coppery tang ignited its taste buds. The wolf wanted more. Wanted to tear off a piece of Frank's flesh and swallow it whole, to feel it slide down its throat and sate its appetite.

Put him down.

The wolf growled.

Michelle and Lisa.

With a whimper, the wolf released its hold on Frank.

The chair fell to the floor and teetered. The thug on the right dashed to steady the wooden frame, and the sudden movement angered the beast.

He barked. Thick strands of saliva flew from its jaws.

"Enough!"

Hearing Victor's voice caused the beast to curl its lanky fingers into fists, the sharp claws slicing the palms of its nightmarish hands.

You did good, Jesse told the beast, *now sleep.*

Reluctantly—and still holding on to the thought of disemboweling Victor—the beast succumbed to Jesse's will. The heavy coat of black fur receded into the bubbling skin; his bones cracked and popped back into place and his muscles deflated.

Jesse stood naked before Victor and his goons—his shame taken from him months ago. He walked over to his pile of clothing and dressed as the thugs cut the restraints off the crying Frank Roche.

"What have you done to me?" he asked in between sobs.

"I've given you the means to fight in my arena," Victor said. "If you win, you continue to fight until your debt is paid."

"And if I lose?"

"I think you know the answer." Victor nodded to his men. "Take him to his cell."

"Feed him. He's going to need his strength," Jesse said. "Steaks. . . medium rare."

"I don't eat red meat," said Frank. "It disagrees with me."

Jesse buttoned his shirt and said, "Not anymore."

As the thugs escorted Frank to his new accommodations, Victor placed a hand upon Jesse's shoulder. "Well done."

Jesse shifted his shoulder and Victor's hand fell away. "It's getting harder to stop the beast."

"I understand." Victor pulled the hem of his gray suit aside and revealed a Colt pistol. The handle plated in mother of pearl with the exposed butt looking to be made of sterling silver. "Just remind it I'll be taking it down with me should it decide to betray us."

Jesse pursed his lips and nodded. "May I go?"

"Yes. But I need you in the morning. I have a meeting that could go south."

"All right," he said, then walked away.

As Jesse put distance between him and Victor, his thoughts lingered on giving into the beast's desires. To allow the creature to rip him limb from limb, rummage through his internal organs and devour his soft, delectable parts and shit him out the next morning. He stood at the stairwell door, the beast's urges bombarding his psyche. *All I have to do is let go.*

"Something wrong?"

Victor's voice cut through him like fingernails on a chalk board. "No," Jesse said. "Just trying to remember if there was something Michelle wanted me to bring home. Good night." He shoved his hand against the lock bar and left without waiting for a reply.

Think about the girls, he thought as he took the stairs two at a time.

Victor Bianchi's reach extended far in the windy city. From pocketed cops to government officials, there was no way he could guarantee his wife and daughter's safety should he slay the mob boss. Someone was sure to retaliate. Running was out of the question as well. How many bounty hunters would jump at the cash Victor could offer? *And what kind of life would that be? My girls deserve better.* There was no alternative worth considering, staying put and benefiting from his affliction was the best course of action for his family.

When he arrived home, Jesse found Michelle and Lisa in the kitchen. His wife washing dishes while his daughter doodled with crayons on a piece of construction paper.

Michelle looked over her shoulder and smiled. "Hey, honey."

Jesse walked over toward her and kissed her rosy cheek. "How was your day?"

"Uneventful," she answered as she scrubbed the coffee pot.

He mussed his daughter's blonde hair. "How's my princess?"

Lisa dropped the black crayon and pushed backward, a sharp screech echoed in his sensitive ears as the chair legs dragged across the linoleum. Without a word, she ran out of the kitchen.

"Don't worry about it," Michelle said.

"How can't I?" He looked down at the paper and sighed through his nose. "Is this how she really sees me?"

Michelle turned off the water and turned around.

The picture Lisa drew was of their family standing beside their house, hands entwined. A bright orange sun cast a dark shadow in the shape of a wolf on Jesse's pictorial image. Eyes red, claws outstretched, and its mouth opened wide to reveal vicious teeth, he could not deny his daughter thought him a monster.

"Well, she did draw us as a happy family."

"Don't patronize me."

Michelle put her arms across his shoulders and rested her head on his broad chest. "She'll come around."

"She's pushing away."

"At least she hasn't told anyone."

"Small comfort," he said.

"I'll talk to her."

"No." He kissed her soft lips. "I'll do it."

She gave him a warm smile, then returned to her dishes.

"Wish me luck," he said with a half-laugh, a feeble attempt at downplaying the situation.

"Good luck," she replied.

He walked out of the kitchen and expected to find Lisa in the living room watching television. With the room deserted, he made his way upstairs to her bedroom. He didn't blame her for being afraid of him. He was just as scared. While Michelle continued to reassure him that she would eventually understand, Lisa distanced herself further. Together they had raised a smart, beautiful young girl and somehow she knew her father was no longer the gentle man who picked her up when she fell, who kissed her boo-boos and magically made the pain go away, and drank imaginary cups of tea with her. He had become the monster he used to check for under her bed.

Though he hadn't transformed in front of her since that first night when Victor's goons held them captive in their own house, he had come home with bullet holes in his shirts, mud on his shoes, and blood on his breath.

Not normal behavior for a Daddy.

The bedroom door ajar, he peeked inside. Lisa lay belly down on her bed facing the other direction. He wrapped his knuckles on the door as he pushed it open. "Honey, may I come in?"

Lisa rolled over and swung her legs onto the bed. She grabbed the sheets and pulled them up to her chin.

"I didn't mean to scare you," he said, approaching her bedside.

"Where's Mommy?"

Jesse's heart ached, the fear evident in his daughter's voice. "She's downstairs."

"Mommy!" She pulled the sheet up over her nose and watched him with unblinking eyes.

"You know I would never hurt you, right?" He reached a hand toward her, hoping to run his fingers through her hair, but her head sunk into her shoulders and a shallow pool of tears glossed over her blue eyes. Jesse pulled his hand back and said, "I'm sorry."

"Daddy," she said as he stepped toward the door.

"Yeah, sweat heart?"

She pulled the sheet down and exposed a quivering lip. "Are you working tomorrow?"

"I have to go in early for something important, but after that, I could leave. Why?"

"Could you take me to the park?"

A smile stretched across his face. "Of course. Would you feel safer if Mommy came too?"

"No. I'll be fine tomorrow," she said and the truth hit him square in the gut.

He looked out through her bedroom window. The full moon cast a soft illuminating glow upon the front yard. *There's still hope.* "Are you sure you don't want to come down stairs and watch something?"

"I'm sure. Can Mommy read me a story?"

Looks like I'll be having some alone time tonight. "Sure thing. I love you."

"Love you, too, Daddy."

As if a weight had been lifted from his shoulders, Jesse bounded down the stairs in a way he hadn't since he was a boy welcoming the first day of summer vacation. A strain in his cheeks from the lasting smile and a warmth in his heart, he grabbed Michelle by the waist line and lifted her off her feet.

"I guess it went well."

He put her down, and then wrapped his arms around her, drawing her close. "Not quite what I hoped for, but at least now I understand. She's only afraid of me during the full moon."

"That makes sense."

"Maybe during these nights it'd be better if I stayed out."

Michelle looked him in the eye. "I'd rather have you home where I know you won't be getting into any trouble."

"I suppose," he said, voice dull and flat as he lost himself in the blue depths of her eyes.

"Overtime, she'll learn it's not the moon that has control, but you."

He broke his gaze, doubt clouding his mind. "I don't know how long that'll be true."

Michelle took his hand in hers. "What happened?"

"Nothing . . . it just took every ounce of strength I had to stop it from ripping into Victor."

With her lips pursed, she breathed heavily through her nose. A *swoosh* caused by the escaping air broke the momentary silence. "I know he demands a lot of you, but he's also provided for this family."

"C'mon," he said, pulling away from her.

"Stop looking at this as if it were a curse and accept it for the blessing it is."

"You have no idea what you're saying. You can't imagine the dark places it takes me to."

"Jesse, you're a good man. Despite the claws and teeth, it's still you." She held his wrist and peered deep into his eyes. "I may not know the stress it causes you, but I do know the stress and anxiety of choosing which bills we can skip to pay in order to have food on the table. To have to say no to your daughter when she asks you for a new toy."

"It's not the same," he said, head hung low. "At any minute I could lose—"

"Shh!" She placed her slender finger upon his lip. "If we live within our means and save all the extra you bring home, we can use it to move far, far away. Beyond Victor's grip."

"Is there such a place?"

"We'll find it. I promise."

In one motion, he grabbed her by the waist and pulled her close. She wrapped her arms around him and kissed him long and soft. Her breasts pressed against his chest, he wanted nothing more than to pick her up and carry her into their bedroom and make love to her, but his thoughts drifted to their daughter and her needs.

He pulled out of her embrace and said, "Lisa wanted you to read her story."

"Is that what you want?"

With her eyes wide and brow wrinkled he knew she felt the same as he. "She's more important than I am right now."

Michelle smiled. "I'll be in the bedroom as soon as she's asleep. Wait for me?"

"Of course." After one last kiss, he watched her as she exited the room.

* * * *

Victor Bianchi had his hand on the revolver hidden under his desk the moment the two men entered his office.

Jesse locked his gaze on them, his attention drawn to their racing heartbeats. Dressed in what looked to be silk suits, the men reeked of cocaine laced with adrenaline.

This isn't going to go well, he thought.

"Please," Victor held out his right hand in gesture toward the seats in front of his desk, "gentleman, sit down."

One made a move toward the chair while the other stood his ground and placed a hand upon the other's shoulder. A telltale sign of which of the two was in charge. "We'd prefer to stand. This isn't a social call."

"Fine. Then speak your peace, my acquaintance here has someplace he needs to be."

Jesse was surprised by the comment; it was the first time the man acknowledge that he had responsibilities beyond Victor.

"With the economy in the toilet, business is slow. And in order to maintain our lifestyle, we cannot afford to continue giving you thirty percent."

"What do you propose?" asked Victor.

The man smiled. "That we keep one-hundred percent of our earnings."

Victor returned the smile, though Jesse doubted his boss was amused. "Dealers such as yourselves are a dime a dozen. You don't like my terms, I can name ten pushers willing to take your place."

"And who's going to take your place?"

The drug dealer's right hand man whipped out a tiny pistol.

Jesse stood ready. *If that's a derringer, he only has two rounds. Four at the most. But…do I let 'im kill, Victor? This could be my chance.*

The idiot fired two shots.

The sound of Victor's finger squeezing the trigger of his concealed semi-automatic weapon rang in Jesse's highly in tuned ear. At the last possible second, Jesse threw himself in front of Victor. Hot lead tore into his chest and shoulder. The force of the near-point-blank shot sent him crashing into Victor, not allowing him to return fire. Both crashed to the floor.

Jesse's adrenal medulla kicked in, his central nervous system synapses fired faster and time seemed to slow to a crawl. Waves of paresthesia surged throughout his body. Breath short, pain mounting, the wolf within called to him and the transformation began.

Victor trembled beneath him as man shifted to beast. He stood on his haunches. Shreds of his clothing clung loosely across its chest and tree-trunk like legs. The bullets rose up out of his flesh, dropped, and clanged against the hardwood floor.

"What the hell?" asked one of the dealers.

"Shoot it!"

"I'm out."

Victor looked up at the beast wide-eyed and mouth agape. *Not him*.

Anxious to rip into human flesh, the beast turned to the two would-be kingpins. With one clawed hand, it tossed the ornate mahogany desk aside.

"We're sorry," said the leader of the two as he stepped backward.

The other goon dropped his pitiful gun and ran to the door. The knob rattled in his hand and the door held firm. "Let us out!"

In a single bound, the wolf leapt and landed on the man's back. He screamed as the beast's powerful jaws clamped down on the side of his neck. The high-pitched wail turned into a garbled mess as blood filled his airway and with the jerk of its head, the drug dealer lost his. The severed head fell to the floor with a wet, slippery *sploosh*. A geyser of blood turned into a trickle before the body crumpled.

"Please," said the other man. "I didn't know he was going to do that. I had nothing to do with it. Honest!"

From the rapid beat of his heart, the wolf knew the man was lying. More than fear was detected by its heightened senses. As the beast stepped closer to him, the man slapped his hands together in prayer and closed his eyes.

"In the name of the mother, the father and the—"

The massive paw grabbed hold of him by the head, its palm covering his mouth. With the pump of its fingers, bone cracked and split and soft, textured tissue plopped up between his hairy fingers. The body dropped to its knees as spasms rippled throughout its limbs.

The door burst open and two of Victor's guards stood in the doorway, guns at the ready. "You all right?" asked one of them.

"Yeah, lower your weapons. Get someone to clean this mess up."

"Boss?"

"Now!"

With the nod of his head, the goon obeyed and lead the way for the other.

"Excellent work," said Victor.

The wolf released its hold on the dead man and turned toward Victor.

Let me handle this. Rest now.

The beast stepped toward Victor, who in turn smiled and took a step forward, closing the distance.

What is he doing? Is he a fool goading you like that?

Jesse felt the beast's rage bubbling up inside like rising bile. Killing the only thing on its mind. Another step closer on the beast's part was met by another from Victor until the two stood with no more than inches between them. Victor's neck craned so as to look into the eyes of the wolf.

"I'm getting tired of this game, monster."

The wolf growled.

Victor slapped the beast across the maw. "Show me what you got."

A clawed hand wrapped around his throat and pulled him closer. Saliva dripped from its upper jaw and splashed on Victor's cheek. The crime boss looked into the abyss and refused to flinch.

That's enough!

Jesse fought for control. His arm trembled as the war within waged. Finally, his will subdued the beast and Victor was released. The transformation reversed and he stood before his boss with torn clothing hanging loosely on his frame. "Are you crazy?"

Victor smiled. "It needed to know that I'm not afraid of it."

"Well, you made your point." Jesse made for the door.

"Where are you going?"

"Like you said, I have somewhere I need to be, but I'll be checking on the fighters before I go."

"Give my regards," Victor said as Jesse exited his office.

Arrogant bastard. Should've let those thugs kill him.

The wolf agreed.

When Jesse arrived at the fighter's cages, he found his spawn stripped of their dignity and treated like animals. Naked and cold, the two men were in adjoining cages. Stainless steel bowls on the floor offered water and their last meals, all that remained were the bare t-bones. Picked clean as if by vultures.

Jesse walked past Frank Roche and approached the new champion's cage. "How're you feeling, Bruce?"

Bruce stood. Under the grime and dried blood, a finely chiseled body and Jesse felt the newcomer hadn't a chance.

"How do you think?" he asked in return. "They treat us like dogs."

"I know. I'm sorry."

"Then let us out," said Frank as he too stood. "I have a family."

"So do I."

"At least tell us how to control it," Bruce said.

"If I could, I would. But you're inherently different."

Bruce rattled the bars of his cage. "Bullshit!"

"It's true," Jesse said, not bothering to step away from the cage. "The circumstances of my transformation cannot be duplicated. I represent the perfect merger of beast and man, united in a single goal."

"And what goal is that?" Bruce asked.

Jesse looked away. "It's not important."

"One way or another, I'll control it, and when I do—"

"I know." Jesse turned around.

"Don't leave us," Frank pleaded.

"I'll kill you," Bruce said. "I swear it!"

The dormant wolf seemed excited by the prospect.

* * * *

In an effort to quell future resistance, Victor leaked word of his powerful bodyguard within his ranks and displayed the unruly drug dealers as a warning to others. Up until the Donovan brothers wanting to branch out on their own, the boss hadn't felt the need; afraid someone with deeper pockets would come along and steal Jesse from him. Only those in Victor's tightly knit group knew Jesse's secret, and they were paid handsomely to keep it.

As the information spread like wildfire through the ranks, Jesse's workload decreased and he was able to spend more time at home, but it came at a price. Those looks his daughter gave him on the night of a full moon were received on a daily basis from Victor's men. No one who didn't know him already trusted him. The men kept a watchful eye on him while they worked, their hands constantly fidgeting for their weapons at the slightest move on Jesse's part. The stares and unease of the men made the dormant wolf anxious, and that frightened him far more than the potential of the weary men carrying silver bullets.

For the first time, Jesse felt excited when fight night finally came around. The idea of his spawn fighting to the death thrilled him, and deep down he knew the reason why. Though Victor refused to give him the opportunity to go off leash, the fight allowed him to live vicariously, and he hoped it was enough to ease some of the mounting tension.

All eyes in the arena fell on him as he escorted Victor to his private seat. Even a woman he had caught looking at him with a sultry stare in the past turned her head in disgust by his presence. He knew her cycle matched that of his. Her aroma tantalized the beast, and often made it difficult for him to concentrate on the fights. *Always thought you were just mildly attractive anyway.* He snubbed his nose at her in retaliation. *As if I'd cheat on Michelle with an over-priced whore.*

"Perhaps it was a mistake to divulge your secret," Victor said as he sat down.

"I understand why you did. And it has helped me more than hinder, so no worries. With less resistance to your rule, the more time I get with my family and to enjoy my pay."

Victor smiled. "See, working for me's not so bad."

"Suppose not. Now if I could just get the rest of your men to trust me."

"They will."

The ceiling above the cage opened and the two, naked fighters dropped inside. The silver muzzles in place. Their bodies crashed against the polyethylene foam mat, the underside covered with needle punch carpet to resist the beasts' sharp claws. Bruce quickly got to his feet and lunged at the steel bars while Frank moaned and tried to rub the bridge of his nose after his face plant.

"Soon, the moon will be high enough," Victor said as the crowd roared.

Jesse nodded, his attention focused on the combatants.

Along the arena, bets were placed. Every man and woman shouted for the Layers' attention to ensure their bets were in before the transformation. Fortunes were won and lost, and everyone wanted a piece.

Frank stood on wobbly legs; even from high in the bleaches Jesse could smell his fear.

"Help me!"

The crowd booed and tossed popcorn at him.

"You damn lunatics! You're the real monsters." Tears streamed down Frank's cheeks as he turned and looked straight at Jesse. "You did this!" He grabbed hold of the bars and shook the cage wall. "You did this!"

The crowd's displeasure with Frank grew louder until the first beam of moonlight struck the center of the ring. An awkward silence blanketed the crowd, and as one they took their seats in anticipation of the night's carnage.

"This is a first," Victor whispered in Jesse's ear as Bruce willingly stepped into the moonbeam.

Interesting. Jesse watched the transformation, only peering away to see the terror etched on Frank's face as he, too, watched.

Bruce's muscles rippled under his skin. His rib cage expanded as auburn hair grew and covered every inch. His ears tapered to a point as his nose elongated. Flat teeth dropped out and fell to the mat to make way for pointy canines. Blunt fingernails lifted away as sharp claws capable of ripping through flesh emerged.

Frank sat in a puddle of his own urine, quivering with fear as the monster stood before him. Arms outstretched and gaze locked on Frank, the werewolf roared.

"Please...no!"

The beast walked over to Frank, ignoring his plea.

"This is going to be over quick."

"We'll see," Jesse said, knowing Victor had no idea what he was talking about.

With its large paw, the reigning champion grabbed Frank by the head. Jesse caught the faint whiff of blood on the air as the razor sharp claws tore into Frank's skin. The man screamed as Bruce hoisted him up and threw him into the widening circle of moonlight at the center of the ring.

Now this is really interesting. Something was different about Bruce. Even the previous champion hadn't embraced the beast within like this. Each fight prior started with the combatants cowering in the cage corners until the moonlight reached them. *Has he learned to control it?*

As Frank's body underwent the change, Bruce grabbed hold of Frank's silver muzzle's lock, and ripped it out of place.

Seeing enough, Jesse turned to Victor. "You've got to stop this."

"Are you kidding me? This could be one of our greatest fights."

"Without the muzzle—"

"There will be more bloodshed."

Victor looked upon him with a stone cold glare. There was no arguing. Jesse turned his attention back onto the ring. He needed to be ready to act should things go further south.

With Frank's transformation complete, he slapped the side of Bruce's face. The lock on the muzzle spun around.

They're working together. But how?

Another hard slap from Frank's clawed hand and the lock gave, breaking in half under his superhuman strength. The crowd cheered as the silver muzzle fell to the floor, the prospect of blood numbing them to the danger.

Jesse stood. "If you're not going to stop this, then I will."

"Sit down!"

"You don't know what you're doing."

Victor stood to meet his gaze. "And you're forgetting your place."

A woman's scream caught their attention. Jesse turned back to the cage. The patrons in the front rows made their way toward higher ground as the two werewolves slammed their bodies into the right side of the cage wall. The steel moaned under their combined weight, but held firm. Dust rained down from the ceiling above. With the cunning eyes of the wolf Jesse took notice of the joints where the steel bars and concrete merged. The stone above cracked further with each violent slam, and soon the cage would be compromised.

"You have to get everyone out of here, now!"

"I don't...," Victor said, his cool countenance crumbling.

Jesse grabbed him by the lapels with one hand, and slapped him across the face with the other. "Snap out of it!" With the rising danger, he couldn't even enjoy manhandling Victor.

"Right. Maybe we should just put them down now?"

"No," Jesse released his hold on the Armani suit, "I need this. And the beast wants it."

Though he expected a look of fury on Victor's face, he was surprised to see one of understanding. "I suppose if I treat you more often, you'll be more inclined to cooperate."

Already giving into the change, Jesse smiled and revealed two rows of needle-like teeth. "Couldn't hurt."

Victor nodded and signaled to his guards to move. "Everyone out!"

A loud clang echoed on the air. Snarls and growls drowned out the screams of the fleeing patrons. Jesse, in the middle of his transformation, watched as his spawn stepped onto the fallen cage wall laid across the seats. An unfortunate, overweight man not fast enough to clear out of the way was slammed in the back and pinned in a chair. The fat of his neck pinched against the back of the seat and pushed upward, giving his bulbous face a toad-like appearance. Eyes bulged from their sockets, Jesse knew the man dead.

Jesse stood before the two werewolves ready to rip them apart and prove its worth. Frank adorned in thick black fur would be his first target. Newly transformed, he would be the weaker of the two. Jesse leapt and traveled over seven rows of stadium seats.

As if sensing his course of action, Bruce reached out with a clawed hand and swatted him out of midair. Jesse's body crashed into the seats, the sound of bone cracking echoed in his ear. A rib broke upon impact with the hard back of the seat, the pain surged, then dulled as it was healed.

Frank ceased the opportunity and swung his right paw. Claws sliced through the air as it descended toward Jesse's exposed abdomen. He rolled out of the way. Foam padding scattered into the air as the seat cushion was decimated.

The moment Jesse's footing was steadied, he launched himself once more, pounced on Frank's back and clamped his powerful jaws on the side of his neck. Warm blood trickled down his throat as fur tickled the roof of his mouth. Frank flailed as he tried to shake Jesse loose, but his teeth were deep into Frank's flesh.

Claws tore into Jesse's hide, but his bite remained. Bruce pulled with all his strength, but Jesse jabbed his claws into Frank's sides and dug in under his ribcage. Frank howled in pain as blood matted his fur.

Realizing the struggle futile, Bruce released his hold and raked his claws down Jesse's back. Jesse wanted to cry, to release his bite and wail to the moon, but he winced his eyes and dug deeper into Frank. Bruce attacked again and again, the instant the torn flesh healed; the wounds were re-opened until finally Jesse could no longer take the pain. He pulled his hands free of Frank, but he didn't come away empty handed. In his right hand a lung and in his left a kidney.

Frank dropped to his knees. Heart beat irregular, breathing heavy, Jesse brought him to Death's door and he only needed another nudge. The explosive crack of a gun whirred in his ears. He felt the whoosh of the bullet blow through his fur. Frank whimpered. A trail of blood hung on the air for that brief moment, then splashed onto a nearby chair as Frank collapsed.

Robbed of its victory, the beast within Jesse roared and slammed its clawed hand into the side of Bruce's face. The auburn wolf dropped to the floor and Jesse leapt over him.

"Stay back!" said the guard foolish enough to intervene. He aimed his shaky gun at Jesse, tears pooling in his eyes.

Jesse grabbed the gun and bent the barrel before knocking it out of the man's hand.

"Please," he begged.

He was just following orders. Probably why he didn't shoot you, too.

The beast growled to relay its displeasure with the man, then turned back around. The guard wasted no time to run away. Bruce stood by his fallen brethren, and looked as though he expected Frank to stand up and continue the fight at any moment.

With its wounds a distant memory, Jesse's beast ran headlong through the aisles toward Bruce, swatting bolted-down, cushioned seats into the air and out of its way as if they were toss pillows. Bruce leapt into the air as though it could not wait a second longer to rip into Jesse. Claws outstretched and mouth unnaturally wide, anyone other than Jesse would have turned tail and ran at such a ferocious sight, but instead, he stopped his charge and caught Bruce by the throat and in a swift motion, drove the beast into the concrete floor.

However, Bruce proved just as fearless and agile. The moment his back hit the ground, Bruce drove his feet into Jesse's stomach and sent him hurling backward through the air. Jesse hit hard, but allowed the momentum to carry his legs overhead. He stood and stared down the aisle. Bruce, already on his feet, charged. Long strands of saliva swung from the corners of his mouth, they broke in mid-stride and splashed on the red cushions.

The charging beasts collided in a furry frenzy. Jaws snapping, barks echoing in the arena, they performed a deadly dance of macabre. The two beasts spun round and round, Jesse giving better than he got, but Bruce's wounds healed just as fast as his own. Claws ripped flesh asunder, blood and fur flew wildly. Bruce made a wide swing and Jesse ducked and raked his clawed hand across Bruce's abdomen. Entrails bubbled up from the wound and before the flesh could fold over and close itself, Jesse grabbed hold of the tubular intestine and pulled. The spongy tissue made slurpy *plops* in his hands as his fingers glided over them; they piled on the floor in a circular pattern like a lasso.

Bruce grabbed hold of his intestines and the two played a morbid game of tug until Jesse swiped his claws across the pinkish tissue and sent Bruce crashing to the floor on his backside. Then, without wasting a second, Jesse plunged his clawed right hand into Bruce's chest. He broke through the ribcage and clamped down on the vital organ. With a twist and a yank, he pulled Bruce's heart free and held it up in triumph.

After a mighty roar, Jesse tossed the muscle into his mouth and swallowed it whole. Bruce's body slumped forward, and for good measure, Jesse dug his black nails into Bruce's neck and pried off his head.

Jesse lifted it eye level and stared into the glossed over eyes of the wolf. *You should've known your place*, he thought.

With no sign of regeneration, Jesse threw the severed head at the wall. Brain matter and blood flew in all directions as it was crushed against the concrete, leaving a crimson stain for the morning crew to clean.

"Well done," Victor said, clapping.

He didn't runoff very far. Jesse remained in beastial form, the desire to kill the crime lord unbearable.

Victor stepped toward him. "All in all, not a bad night considering. We only lost fatty there. Mostly everyone else is just bruised and shook up."

Lord I wish I could rip your heart out through your ass.

"C'mon," Victor waved him over, "we need to find new fighters."

With Lisa and Michelle on his mind, Jesse reversed the transformation. *One day, I will make* you *my bitch.*

ABOUT THE AUTHOR

Keith Gouveia is an accomplished horror and dark fantasy writer and fierce advocate of independent and artisanal publishers. His other recent releases are *The Screaming Field*, *The Black Cat and the Ghoul*, and *The Dead Speak in Riddles*. He is also editor of the horror anthologies, *Bits of the Dead*, *Skeletal Remains*, and *The Snuff Syndicate*.

Keith was born and raised in Fall River, Massachusetts, but now lives in Orlando, Florida.

You can keep up to date with all of Keith's projects at by friending him on Facebook.
www.Facebook.com/KeithDBZ